Conversation *with* Grandfather

EUGENE H. STRAYHORN JR.

ISBN 978-1-966540-10-6 (softcover)
ISBN 978-1-966540-17-5 (hardcover)
ISBN 978-1-966540-11-3 (ebook)

This book is a work of fiction. Names, characters, places, and incidents are the product of the author's imagination or are used fictitiously. Any resemblance to actual locales, events, or persons, living or dead, is purely coincidental.

Printed in the United States of America.

Conversation with Grandfather

EUGENE H. STRAYHORN JR.

CHAPTER 1

On a remarkably hot August day, exactly one week after his thirteenth birthday, Mathias Reslin pedaled his new bicycle slowly down the long driveway that led to his house. As he followed the graveled ruts that cut straight to the heart of the Reslins' ten-acre parcel of land, he sensed that something was out of kilter. Troubled, he wondered if the scorching heat was responsible for his uneasiness. The sun beat down with such ferocity that the forest had fallen silent. Only at dusk would the finches and sparrows emerge from the shaded branches of the lodgepole pines and begin twittering again.

Looking ahead, Mathias could see his home—a simple two-story, cedar-sided, south-facing structure. Small windows and a steeply pitched metal roof stood as strong defenses against the harsh winters of northwestern Montana. Yet those same features could create a problem in summer. By trapping heat, they could turn the interior spaces into slow-bake ovens. The humble dwelling also happened to be the first and only house his father had ever built.

Ribbons of dust kicked up by the bicycle's tires rose inches off the ground to hover lazily in the quiet air. Mathias listened. No breeze stirred the tops of the surrounding trees. No sounds suggested a reason for his uneasiness.

After arising early, he had hurried through his morning chores before heading out. His destination had been Regford Park, where he had arranged to meet up for a spirited two-on-two game of soccer. As was his custom, he had partnered with his best friend and classmate, Trent Blaine. Trent, Mathias, and their two opponents would enter high school as freshmen in the fall. Their competition had begun as a lively rivalry, but as the sun arced higher in the sky, enthusiasm had waned. Before noon, both teams had agreed it was too hot to continue. Trent and the other two boys had opted to head for the swimming hole carved into the banks of Tanner's Creek. Something had prevented Mathias from joining them. Premonition perhaps.

Looking ahead, Mathias's uneasiness increased when he noted the stranger standing on the front porch. He tried to imagine why an aged scarecrow of a man would be conversing with his mother. He dismounted and began cautiously walking his bicycle down the driveway.

Could their visitor be a traveling salesman or one of those resolute zealots who piously peddled religious tracts and leaflets? He searched his memory for the last time a salesman had appeared at their front door. It had been a while. Outside the city's limits, houses were too far apart. Traveling long distances to deliver a sales pitch made turning a profit difficult. Even more of a hindrance, rural folks had a habit of strongly objecting to strangers hawking things that weren't needed or were too expensive.

The zealot notion didn't fit either. Those guys tended to travel in pairs and were usually younger. Plus, they were always neatly dressed. The stranger gabbing with his mother looked to have slept in his rumpled suit for at least five nights straight.

Peering ahead, Mathias knew that he had never seen the man before. He would have remembered his close-cropped salt-and-pepper hair, his narrow chin shadowed by gray stubble, and his slightly hooked nose. There was, however, something about the man that reminded him of his mom. Mathias labored to put a finger on what it might be.

Recognition came when the visitor again tugged on an earlobe. That same subconscious gesture generally signaled his mother's rising sense of frustration. What was the probability that both adults would independently adopt that particular mannerism?

A new jolt of concern struck Mathias when he noted the brown suitcase on the porch at the man's feet. It wasn't a peddler's case. Scuffed and battered, the leather valise seemed larger than the carry-on Mrs. Udall had brought with her when she had stayed over to comfort the family after his father's passing. Like the stranger, the suitcase had clearly seen better days.

Quietly closing to within a dozen feet of the porch, Mathias listened intently, doing his best to snag snatches of conversation.

The man said sharply, "After all this time, why?" He raised a hand, palm up for emphasis, and added something Mathias couldn't quite make out.

A bit later, Lauren Reslin, Mathias's mother, exclaimed, "It absolutely was your fault!" Her words rang with a timbre that her normal speaking voice lacked. Mathias noted that his mother stood straight and tall with her shoulders squared. He recognized her posture. It signaled a sense of confidence that her opinion was correct, and she was prepared to defend it—whatever the cost.

In most people's eyes, Lauren Reslin was a beautiful woman. Mathias had no opinion one way or the other, being constrained by age and a lack of worldly experience, but mostly because she was his mom. Thinking in such terms would have been unseemly—not to mention embarrassing. Only in recent months had she began showing signs of infirmity—creases at the corners of her mouth, shadows under her eyes, and hollows in her cheeks. Gone as well was the liveliness in her step that had marked her zest for life. In years to come, Mathias would blame himself for having failed to recognize these and other warning signs.

Lauren faced the stranger and wagged her finger from side to side. "That is not the reason I got in touch."

Mathias advanced another hesitant step. He tried to remain inconspicuous, but his movements must have caught his mother's attention.

She stopped speaking midsentence and looked down as if startled. "You're home early. Is something wrong?"

The boy shook his head but kept his gaze fixed upon the stranger. Up close, the man seemed even more disheveled. Yet despite the heat, he wasn't perspiring. When the man turned his head, Mathias noted he had piercing eyes—same as his mom's. Except Lauren's eyes were blue green, like the deep parts of a stormy ocean. The stranger's were lighter blue, like an empty sky on a sunny day.

Lauren held a hand out to her son. "Come up here. There's someone I'd like you to meet."

Uncertainty rooted Mathias in place. As a rule, being introduced to an unfamiliar adult was a straightforward affair. He had learned to smile, shake hands, and keep his mouth shut. When they started chattering away, his imagination was free to chase whatever fantasies came to mind.

Lauren stretched her hand out with more insistence. "Come on. It's all right. He won't bite." She glanced at the man, and her smile hardened ever so slightly, as if issuing a warning.

Still, Mathias hesitated. One of his father's homilies had come to mind. *Rule 18: Never tell folks your dog don't bite. When he does, they'll hold you accountable.*

The mental image of his father dredged up a familiar emptiness. Losing a parent is tough when you are eight. Turning thirteen hadn't softened his sense of loss in the slightest.

"Mathias." Lauren's tone indicated her growing impatience. Any further delay would border on rudeness, which would not be tolerated. Of course, running away would evoke an even harsher reprimand.

Trapped and with nowhere to turn, Mathias ambled up the porch's two steps. At length, he settled into a position to the side of, and slightly behind, his mother, careful to remain just beyond the stranger's reach.

Lauren rested a hand on her son's shoulder. From his new vantage point, Mathias became aware that, except for his bicycle, the graveled driveway was empty. He assumed the family truck was parked in the garage, as was customary.

With his attention focused on the stranger, Mathias failed to appreciate the fact that no vehicles were in sight.

"Ward, this is your grandson, Mathias Tyrone Reslin." Lauren beamed with obvious pride. "Mathias, this man is your grandfather, Ward Stanford. You remember me telling you about him?"

For Mathias, three things became immediately apparent. First, his mother wanted to make a good impression. His middle name hadn't been spoken aloud in years, except when he was in hot water. But never during an introduction. Second, his mother had just lied. To the best of his knowledge, she had never mentioned her father. Not once. Third, he actually had a maternal grandfather. Of course, he knew everyone had two grandfathers, and he had once met his father's father before his father's accident. But to be introduced to his mother's father? The possibility had never crossed his mind.

He tried to decide how he should feel. An odd impression struck him. It seemed as if a man who did not exist had suddenly materialized on their front porch.

Ward looked down. His expression remained severe. "I thought he'd be bigger."

"Mind your manners," Lauren snapped. Her tone softened as she nudged her son's arm forward. "Mathias," she prompted.

The boy understood what was expected of him. Yet rather than proffer a handshake and the obligatory "Hello, sir," he fashioned a scowl that he hoped equaled his grandfather's. "I thought he'd be younger."

An uncomfortable silence followed. Then the stranger tilted back his head and laughed. "Touché," he said as he extended his hand. "Pleased to meet you, boy." His chin dipped in acknowledgment.

Despite himself, Mathias grinned and returned the handshake. The skin over the old man's bony fingers felt rough, like a baseball mitt left out in the rain.

Lauren breathed a sigh of relief. "Good. Let's go inside and get acquainted." She stepped toward the screen door and held it open.

Her father bent down to retrieve his suitcase.

A single question troubled Mathias as he trailed his grandfather into the house: why had this man come to Rockridge?

A tidal wave of heat cascaded over Mathias as he stepped inside the house.

Lauren ushered her father through the entryway and into the living room, but then paused as if figuring out what to do next. When she noticed the suitcase in her father's hand, she turned to her son. "Put your grandfather's bag in the guest bedroom. Please."

That answers one question, Mathias told himself. *He's spending the night.* On deeper reflection, he realized that the likelihood should have been obvious from the beginning. He reached for the bag and was surprised when Ward hesitated in letting go. A minor tug-of-war ensued. Mathias had his marching orders, and he wasn't about to back down. Stiffening his legs, he was about to give a determined yank when his grandfather relaxed his grip and stepped away.

As Mathias carried the bag toward the back of the house, he wondered about the incident. Could there be contraband in the bag? Was his grandfather afraid someone might steal his worldly possessions? The possibility that the old man might have second thoughts about staying never entered the boy's mind.

Mathias set the bag down beside the bed in the guest bedroom and looked around. The space had an austere feel to it, even by rural standards.

There was a bed, a nightstand, a tall chest of drawers, and an armoire that served as a closet. A solitary picture hung on the wall opposite the bed—a faded print showing a venerable clipper ship venturing into a storm. Both the bedspread and the wallpaper bore bold floral designs. The low-pile carpet was a soft beige color. Though no one had slept in the room since shortly after his father's passing, all surfaces were free of dust—testimony to his mother's flair for housekeeping.

When Mathias returned to the living room, he found that he had two choices as to where to sit. His grandfather had claimed one end of the couch, leaving the opposite end available. His mother had settled demurely into the easy chair by the fireplace. That left the straight-backed chair in the corner as the only satisfactory option. Briefly, he toyed with the idea of plopping down on the floor, though, no doubt, his mother would object. In the end, he chose the uncomfortable chair with its thinly cushioned seat.

As he sat down, Mathias glanced toward the rear of the house. The dining nook beside the kitchen was normally where his mother entertained guests. That she had settled her visitor in the living room gave evidence that his grandfather's visit was more than a social call.

Within moments after Mathias was seated, Lauren rose and addressed her father. "I am sorry. I'm being a terrible hostess. Guess I'm a little out of practice. Can I get you something? Water, coffee? I think there might be tea bags in the cupboard. I can check. Or would you rather freshen up after your trip?"

Ward folded his hands in his lap. He sat upright with both feet flat on the floor. "A glass of water would be appreciated, with ice if you have it."

Lauren headed toward the kitchen. In her absence, Ward openly studied his grandson, looking him up and down in the way a man might judge a racehorse before placing a bet. The intensity of his inspection made Mathias uncomfortable. Rather than chance making eye contact, the boy fixed his gaze on the well-worn Bible lying on the coffee table.

When his mother returned, she carried two glasses of ice water. Accepting one glass from her hand, Mathias downed a long grateful swallow.

Ward also took a sip. "You're not having any?" he said to Lauren as she sat down.

"Maybe later," she replied. "I'm feeling a mite nauseous." She flicked a glance in Mathias's direction and just as quickly looked away. Returning her attention to her father, she said, "I apologize for it being so hot. I was hoping we'd have a cool spell for your visit. We've been thinking about putting in air-conditioning, but…"

Well, that answers another question, Mathias thought. *She knew he was coming, and she didn't say a thing, but she's right about the heat.* With most of the windows in the house standing wide open, there wasn't even the hint of a breeze. The air in the room seemed to hang suspended, as if the flow of time itself had ceased.

"I don't mind being overly hot," Ward said, "not like I used to. You get older, and your metabolism slows down. Makes you feel cold all the time. It's better to be warm. Right, boy?" He peered at his grandson.

"His name is Mathias," Lauren interjected.

"Indeed. Tell me, *boy,* they ever call you Matt or Mattie?"

"No, sir," Mathias said.

"Right. Mathias it is then."

"To be honest," Lauren admitted softly, "I wasn't sure you would come."

"You did invite me, though I'm still not at all clear why." Ward sat quietly, keeping his hands in his lap as if waiting. His ice water sat on a coaster on the coffee table. A ring of condensation was already forming around the bottom of the glass.

Lauren responded lightheartedly, "Of course I invited you! Why shouldn't I? You are my father."

"Well, for starters," Ward exclaimed, "how about the fact that the day you took off, you screeched in my face that you wished I was dead and that you never wanted to see me again? That hurt more than you can imagine."

"I meant it to hurt. And what I said was true. I never wanted to see you again."

"So what's changed?" Ward inclined forward slightly, still waiting. "Why am I here?"

Lauren stared at the floor as if gathering her thoughts. "What's changed? Circumstances, life, me. I changed." She looked up again, straight into her father's eyes. "Why did you come if I hurt you so badly? I was under the impression those feelings were mutual."

"Like I said, I'm here because you invited me and maybe because I'm a little curious. Why, after nearly fourteen years, would you send a letter that basically says, 'Hey, if you're not doing anything, how about visiting me in Montana?' I felt like I'd been handed a puzzle with a bunch of pieces missing. Now, you want to tell me what's really going on?"

Lauren's fidgeting gave evidence that she was feeling increasingly ill at ease. To her father, she said, "I know you have questions, but hang on to them for a time." She stood and turned to her son. "I was going to wait till it cooled off this afternoon, but now is probably better. I need to talk with your grandfather in private. So, do you think you could do something for me?"

"Mom, what's going on?" Mathias rose to face her. "Why can't I stay? If you have something to tell him, I should hear it too."

Lauren reached out and gently combed her fingers through her son's flaxen hair. "My, look at how you've grown. You're going to be a fine, strong man. We'll talk tonight. But first, there are some things I need to work out with your grandfather. Besides, I need you to gather some mud for me. The Silver Rose called. They've taken in an order for a dozen place settings. They need me to get them out the door by the middle of next week. Think you can handle fetching about eight bucketfuls?"

The Reslins' primary source of income was the modest pottery business Lauren ran out of the studio behind their house. As her skill in crafting dinnerware had increased, so too had the demand for her creations, at least locally. Initially a hobby, her business had taken off when she had discovered special mud deposits along the banks of Tanner's Creek. The finely textured clay was exactly the right consistency, and its high iron content imparted a rich dark red color to her creations. Mathias's contribution to the family business was shoveling clay into five-gallon buckets and hauling them from the creek at the edge of the property to the studio. Each bucket could weigh up to sixty pounds, sometimes more.

Mathias groaned. "Sure, Mom. No problem."

"That's my boy. When you come in, I'll fix us some ice-cold lemonade. Now, best get started." Lauren regarded her father. "You can have lemonade too if you'd like."

Ward tilted his head slightly. "What a charming offer. Got anything to put in it? A little JB perhaps?"

Lauren's eyes narrowed. "No spirits in this house. We don't allow them. You'd be wise to keep that in mind."

Ward recoiled. "I will."

Seated in the easy chair, Lauren called out as her son was about to exit through the screen door at the rear of the house, "By the way, if I catch you eavesdropping, I'll tan your backside so you won't be able to ride your bike for a month. You got me?"

"Yes, ma'am," Mathias muttered. As he stepped out onto the back porch, his thoughts were on the agony of gathering mud on such a hot day. Without question, his task would be pure torture.

His mother then called out, "And don't"—the screen door slammed shut—"slam the door."

A squirrel chittered down at Mathias from the branches of a grand fir thirty feet away. No doubt the furry rodent regarded the tree and the surrounding property as his private domain.

"Shut up," Mathias spat out. He fetched a smooth rock of medium size from the flower bed near the back door. After hefting it to judge its weight, he hurled it in the squirrel's direction. The stone flew wide by several feet. The backyard sentry redoubled its protests, as if mocking such poor marksmanship.

Roused by frustration and anger, Mathias sailed a second stone at the squirrel but again missed. The noisy varmint was his target, but not the trigger for his hostility. His mother's dismissal had stirred up painful memories clouded by feelings of isolation and abandonment.

Similar emotions had troubled him two weeks earlier. After a summer picnic, he had been mistakenly left behind by the church's youth group. The associate pastor had miscounted heads as kids were boarding the bus. His rescue had arrived in less than an hour, but in the interval, his ire had grown so intense that he had refused to speak with anyone during the ride home. There had been other instances as well, reaching all the way back to when his father had died. The feelings of abandonment caused by his father's passing had left scars that might never heal.

A third rock bounced off the tree trunk a foot from the squirrel. The animal skittered to a higher perch where it resumed its tirade.

Mathias considered a fourth assault, but then dismissively gestured in the squirrel's direction and continued on his way to the studio. It was too hot to be a perfectionist, and besides, his aim just wasn't that good.

For a moment, he toyed with the idea of sneaking around to the front of the house and settling in beneath an open window. Still troubled by an uneasy feeling, he desperately needed to hear what his mother was telling her father. How else was a child supposed to gather information? Eavesdropping on adult conversations had proven enlightening on numerous occasions. The problem was that his mother hadn't delivered her warning as an idle threat; she had meant what she had said.

Sporting a scowl of frustration, he continued on. As his father had once said, "Sometimes discretion actually is the better part of valor."

Mathias opened the studio door and stepped inside. With all the windows closed, the room seemed even hotter inside than out. A fine layer of dust gave the interior a hoary look, like powdered sugar sprinkled on cookies or the first faint flurries of new snow. Keeping a pottery shed dust-free was virtually impossible, even for a woman with his mother's fastidious nature.

A variety of special racks filled the floor-to-ceiling shelves along one wall. Pegs in each rack had been precisely placed to accommodate a particular type of pottery—cups, dinner plates, saucers, bowls, mugs, platters, serving dishes, bread plates, etc. A number of racks were already filled with crockery, items to be delivered as part of his mother's latest order. On the table nearest the industrial-sized kiln, stacks of greenware waited to be glazed and fired.

Mathias noted a bulky mound of unformed clay centered on the potter's wheel. Normally the wheel was cleaned and serviced after each day's use. It appeared that his mother had been interrupted while fashioning something large, like a soup terrine or serving bowl.

Jake Reslin, Mathias's father, had begun constructing the studio even before adding the finishing touches to their house. His goal had been to create a workshop where he could design and assemble custom-made furniture. Ultimately, he had planned to supplement his logging income by marketing his creations online.

A collection of hand tools hung on pegboard hooks above the workbench in the far corner of the room. Along with a drill press, a radial arm saw, and a few power tools, they were all that remained of Jake's dream. The rest of his tools had been sold at auction so that Lauren could launch Clay Slinger Designs.

By default, the workbench and the surrounding floor space were Mathias's domain. His job was to repair, whenever possible, any mechanical devices that ceased to function. Both he and his mother had been pleased to discover that he had inherited his father's skill as a fix-it man.

Two stacks of nested five-gallon buckets stood beneath the workbench, seven buckets per stack. Mathias crossed the room in that direction. After freeing the top bucket from one stack, he added it to the other stack. Wrapping his arms around the nested buckets, he half waddled, half carried his load outside. Freeing the top two buckets, he placed them in an old-time Radio Flyer wagon, which he tugged toward Tanner's Creek. With the buckets empty, the wagon jostled and bounced along ruts laid down by innumerable trips.

Halfway to his destination, he realized that he would also need a shovel. Irritated because of his lack of foresight, he spit out a four-letter expletive that would have compelled his mother to box his ears. After retracing his steps, he entered the shed beside the studio where the gardening tools were stored. Shovel in hand, he resumed his trek.

When he again thought about his grandfather, Mathias realized he had no idea how to properly address his relative. Grandfather seemed too personal for a stranger he'd just met. Gramps was too mushy, Old Man too demeaning—as were Geezer, Scarecrow, and Old Fart. The only word that seemed to fit was his given name. Ward it would be then, and if he didn't like it, well…

As Mathias neared the creek, his thoughts returned to the nature of his grandfather's arrival. He set his mind to puzzle out an explanation as to why the empty driveway was devoid of any form of transportation. What seemed obvious was that Ward hadn't driven himself and then parked his vehicle away from Reslin land. It also seemed unlikely that his mother had picked him up from somewhere else and brought him home. If she had, she wouldn't have left him standing on the front porch while she pulled the truck into the garage. She was too polite by nature. Nor would there be a mound of clay hardening on the potter's wheel. She would've cleaned up before heading out to fetch him.

Someone could have given the old man a lift, brought him to the house, and then departed. To Mathias, that possibility seemed implausible because he hadn't passed any cars while pedaling home. In the same vein, Rockridge was too small to host a taxi service.

That meant Ward had walked, but from where? Certainly not from the regional airport the town shared with Flint. That would have entailed a twenty-mile hike. He could have come by train or by bus. There were terminals in town for both modes of transit. In either case, he still would have faced a five-mile slog on one of the hottest days of the year. The man just didn't seem that fit.

It was a puzzle, the kind most thirteen-year-olds would shun. Not Mathias.

Upon reaching the creek, he temporarily put the matter aside but promised himself he would take it up again when he had gathered more information.

Mathias positioned one of the plastic buckets beside the creek and began shoveling in scoops of mud. Each spadeful lifted from the riverbank made a sucking sound. Already perspiring from his quarter-mile trek, the exertion of filling the buckets evoked a torrent of sweat. In no time, the collar of his shirt, under his arms, and the areas around the small of his back were soaked.

Pausing, Mathias looked up at the sky. The sun had begun its descent toward the distant mountaintops. A faint breeze was beginning to stir. Perhaps the heat wave might break soon. One could hope.

On his final trip back to the studio, feeling tired and hungry and more than a little irritable, his mind turned once more to his grandfather. Why had the man come? What were his intentions? Goaded by a host of uncertainties, Mathias tried to visualize the future, but there were simply too many unknowns. As he tipped the wagon up against the studio's rear wall, the only thing that seemed certain was that his life was about to change in ways he could not foretell.

He washed the mud off his sneakers with a garden hose, careful to remove every last speck as he had been taught. When he entered the house, Ward and his mother were still seated in the living room. They fell silent when the screen door slammed shut.

From the kitchen, Mathias called out, "What's for dinner? I'm starving."

***

The screen door slammed as Mathias left the house to gather mud as his mother had requested. Seated in the easy chair, Lauren watched him hurl rocks at a squirrel before continuing along the flagstone path that led to the studio. For his sake, she hoped her son would heed her warning not to eavesdrop. She hated sending him out on such a hot day, especially on a task that could have waited till the cool of evening. Her father's unannounced arrival had virtually guaranteed that she would not resume crafting pottery that day or the next.

Ward sat quietly, having shifted his position hardly at all. She remembered him as being more robust, more muscular, and considerably more animated, though they had been apart for a long time—at least for her, it had seemed like a long time. Memories of how she and Jake had struggled to build a life together came to mind. She drove each one away in turn. At the moment, the last thing she needed was to succumb to nostalgia and lose her objectivity.

Lauren scanned the yard beyond the screen door, making certain that her son was out of earshot. She estimated he would be gone at least an hour. The distant timberline caught her attention.

For some, ten acres might seem like a sizable parcel of ground, and in many respects, it is. Reslin Ranch, as Jake had named the place, was large enough to feature regional variations in vegetation and topography. Pine trees stood as the dominant species, but larch, dogwood, poplar, and cottonwood grew here and there. A towering red maple guarded the sunny side of the house. The stately hardwood threw down shade in summer and a thick blanket of leaves in late fall. It usually fell to Mathias to rake the leaves into piles to be burned. She pictured her husband and her son toppling trees and pulling stumps to clear what was now their backyard. This memory too she hastily put away.

Turning again to her father, Lauren said in her best hostess voice, "How was your trip?"

"Long. It's a stretch riding from LA to Rockridge, even in an air-conditioned bus."

"You might've called when you got in. I would've picked you up."

"Thought about it, but I'd lost the letter you sent me, the one with your phone number and your address. There was a guy at the station.

Nice fellow. Fortunately, he knew where you lived. He gave me a lift partway, dropped me off about a mile out. I walked from there."

"I'm sorry you had to do that on such a hot day."

"It is hot. I'll grant you that."

"I'm pleased you got my letter. I wasn't sure you would. And I'm glad you're here."

"Are you?" Ward tilted his head and peered intently at his daughter.

"Yes, I am," Lauren declared decisively. "I think it's time we put the past behind us." Even as she spoke the words, she wondered if she'd be able, or was the gulf that separated them too wide? "So, tell me about yourself. What have you been doing these last…how long has it been?"

"Thirteen years, six months, and five days. I figured it on the way up. That's starting from the day you and your boyfriend took off."

"His name was Jake, and he was my husband."

"So I gather. He's dead, right?"

"Yes."

"How?"

"How did he die?"

Ward nodded an affirmation, though his facial expression remained unreadable.

"He lost his life in a freak accident. Montana's logging industry had hit a slump. Jake was having a hard time finding work. After consulting with some of our neighbors, he took off for the Bakken oilfields in North Dakota. One day, his employers sent him to Williston to check up on some parts they were expecting. Jake would have driven himself, but the power steering on his truck had just gone out. So he hitched a ride on an eighteen-wheeler. It had been raining hard for a couple days, and a huge boulder cut loose on their winding road. It happened in a place where there was a high cliff on one side and a steep ravine on the other. The boulder caved in one side of the semi. The driver tried to compensate, but the entire rig, cab and all, was pushed over the edge. The driver survived. Jake didn't."

"That was five years ago?"

"Yes. Mathias was eight. It was hard on him, losing his father. It was hard on both of us. As a family, we were just getting our feet on the ground."

"I'm sorry for your loss," Ward said flatly.

"Are you?" Lauren regarded her father. "Let's agree on one thing, shall we? We need to be honest with each other. Otherwise, there's no point in your being here. As I said in my letter, I want to put the past behind us. We can't do that if we're not open and honest."

"You want the truth? Fine. Maybe I didn't like Jake."

Lauren stiffened. "The reason you didn't like him is because you never got to know him."

"You never gave me a chance. You two eloped before I knew what was going on."

"You could have known…if you'd ever been home."

"I had a business to run."

"You had a mistress to cuddle!" Lauren forced herself to relax. "Sorry. I promised myself I wouldn't do that. I didn't invite you here so we could fight. I apologize. I'll try not to let it happen again."

"Apology accepted." Ward sat back and rested a hand on the couch's armrest. "What I was about to say is maybe I didn't like Jake, but I am sorry he died. Despite what you may think of me, you are my daughter and my only child. I care about your welfare, probably more now than when you were living at home. That's the truth. I guess people change when they have time to think. Besides, I know what it's like losing a spouse. Everything was different after Lily died. I do have some idea what you've been going through."

Lauren bit her tongue to keep from screaming at her father. There was no doubt in her mind that his infidelities had driven her mother to commit suicide. In fact, her father's repeated cheating was the main reason she had asked Jake to help her run away from home. How can any woman, even a daughter, live with a man she cannot trust, a man who tramples on his wedding vows, a man who treats his oath before God as nothing? Instead of lashing out, however, she glowered at her father and remained silent.

Ward, for his part, stared at the floor.

Lauren noted a look in his eyes that lasted but a moment. Yet in that brief interval, what she saw caused her to wonder, *Was he sincere? Had he truly felt the pain of losing someone he cared about deeply?* But then the look faded, and his expression again became placid.

Lauren stood up. "Let me freshen your ice water." Without waiting for a reply, she gathered up his glass and coaster from off the table. She carried them into the kitchen where she paused to regain her composure. This was going to be far more difficult than she had imagined. She despaired at the thought of continuing their conversation, but then remembered what was at stake.

After refilling her father's glass and adding several ice cubes, she wiped the coaster free of condensation. Carrying both, she returned to the living room to set them down on the coffee table in front of her father. Still standing, she gestured toward the backyard. "So, what do you think of your grandson? What's your first impression?"

Ward shrugged. "He seems okay—doesn't talk a lot."

"He can, once you get to know him. Anything else?" Lauren settled into the easy chair again and crossed her legs. Her denim jeans and sleeveless cotton blouse bore smudges of pottery dust, but then she hadn't been given time to change.

"He's not as stout as I thought he might be. Of course, I haven't known many thirteen-year-olds."

"He's just starting his growth spurt. He'll fill out."

"I assume his father had brown eyes?"

"He did. Mathias takes after his dad in a number of ways."

"It's obvious that you loved the man."

"I did," Lauren admitted flatly. Unwilling to continue down that path, she said, "Look, I hope this doesn't distress you or cause any offense, but there's something I need to ask. I heard that you were in prison for a time. Is it true?"

Ward's hand balled into a fist. When he caught himself, he flattened his fingers out on the arm of the couch. "Who told you?"

"I don't remember specifically." Lauren's shoulders lifted in an expression of uncertainty. "I think I found out a year or two after learning that Mom had passed away." Another old wound reopened. The news of Lily's tragic demise had been delivered via a third party months after her mother's passing, denying Lauren the opportunity to attend her funeral. There had been no closure, no chance to say goodbye, and for that, she blamed herself. True, she might have stayed in touch, but what would have been the point? Her mother's alcoholism had rendered every meaningful relationship unworkable.

But she also blamed her father. Lily had begun drinking only after learning of her husband's philandering. From a certain point of view, Lauren had lost two parents on the day her father's cheating had been revealed. She closed her eyes and fought back tears that were beginning to form.

"Yes, it's true," Ward acknowledged, his voice devoid of emotion. "As you probably already know, I spent eighteen months inside."

"For embezzlement?"

"That's right."

"And that's why your business failed?"

"Among other reasons."

"Such as…?"

"Let's say I lost interest—couldn't muster the motivation to keep the doors open. It's flattering to know you've been checking up on me."

"It seemed wise to understand the man you've become."

"Why? Filial affection?"

"Hardly."

"Ouch. I'm not sure I like this honesty gig. So why am I here? Your letter wasn't especially forthcoming."

"Before we get to that, there are a few more things I need to know." Lauren posed a series of pointed questions and received equally blunt answers. Ward's willingness to respond candidly impressed her. She remembered a time when he would've gotten up and stormed out of the room.

Her interrogation revealed that he had recently rented a one-room apartment in Santa Monica. Before that, he had spent half a decade living on the streets as a homeless person. She also learned that he now earned his living working in a supermarket as an apprentice grocery clerk. The work seemed trivial when compared with his once having owned a mortgage company and served as its chief executive officer. Also, she confirmed that he was in stable, though not excellent, health. Or so he claimed. As she sat facing him, she had her doubts. Most important of all, he had fulfilled his parole obligations and was currently free of any and all legal entanglements.

Ward eased forward on the couch and, for the first time, showed a modicum of curiosity. "All right, I've answered your questions. Now answer mine. What's going on? Let's have a little of that honesty. Why am I here?"

"You are here because I need you. More precisely, you are here because your grandson needs you."

"And why is that after all these years?"

"Because I'm dying." Lauren flinched at hearing herself speak the words aloud. "I only have a month to live, maybe two."

The screen door slammed shut. From the kitchen, Mathias called out to ask about dinner.

Lauren and Ward sat facing each other. In panicked silence, she raised an index finger to her lips and mouthed the words, "He doesn't know."

***

Feeling antsy and a little claustrophobic, Ward Stanford paced the floor in the guest room. Visible through the window, a shaft of late afternoon sunlight illuminated the towering mountain peaks. A reflected glow filled the room. He squinted against the glare and would have drawn the shade had his mind been less distracted.

Twice he had pressed his daughter for details about her medical condition, and twice she had refused to discuss the matter while her son was within earshot. Instead, she had shared interesting facts about Rockridge, not that he cared one whit about life in the Montana boondocks.

With the sleeve of his shirt, Ward mopped his brow against the stifling heat. When he tried opening the window, he found it was painted shut. Leaving the guest room door ajar seemed pointless; the rest of the house was sweltering as well. He wondered if there might be a fan available and briefly considered searching for one. He abandoned the idea when it occurred to him that although related by blood, he was a stranger. Scuttling room to room, poking about in cupboards and closets would seem like snooping.

Ward halted his pacing in the middle of the floor and looked around, having imagined himself back in prison, robotically tracking the limits of a six-by-eight cell. A shiver ran through him despite the heat.

Leaving the guest room to enter the living room and then the kitchen, Ward soon found himself out on the back porch, gazing out at a gathering sunset.

Why had he come? He wondered. What was the real reason? What could possibly have been his rationale? He rejected the notion that he had traveled such a far distance for sentimental reasons. He didn't know these people nor did he owe them a thing. Or did he? Was it guilt? Was that why he had opened Lauren's letter rather than toss it in the trash immediately?

A flash of movement at the edge of the forest startled him. The possibility that a bear might be nearby brought a moment of panic. He had heard terrible stories about grizzlies and their lethal ferocity. He reached for the screen door's handle to go back inside but relaxed when a yearling doe emerged from among the trees. The tawny animal peered at him with liquid brown eyes. The fawn seemed all neck and legs. *How could something so frail survive in such a rugged environment?* he wondered.

Ward waved his hand at the deer in an uncharacteristic show of empathy. The animal startled and disappeared into the forest so swiftly that, for an instant, he considered that maybe it hadn't been there at all. He looked for other deer but saw none. Was the yearling an orphan?

A tangential thought came into his mind so suddenly that he recoiled. What would it be like to raise another child? He had done such a ghastly job the first time.

The sound of truck tires crunching down the graveled driveway spared him further speculation. He reentered the house and stepped into the living room under the assumption that Lauren and his grandson would enter through the front door. Instead, they came into the kitchen by way of the screen door. "How was shopping?" he said, turning around to greet them.

Lauren set her groceries down on the table in the dining nook. "Exasperating. Sorry, we're running late. Sterling's was out of hamburger meat. We had to go to the Grand Feast. Then this one"—she tilted her head toward Mathias—"decides he needs hooks and worms to go fishing tomorrow. That meant a trip to the Best Shot, our local sporting goods store. Fortunately, we got there just before it closed."

"Going fishing, are you?" Ward said, primarily to make conversation. "Where?" He remained standing in the living room for fear of overcrowding the kitchen.

Mathias hefted the grocery bag he carried and then eased past his mother to set it down on the counter beside the sink. "Horse Collar Lake. It's in a saddleback valley partway up Starfall Mountain." He pointed out the window toward a far peak. "It's a hike, but it'll be cooler in the morning."

"You're going alone?" Ward's eyes narrowed. "Aren't you worried?"

"About?" A look of defiance spread across Mathias's face as if his masculinity had been challenged.

"Well, how about bears or poisonous snakes for that matter?"

"No way. We don't have poisonous snakes in Montana. Besides, Trent's going with me. We—"

"He'll be fine," Lauren interjected. "He's been fishing these parts since he was six. Jake took him the first couple years till he learned to fend for himself. Here"—she turned to her son—"deal with these." She fetched a package of fishhooks and a polystyrene container out of her grocery bag. She seemed unfazed that the worms had been resting atop the hamburger meat. "You might want to put those with your tackle box now so you won't forget them—again." Over her shoulder, she commented to Ward, "The last time they went up, they had to scrounge grubs and grasshoppers."

Disgusting, Ward thought, but he kept the comment to himself.

When Mathias left the room, Lauren moved toward the back door and crooked a finger at her father, summoning him to join her. Without opening the door, she pointed out through the screen. "See that tree there, the leafy one close to the garden? That is a pear tree. How would you like to pick a couple ripe ones so I can put them in our salad?"

"I can do that," Ward confirmed. He stepped outside.

As the screen door closed behind him, Lauren called out, "Try not to rile the bears. They leave such a mess."

"Real funny," he hollered back. Ward's rational mind told him there was no reason to worry. Still, he kept a sharp eye on the line of trees beyond the garden. As he plucked two pears that he guessed were ripe, he tried to bring to mind his daughter as a teenager. His recollections were fuzzy, but as far as he could remember, she had never displayed a morbid sense of humor. In fact, she had been a rather happy child, that is until—

Don't go there, he reminded himself sternly as he returned to the kitchen.

"Those will do." Lauren nodded as she accepted the pears from Ward's hand. "Now, if you'd be so kind, could you set the table?" She aimed her chin at the cupboard above the kitchen counter.

Ward took down three dinner plates. "Are we having bread?"

"No, but we are having dessert—apple pie."

He retrieved three dessert plates as well. "Cups, saucers?"

"Only if you want coffee with your meal."

"I'm good with whatever you're having."

"Water then. You'll find glasses in that cupboard." She pointed with the spatula in her hand.

Ward deposited the dinner plates on mats already on the table. The dessert plates he left on the side counter, figuring his daughter would divvy up the pie in the kitchen. After completing his task, he sat down in the chair that faced into the room. Out of habit, he kept his back to the wall. A moment later, he glanced down at the dinnerware to give the settings a closer inspection. "You made these, didn't you?" There was genuine admiration in his voice.

"I did. That's how I earn my living."

"They're beautiful." Individually hand-painted designs with rustic themes decorated each plate. "You have genuine talent. I especially like the earthen colors."

Lauren spun around to face her father. "Why are you being so polite?"

"I'm a guest. I thought it would be appropriate. Like you indicated earlier, I didn't come here to fight."

"You're making me nervous."

"Sorry. I can go back to being an asshole if you want."

"Watch your mouth," Lauren snapped. "We don't allow that kind of language in this house."

"Well, if I can't be polite and I can't be vulgar, what should I be?"

"Genuine."

"Fine, assuming I can remember how. So, what do you want to talk about? How about telling me—"

"When the time is right," Lauren interjected curtly.

"Right for what?" Mathias asked as he entered from the living room.

"Having dinner," Lauren responded brightly. "Grab your plate and build your own." She opened a package of buns and positioned them between the platter of hamburger patties and the platter with the sliced tomatoes, cheese, onions, and pickles. She fetched squeeze bottles of mustard and ketchup out of the refrigerator and set them on the counter as well. Next, she ladled a serving spoon into the pot of beans on the stove. "It's not fancy, but it'll fill you up. If there's anything you want but don't see, tough." She chuckled as if it was an inside joke.

Ward rose from the table and joined his grandson in the kitchen, where they began assembling their hamburgers.

Ward looked to his daughter. "Mayonnaise?"

She shook her head. "Forgot to get some."

"No worries." After scooping beans onto his plate, Ward returned to the table and sat down. He then waited until the others joined him. About to take his first bite of hamburger, Lauren stopped him by laying a hand on his forearm.

She smiled. "If you don't mind, I'll ask Mathias to say grace. If you would, son?"

"Sure." The boy bowed his head and closed his eyes. "Heavenly Father, thank you for this meal we are about to receive. Bless it to the nourishment of our bodies. Forgive us for whatever wrongs we have done, and lead us along the narrow path we are to follow. Amen."

"Nicely done," Lauren said supportively.

Ward added his own amen. Being polite again? He bit into his hamburger and tried to recall the last time he had prayed over his food. Giving up, he looked at his grandson. "I understand you had a birthday recently?" When he checked with his daughter for confirmation, he noted that her smile had faded. Why? Because he had spoken with his mouth full or for a more serious reason? He swallowed and added, "You're a teenager now, right?"

Mathias nodded with pride. "Thirteen."

"What did you get for your birthday?"

"A bicycle."

"The one you rode home on? Looks like a nice one."

"It's okay."

"Just okay?" Lauren exclaimed. She seemed hurt.

"No, Mom, it's cool. I like it, really—a lot."

"I should hope so. I got the best one I could afford."

"I know, and I love it. It's really neat. I mean it."

Ward focused his attention on his plate. Obviously, the kid had hoped for something else but would settle for what he had received. There were adults who would not have been so gracious. His opinion of the boy edged up a notch, but then he found himself at a loss. How do you talk to a teenager with whom you have absolutely nothing in common, especially one who considers you an intruder?

Returning his attention to his daughter, for the first time, Ward noted how pale she seemed. Maybe it was the light, or maybe he hadn't looked that closely before. No pink blush highlighted her lips and cheeks, and her skin had a sallow hue. While he was studying her features, a small drop of blood appeared beneath her right nostril. He caught her attention and tapped an index finger to his own nose.

Lauren immediately grabbed her napkin and pressed it to her face. In haste, she rose from the table and murmured, "Excuse me. Go ahead and eat. I'll be right back." Without hesitation, she fled from the kitchen.

Mathias watched his mother leave but said nothing.

Left alone with his grandson and feeling ill at ease, Ward ate his meal in silence.

CHAPTER 2

The next morning, Mathias awoke with his cell phone's alarm softly chirping in his ear. Forcing one eye open, he checked the time. His phone told him it was 5:00 a.m. He wondered if Trent was awake or if he would be late as usual. He considered closing his eyes and drifting off for a few minutes, but because he wanted to reach the lake as early as possible, he decided it would be better to wait for his friend rather than the other way round.

Outside, a purple glow silhouetted the serrated mountains. Mathias climbed out of bed and tugged on a pair of shorts, an old T-shirt, and tennis shoes suitable for hiking—his standard uniform in summer except on Sundays. Winters were a different matter when the thermometer dipped below zero and stayed there for a week. Although winters could be brutal, they were Mathias's second favorite season. He loved being out of doors when the world turned white and everything seemed clean and pure. Still, summers were better; there were more fun things to do.

A surprise greeted Mathias when he leaned close to the window and looked down. The ground was damp—evidence of an unexpected rainstorm during the night. A layer of gray clouds still hung in the sky, barely visible against the dawn. Not only would the day be cooler, but some of the best fishing was to be had right after a rainstorm when falling droplets knocked gnats and other flying insects into the water.

He moved to the corner of the room where he had stowed his fishing pole, tackle box, and the knapsack he had set out the night before. His knapsack contained items essential for tramping through the woods: folding knife, flashlight, whistle, compass, first aid kit, sunscreen, medium-duty rope, slip ties, matches, and lip balm. The polystyrene container that held the earthworms sat beside his pack. He popped the lid to make certain the dozen or so night crawlers were still alive. Satisfied, he carefully positioned the container in the bottom of his knapsack where it would not tip over.

Just in case, he grabbed a lightweight water-resistant jacket out of his closet. As he tiptoed downstairs, careful to avoid the steps that squeaked, he remembered something his dad had said: "In the woods, people get into trouble because they're too lazy to think ahead or too proud to imagine that something bad can happen to them."

At the foot of the stairs, Mathias paused to listen. He heard the faint sound of breathing, but could not tell if it came from the front of the house where his mother slept or the guest bedroom toward the rear. He continued on. His mother, being an early riser, might soon awaken, and he wanted to be gone before that happened. She would smother him with unwanted advice and bludgeon him with a litany of chores that needed doing when he got home.

In the kitchen, he slapped together a couple peanut butter and jelly sandwiches: one for himself, the other for Trent, who undoubtedly would forget to bring his own lunch. He also grabbed two apples, two granola bars, and a baggie of trail mix. After topping off his water bottle, he set out, careful not to let the screen door slam shut behind him.

An easy three-eighths-of-a-mile stroll separated the trailhead for Horse Collar Lake from the Reslins' front door. Mathias arrived at the rendezvous spot just as the first rays of dawn clambered above the eastern peaks. Shafts of hazy light collected in amber pools amid fallen pine needles. Trent was nowhere to be seen. Disappointed that his prediction had been confirmed, Mathias sat down on a gnarled log to wait, hoping his friend hadn't entirely forgotten the plans they had made.

A two-mile trek, most of it uphill, would take them to their favorite fishing spot. With his eyes, Mathias tracked the dirt path they were to follow until it disappeared into the surrounding forest. Like a compressed oval, Horse Collar Lake was flatter at one end than the other. An ancient glacier had gouged a thirty-acre hollow into the side of Starfall Mountain. The stream-fed lake was known for its exceptional fishing, especially in late summer, after its crystal clear water had warmed a bit.

A twig snapped. Mathias looked around to find Trent tiptoeing in his direction, still ten yards away.

"Yep," Mathias said. "One thing's certain. You ain't got an ounce of Indian blood in you."

"You say that like it's a bad thing." Trent sauntered forward to join his friend.

"You're late." Mathias bent down to retrieve the gear he had deposited beside the log. When he straightened up, he noticed an angry red welt beneath his friend's eye. Big as a half-dollar, the mark was already turning deep purple. "What happened to you?"

"Nothing."

"Pick a fight with a door?"

"I said it's nothing. Leave it be." Trent's rancor cut through the crisp morning air.

"No problem." Mathias settled his knapsack on his shoulders. "All right then. Let's be on our way." He cupped a hand behind his ear. "Hear that? A huge rainbow trout is calling my name."

Before starting off, Mathias made doubly sure the latch on his tackle box was securely fastened. On a prior trip, it had sprung open, spilling every lure, sinker, hook, and spinner onto the ground.

As they headed up the trail, he wondered about the bruise. He recalled Trent setting off to go swimming after their aborted soccer game. Maybe he had fallen or gotten into a fight. His friend could be like that when the mood took him. But the bruise looked too fresh. With no way of knowing for sure, he put the matter aside. Trent would tell eventually if he chose to.

By steadily pressing ahead, the two boys made good time. At the bend of a long switchback, they halted to take in the view. Standing on a yard-wide shelf, they gazed down on a remarkable panorama. The town of Rockridge lay nestled peacefully in the valley below. Morning light was just reaching the scattered rooftops. An older-model pickup rattled down Main Street, one of half a dozen vehicles already out and about. A wisp of smoke curled upward from one of many brick chimneys all the color of Lauren's earthenware mugs. Mathias wondered about the sanity of someone who would light a fire in the middle of August.

Since setting out from the trailhead, Trent had spoken hardly at all, but not from exhaustion. Neither boy was even breathing hard. As an only child—like Mathias—Trent could keep his own counsel when it suited him. He could also chitter away like a frenzied squirrel and often reminded Mathias of Rule 5: "Don't talk when you have nothing to say."

Jake Reslin had begun collecting rules even before his son was born. Lauren had added to their number over the years. Eventually, they had become known as Reslins' Rules. Mathias's favorite was Rule 7: "Never kick a grizzly unless you can run faster than the guy next to you."

The fluorescent lights inside the Best Shot Sporting Goods store flickered on. Mathias pointed. "Looks like Old Man Sullivan is getting a running start on his day."

Trent shifted his gaze and squinted. "You wouldn't believe how often that fool forgets to lock his back door."

"How would you know?" Mathias studied his friend's face.

A faint gust of wind tousled a lock of Trent's sandy-colored hair. He combed it away from his forehead with his fingers. "Because I've watched him leave and then tested the latch—more than once. I've even been inside."

"You didn't steal nothing, did you?"

"Not yet…"

"Weren't you afraid you'd get caught?"

"Nope. The light in the alley behind his store is burned out. Unless there's a moon, no one can see you."

"You're not thinking of robbing him?" Mathias said with incredulity. The notion seemed unimaginable.

"Why not if he's so careless? Why shouldn't I take advantage?"

"Because stealing is wrong."

"Who says?"

"The law says. So does the Bible. Come to church with us tomorrow. You can ask Rev. McAllister if you don't believe me."

His friend ignored the invitation, just as he had a number of times before. "According to the law," Trent said, "it's only wrong if you get caught. As for the Bible, you don't really believe all those fables and stuff, do you?"

"A lot of people do," Mathias declared defensively, although unsure how he truly felt. Both his parents had striven to impart their strong spiritual beliefs. As a result, he had been well schooled in the Scriptures but had not yet made a formal commitment of his own.

"Next time I go in, you could come with me." Trent eyed his friend as if to measure his grit.

"Like that's ever going to happen." Mathias collected his fishing pole and tackle box. "Let's go. I need to catch me some fish."

"Look," said Trent. "I'm only kidding. Okay? You need to lighten up." He fell in behind, spouting other words of denial and commenting on the fact that some people are truly gullible.

Mathias trudged up a stair-step incline and ignored his friend's chatter. Ahead, he recognized the stony crest where the trail would begin its descent toward the lake. They were nearly there.

A host of small coves serrated the shoreline of Horse Collar Lake. All were decent fishing sites, some better than others. Trent had his favorite. So did Mathias. Trent's was closest, so they decided to start there. The sun was in their eyes till they rounded the south end of the lake where the trail began to thin out and the forest became less dense. They continued on until they reached their destination.

A deep sigh of anticipation issued from Mathias's throat as he stood facing a rocky cove cut into the shoreline. Smartweed, sorrow grass, and a smattering of cattails grew in the water. Milkweed, manna grass, and wild iris sprouted along the shore. He turned around to check the terrain behind him. Twenty yards away, an avalanche chute had notched the hillside. Gray rocks, some the size of his head, littered the shallow gully. *Perfect*, he thought. Runoff from the rainstorm would have washed beetles and ants into the lake. The introduction of even a few insects would lure fish toward the shore.

A tree, its needles brown and starting to decay, lay on its side at the edge of the chute. *How much force*, Mathias wondered, *does it take to snap a Douglas fir clean in half?* Partway up the mountain, he noticed a shallow cave. "You don't suppose there's treasure buried around here, do you?"

"What kind of treasure?" Trent said without looking up from where he had squatted down. He scrunched up his mouth as he tied a hook on the end of his fishing line.

"Gold bars, rubies—diamonds."

"Pirate treasure?"

"Yeah."

"For real? Are you serious? Why would you think that?"

Mathias pointed to the cave. "Seems like a great place to stash some loot."

"Don't be stupid," Trent scoffed. "There ain't no pirates in Montana. Outlaws maybe, but not around here. They were east of the Rockies. Check it out if you think it's worth the trouble."

"No, you're probably right."

"Of course I'm right. By the way, you wouldn't care to place a friendly wager on today's fishing, would you?"

Mathias set about to prepare his own gear. "That would be foolish. You're a better fisherman than me." He knew his assertion was not true, but he had remembered Rule 10: "Never bet what you can't afford to lose." Falsely flattering his friend had seemed less traumatic than admitting his poverty. He fished an apple out of his backpack and tossed it to his companion.

Trent snagged the apple with one hand. "Well said. A man has got to know his limitations." As a fisherman, Trent's principal flaw was that he lacked patience. He would rather skip stones across calm water than sit quietly waiting for a strike.

Mathias looked up at the sky. The tracery of clouds left by the storm had finally dissipated. Above the trees, a translucent blue canopy arced high overhead.

"Gonna be another hot one," Trent commented, having looked up as well.

"Not as hot as yesterday," Mathias said hopefully. He knew that on really hot days, clawing through the forest could feel like slowly roasting to death. With care, he drew a new lure out of his tackle box and tied it onto the end of his fishing line, making doubly sure the knot was tight.

As if in anticipation of the heat that would soon descend upon them, Trent stripped out of his T-shirt. When he turned away to drape it over a low-hanging bough, Mathias noticed an angry red mark running diagonally between his shoulder blades. Like the bruise beneath his eye, the inch-wide stripe was also turning purple. The two injuries had to be related.

Mathias averted his gaze. A single wound could be explained away. Not two. He thought about telling his mother, but without knowing the facts, any meddling might do more harm than good. He decided to wait to see if he could ease Trent into a conversation later.

Hardly a ripple disturbed the lake's glassy surface. A hawk lazily soared above the trees. Mathias crept forward until he stood at the water's edge, as close as he could get without soaking his tennis shoes. After drawing back his fishing pole, he whipped it forward, slinging lure and line far out into the lake. Without hesitating, he began slowly turning the reel's handle at precisely the right speed to seduce a hungry trout.

Mathias startled when a second splash sounded nearby. Something small and flat had hit the water. His first impression was that Trent had begun skipping rocks. His second impression was that a fish had broached the surface, but there were too few ripples. His third guess was that Trent had cast his own line, but out of the corner of his eye, he saw that his friend was still fiddling with his gear.

A series of concentric wavelets expanded outward from the bay to the north. The ripples announced that they were not alone.

Like most fishermen, Mathias preferred to fish by himself or with a single companion. He would grudgingly share a lake with others, but only if he knew who they were and where they were. Every schoolkid had heard campfire stories about the weirdos who live in the north woods.

After reeling in his line, Mathias retreated toward the mouth of the ravine. He lay his fishing pole down beside his tackle box. Signaling Trent to be quiet and stay put, he slipped forward one step at a time, careful to avoid brittle twigs and loose stones. Advancing cautiously, he reached a spot where he could peer between the trees. At first, he couldn't see clearly, but after shifting sideways, he recognized a boy he knew from school.

Mathias breathed a sigh of relief. It appeared that he wasn't on the verge of being slain by a deranged backwoods maniac after all. He also felt a sense of disappointment. The lad was a year younger and not very popular—not the sort you want to hang with. For a time, Mathias stood motionless and waited. The boy gave no indication that he was aware he was being watched.

Again moving slowly so as not to make a noise, Mathias returned to where Trent waited. He drew close enough that he could whisper. "It's Fat Abe," he confided, his voice barely audible. "I don't think he knows we're here." When he thought about it, he realized that his assumption was probably wrong, unless Abraham Finkel was both deaf and blind as well. Surely they must have been observed on the trail or at least overheard. Sound waves travel huge distances over water. So why hadn't Fat Abe greeted them? Perhaps the boy treasured his solitude as much as they did.

"Fat Abe?" Trent exclaimed, making no effort to keep his voice down. "How the hell did he get all the way up here?"

Good question, Mathias thought. For a young kid, Abe was huge. Mathias recalled steep stretches of trail that climbed the side of the mountain, rugged enough to challenge even seasoned hikers. As he turned away to gather up his gear, he tried to picture how hard Abraham must have struggled.

"Where're you going?" Trent said.

Mathias halted and returned to where he had been standing. "Keep your voice down."

"Why?"

"I don't want him thinking he can join us. If he hears us talking, he might feel like he has to be neighborly. Come on. We can find a spot farther away."

"Hell no. Let's go see if he's caught any fish." Trent headed off through the woods, leaving his fishing pole and tackle box where they lay.

Mathias abandoned his gear as well, having perceived that they weren't about to resume fishing anytime soon. He hurried to catch up.

Abraham startled as the two boys burst out of the woods. He looked around as if searching for an escape route.

"Hey, fatso," Trent bellowed, "catch any big ones?" He spread his hands wide apart, more than twice the length of even the largest record-setting trout.

"No," Abraham scoffed as if the notion were ridiculous. Aware of Trent's scrutiny, he seemed to grow increasingly nervous and more than a little frightened. For a moment, Mathias wondered if Abe and Trent had crossed paths before.

"Really?" Trent's voice dripped sarcasm. "You must not be much of a fisherman. What are you using for bait?" He stepped forward.

"Grubs." Abraham backed away defensively and cast a glance at the cardboard box sitting on a flat rock nearby.

"Grubs?" Trent sneered. "There's your problem. Nobody fishes with grubs. Didn't you know that?" He tracked Abraham's gaze till he caught sight of the shoebox. With a tight smile, he moved forward to retrieve it. "You up here alone, fat boy?"

Too frightened to speak, Abraham shook his head.

"Don't lie to me," Trent bellowed.

There was no response.

"You are, aren't you? You are alone." Trent snatched up the shoebox and ripped off its lid, which he roughly cast aside. He stared directly at Abraham. "Aren't you?"

Sheepishly, Abraham nodded.

Mathias remembered that other children tended to tease Abraham as much for being shy as for being fat. Come fall, Abe would enter the eighth grade, and though he outweighed Trent by forty pounds, in a fight, he wouldn't have stood a chance. Trent was stronger, faster, and more agile.

It seemed Fat Abe had calculated the odds as well.

"Come on, Trent," Mathias pleaded. "Let's get to fishing. It's not like we've got all day. I have chores waiting at home, and Fat Abe here hasn't done us any harm."

"Relax, dude. I'm just trying to help. Has to be a reason why he hasn't caught any fish." Trent began poking around in the shoebox but then abruptly tipped it over, spilling its contents onto the ground. Trent looked up with exaggerated regret. "Hey, man, I'm sorry. Let me help you pick your stuff up." As he bent down, his foot came forward, scattering hooks and sinkers into the piney underbrush and knocking other bits of tackle here and there. "Damn, I am so clumsy." He gave another swipe with his foot.

Driven by a rush of sympathy, Mathias stepped forward. "There was no call to do that."

Trent faced his friend and held his hands out, palms up. "Hey, I said I was sorry." He surged past Mathias to snatch the fishing pole out of Abraham's grasp. "Maybe this is your problem." He held the pole up and inspected it end to end. "Yep, that's what I thought. You can't catch fish with a dry pole." In one swift motion, he tossed the pole into the lake. It promptly disappeared below the surface. With a menacing glower, he turned to face Abraham. "Go get it, fat boy."

"Enough!" Mathias exclaimed. "Leave him alone." He sprang forward. Before Trent could follow through with whatever he had intended, Mathias had placed himself directly in the line of fire.

Trent hesitated. The two boys had roughhoused and tussled on previous occasions, testing each other's strengths and weaknesses. After all, what are friends for? But they had never actually come to blows, which raised an interesting question: Who would win? The answer seemed unclear to both of them.

When Trent saw that his companion was serious, the look on his face lost some of its hostility. In its place, a look of amazement emerged. "You're not standing up for this kike, are you? I don't believe it."

"Look, man, I know you're upset. You haven't been right all morning. That doesn't mean you should take it out on Fat Abe. Why don't we forget about fishing for today? Looks like it's going to be hotter than we thought. All the fish will head to deep water."

Trent stood quietly for a moment, as if trying to make up his mind about how to handle the situation. For a space, it seemed he might actually take a swing at his friend.

Mathias tensed his muscles and stood ready, having perceived that if he were to back down, things could get really ugly. So he waited.

"I don't believe this." Throwing up his hands, Trent turned and stalked off, shaking his head. A string of expletives trailed in his wake.

Mathias stayed where he was and watched him go. When he and Fat Abe were alone, he stripped off his T-shirt, slipped out of his tennies, and pulled off his socks. He then began unbuttoning his pants.

"What are you doing?" The quaver in Fat Abe's voice indicated that he was more than a little shaken.

"Can you swim?"

Fat Abe shook his head.

"That's what I thought."

Wearing only his undershorts, Mathias waded into the lake. The water was colder than he had expected. Gritting his teeth, he ducked below the surface and dove toward the spot where he thought the fishing rod had landed. On his third try, his fingers closed on its cork handle. He hauled the pole to shore. That's when he noticed that the rod and reel looked expensive and were certainly in better condition than his own.

Mathias returned the fishing pole to its owner. "You might want to oil everything down so it doesn't rust."

"Thank you," was all Abe said. Clearly, he felt embarrassed.

What would it be like, Mathias wondered, *being physically incapable of defending yourself?* "You'd best stay away from Trent for a while." He slipped into his pants without waiting for his legs to dry. Then he sat on a rock and tugged on his socks and shoes.

When he looked up, Fat Abe was on his hands and knees, salvaging what tackle he could find. He didn't speak as Mathias walked away. It seemed he was trying to pretend that nothing had happened.

Mathias kept walking, slipping on his T-shirt as he went. It stuck to his skin as he pulled it over his shoulders. As he drew near the avalanche chute, he noted that both Trent and his gear were gone. His own stuff, however, was exactly as he had left it, and for that, he felt a measure of gratitude. Apparently, Trent's hostility had not compelled him to lash out and damage someone else's property other than Abe's. That suggested there might be a chance they could salvage their friendship.

Struggling with feelings he found hard to identify, Mathias decided to head for home. The thought of fishing alone had lost its savor.

Downheartedly, he made his way along the trail as it curved around the south end of the lake. At a spot where the trees opened up, he could see the shoreline. He stopped to admire the glimmering expanse of icy blue water. *What a wasted morning*, he thought, but then recalled something his mother had once said about how everything fits together. He resolved to puzzle out how recent events were connected. Yet by the time he finally regained the trailhead, he was still a long way from recognizing the fragile bonds that joined cause to effect.

***

Ward Stanford lay in bed and stared at the ceiling. His body ached in diverse places as if he had endured a mugging several days before.

The guest bedroom was directly below Mathias's room. Half an hour earlier, Ward had awakened to the sound of his grandson getting dressed and gathering his fishing gear. Always a light sleeper, Ward's sensitivity to strange noises had intensified during his homeless years. After having been robbed on several occasions, he had learned to sleep with one eye open to protect what little remained.

When Mathias had finally set out to go fishing, Ward had curled up on his side in hopes of getting some additional shut-eye but was again awakened when Lauren had begun her morning routine. In short order, she too had headed outside. With the house silent once more, he had again tried to sleep but was too keyed up.

Finally acknowledging that he was awake, Ward rolled out of bed, planted both feet on the floor, and stood up. With his vision still clouded by sleep, he looked out the window. For a moment, it seemed that the gathering dawn had set the eastern horizon ablaze. The glorious sunrise was not at all the same as when morning light cascades off the tops of downtown skyscrapers.

He attempted to guess the time. Lacking a watch, all he could deduce was that it was ridiculously early. "Good lord," he muttered in a graveled voice, "I've traveled thirteen hundred miles to live with crazy people."

When it occurred to Ward that what he really wanted was a cigarette, he reached for the pack he habitually kept at the bedside. When his hand came away empty, he recalled that he hadn't been able to find his smokes the night before either. He suspected Lauren had covertly tossed them.

Scratching sundry places that itched, he resigned himself to his fate and set about to begin his day.

Feeling somewhat better after having showered and shaved, Ward finished dressing. Now fully alert, he left his room. As he moved through the living room, he thought about the luxury of sleeping in a real bed, a thing most people take for granted. After being released from prison, he had spent five years burrowing in between dumpsters, shivering over steam grates, or hunkering down under bridges and overpasses. After finally pulling himself together, he had landed a menial job at minimum wage. His earnings barely covered the rent he paid on his studio apartment above a garage. In truth, the place was a hovel, but it had a bed.

In the kitchen, Ward set about scrounging breakfast. After checking the refrigerator and finding nothing ready to eat, he elected to wait. Besides, he wasn't particularly hungry. Maybe the family would gather for brunch. Surely he could wait that long. At least Lauren had brewed a fresh pot of coffee. He poured himself a cup. Standing by the counter near the sink, he gazed out the kitchen window.

The lights were on in the pottery shed. He assumed that was where Lauren had gone. He headed outside to investigate. The scent of pine trees filled the air as he walked the flagstone path.

Lauren sat in front of a spinning potter's wheel. She wore a workman's apron over her jeans and pale blue cotton blouse. The apron's coarse material covered her torso from her shoulders to just below her knees. Pitched forward at the waist, her hands circled a glistening lump of ocher-colored clay, molding it into something that was as yet unrecognizable.

"Good," Lauren said as her father entered the shed. "You're up. I was beginning to wonder."

"What time is it?" Ward stepped fully into the room. The door swung shut behind him.

"You don't have a watch?"

"I pawned it years ago." He looked around as he tried to stifle a yawn. The room seemed to have been divided into different work areas, each with its own special function. Pottery items in various stages of completion crowded most of them. "You've got quite a little enterprise going."

"It puts food on the table."

"Speaking of which…"

Lauren glanced up. "If you're hungry, fix it yourself. I don't have time."

"That's no way to treat a guest," Ward declared lightheartedly so as not to give offense.

"Yesterday you were a guest. Today you're family."

"You sure about that?"

Lauren paused a moment to consider her response. "Biologically speaking, absolutely. Growing up, there were times when I fervently prayed it wasn't true, but Mom convinced me otherwise. From a relational point of view, I guess the jury is still out. I sincerely hope we can make this work. The fact that you are here counts for a lot."

A tall stool stood in the corner diagonally opposite where Lauren shaped her clay. Ward crossed the floor in that direction. As he passed by one of the workstations, he reached out to touch a muddy-looking plate, one of a dozen arrayed in rows on the well-used table.

"Don't touch that," Lauren snapped. "That's greenware. It hasn't been fired yet. You can break it by staring at it sideways."

"Sorry." Ward sat on the stool and drew up one leg. "What are those?" He pointed to a different workstation where a line of earthenware cups reminded him of small flowerpots.

"Bisqueware."

"Sorry, I don't know that word."

"Bisqueware is clay pottery that's been through its first firing. *Bisque* is French, I think. It means 'biscuit'—has to do with the rough porous texture pottery gets before it's glazed."

"I see. You learn something new every day." Ward watched his daughter's fingers deftly shape the clay. Her movements were precise and her skill undeniable. In no time at all, she had transformed the featureless lump into an elegant dinner plate. Pausing occasionally, she moistened her hands so the mud wouldn't stick. With a long caliper, she measured the plate's diameter and then used a craftsman's knife to trim the edge by an eighth of an inch.

"How long did it take you to learn your trade?" Ward swept a hand in an arc, indicating the studio.

Lauren straightened up and flexed her lower back. "I took it up not long after Jake and I bought this place." She set to work again. "Pottery was a hobby at first. After Jake died, I had to do something to make a living." She dipped a sponge in the bucket at her side, then she squeezed out the excess water. With care, she drew the sponge across the plate's surface, wiping away imperfections. "This studio used to be his workshop. His intention was to make lodgepole furniture. I converted it into what you see now. Before that, I had to drive into town to the pottery shop where I took my first lessons."

"Obviously, you must have been paying attention." Ward wondered how he would have fared under similar circumstances, having pretty much failed at everything he had ever attempted. He had stolen money from his own business and driven it into bankruptcy. He had cheated on his wife and ruined their marriage. He had so thoroughly ignored his only child that she had cast him out of her life. Until now.

"So…?" Ward adjusted his perch on the stool to take the pressure off knobby places on his pelvic bone. In the last few months, he had regained some, but not all, of the weight he had lost while living on the street. "You want to tell me about this dying gig you got going on now that we're alone?"

Lauren heaved a deep sigh. Her pained expression made clear how desperately she wished to avoid what she knew was coming. "Very well, but let me finish what I'm doing before we get into it."

Ward waited while Lauren drew a thin wire beneath the plate, separating it from the throwing wheel. The wire had handles on either end like a garrote. With care, she slid a broad flat potter's rib under the plate so she could transfer it to the greenware table. Ward noted her hands were smeared with mud, some of which was already dry.

Crossing the room again, Lauren picked up the bucket beside the throwing wheel. "I'll be right back." She stepped outside. When she returned, her hands were clean, and there was fresh water in the bucket. She set it down and turned to face her father. "What do you want to know?"

"Let's start by telling me what's going on. You send me a letter inviting me to get reacquainted, but you don't mention why. When I arrive, you greet me as if I have leprosy, which is understandable given our history. Next, you introduce me to this scrawny kid and tell me he's my grandson."

Lauren stiffened.

Ward held up a hand. "Relax," he said soothingly before she could protest. "I realize he hasn't started his growth spurt, and one day he'll fill out. That's not the issue. The problem is the kid looks at me like I have a third eye in the middle of my forehead, which is also understandable, I suppose. But then you tell me that you're dying, except there's no emotion, no tears, nothing. It's like you're ordering pizza. And looking at you now, you seem tired but not terminal. Is it any wonder I'm skeptical? So fill me in. What makes you think you're dying? What's your diagnosis?"

"I haven't been to see the doctor."

"Really?" Ward exclaimed with amazement. "Then how—"

"Because I know. All right? I can feel it. I can't sense how long I have, but it will be soon."

"You don't feel well, so you think you're dying—"

"I know I'm dying. There's a difference."

"How do you know? Did you have a dream? Did you read your symptoms in a book? Did you consult a palm reader?"

"Don't you dare mock me."

"Sorry. I didn't mean for it to come out like that. Tell me then, how do you know?"

"You won't believe me."

"I might."

"The Holy Spirit told me," Lauren declared evenly.

"The Holy Spirit? You can't be serious."

"See. I told you." Lauren chewed her lower lip in frustration. "Look, I don't expect you to understand, but I do expect you to consider the possibility that what I'm saying is true."

"Are you telling me that God Almighty spoke to you in person?"

"Through His Spirit, yes. That's exactly what I'm saying."

Ward found himself at a loss for words. He stared out the window at the garden fence. A moment later, he refocused his attention on his daughter. "All right, let's assume for the sake of argument that I do believe you. What is it you want from me?"

"I want you to get to know your grandson."

"Very well, let's say I can do that. What then?"

"I want you to promise me that you'll raise him as your own, but this time you'll do a far better job than you did with me."

Ward shook his head and then stared at his daughter in disbelief. "You expect me to become Mathias's parent?"

"His legal guardian. I've already drawn up the papers. All you have to do is file them with the court after I'm dead."

"Are you crazy?" Ward tugged on an earlobe. "So what if he's my grandson? You think I'm fit to raise a teenager at my age?"

"Surprisingly, I do. Because you must. You're the only family he'll have. There is no one else. Besides, you owe me for the life I never had, or have you forgotten?"

"I haven't forgotten. There's not a day that goes by that I don't regret driving you away."

Lauren intently studied her father. "I hope you mean that. If you do, here's your chance to make up for being a lousy dad—to do something worthwhile for a change."

Ward shifted his position on the stool. "I don't know what to say. This all seems too unreal. I need time to think."

"You can have as much time as will be given to me. Look, if there were any other way, you wouldn't be here. I know this is unsettling—"

"Unsettling? The word hardly comes close to describing how I feel."

"One more thing. It's essential that you raise your grandson as a Christian."

"Me? You know I'm not—"

"I know." Lauren sighed. "Maybe we should take this one step at a time. For now, how about getting to know Mathias? He's a good kid. He'll warm up to you if you give him half a chance."

"What do you suggest?"

Lauren's feeble smile indicated that their conversation was going about as she had expected. "Spend time with him. Hang out together. Learn what he likes and doesn't like. You know, be his friend."

"I don't have friends," Ward admitted.

"Then it's time you learned how."

"I'll think on it." Ward stood and headed for the door. In his heart, he sensed that he would rather be anywhere else than in Podunk, Montana, being challenged by a daughter with whom he was only beginning to get reacquainted.

"One more thing." Lauren grasped her father's forearm as he passed by. "While you're living under our roof, we will expect you to be part of this family."

"Meaning?"

"You'll need to pull your weight. For starters, you can weed the garden. There's a hoe in the toolshed. Just dig up anything that doesn't look like food."

"This is all a colossal joke, right?"

Lauren stared at her father. The resolve in her eyes left no doubt that she was absolutely serious.

***

The Reslins' pickup rolled slowly down Main Street, with Lauren driving just under the speed limit. The family was on their way to church. With over 180,000 miles on the odometer, the nine-year-old truck was showing its age. Mathias held the middle position on the bench seat. Ward, having called shotgun, sat closest to the passenger-side door. All three wore their Sunday's finest, which for Ward had meant putting on a clean pair of slacks and his only dress shirt. He owned neither a sport coat nor a tie.

The truck glided past a patchwork of Western-style buildings as it cruised through the middle of town. Virtually every retailer was shuttered for the Sabbath. Ward noted only two establishments that were open for business: the Tall Timbers Tavern and the Leaky Canoe, Rockridge's only sit-down restaurant. *Is there some Montana law*, he wondered, *that mandates the use of quirky names?* Of course, he had christened his own enterprise Respectable Mortgage, not realizing how ironic the name would seem when his firm was ultimately shuttered due to bankruptcy.

More than a few of the buildings they passed looked to be in poor repair, leaving Ward to wonder about the town's financial health.

"That's Regford Park," Lauren commented, pointing to an expanse of lawn. Flat at the front, the five-acre park rose in a slight incline toward the back. Here and there, the August heat had withered patches of grass. In comparison, mature trees populated a verdant area along the side of the park. Leafy foliage shaded picnic tables and metal fire rings useful for either barbecues or campfires. Near the entrance to a small parking lot, a lacquered sign with engraved lettering declared "Reginald Fordyce Memorial Community Park." Ward chuckled under his breath. No wonder common usage had shortened the park's name.

Lauren continued. "That's where the town holds its Independence Day picnic. Festivities start right after the parade and last all day. At night there's fireworks and dancing."

"Do you dance?" Ward asked and then cringed. Having intended an innocent question, he had inadvertently asked if she was actively dating.

"I used to when Jake was with us," Lauren responded, simultaneously answering both the direct and the implied questions.

Ward noted the wistful expression on his daughter's face. He looked more closely, as he had often done over the past twenty-four hours. The telltale signs of fatigue could be easily explained: she was a single mom, the sole breadwinner, and the only adult holding a rural homestead together. No wonder she seemed tired. Her pallor was also understandable. Lily, her mother, had been fair skinned. In fact, Lily's ivory complexion had been one of the first things to attract Ward's attention.

"We run in the three-legged race every year, Mom and me," Mathias volunteered.

"Mom and I," Lauren corrected.

"Right. We almost won last year." It was the first time the boy had spoken since leaving home.

"Is that right?" Ward responded brightly. "A three-legged race. Isn't that where you tie your legs together and…" With two fingers, he made a running gesture.

His grandson gave an ambivalent nod and resumed watching the road ahead.

Lauren had insisted that they go to church—the three of them together, like a real family. Ward had struggled to find an excuse to refuse, but she had overridden his every objection. Rather than escalate their disagreement into a contest of wills, he had discreetly relented. To his dismay, he was learning that his daughter could be incredibly strong-willed.

"Tell me something, Dad," Lauren said.

Mathias startled and looked at his mother as if amazed that she would address them in such a fashion.

"Why are we here?" Lauren continued, ignoring her son's implied commentary.

"Here we go…" Mathias mumbled under his breath. He kept his eyes fixed on the road ahead.

"Because we're on our way to church," Ward responded. "This was your idea, remember?"

"No, I mean why do we exist? Any of us? More than that, why are we aware of our own existence? I guess what I'm asking is, What's the purpose of life, in your opinion?"

"All life?" Ward said.

"Human life." Lauren turned her face toward the side window to wave at an elderly gentleman walking in the same direction they were headed. The old man smiled broadly and waved back. Dressed in a suit and tie, he too looked to be on his way to church. "It's good to see Mr. Tolliver up and around. He's had a rough go after his prostate surgery. I'd offer him a lift, but I doubt he'd be comfortable riding in the back."

The man's attire caused Ward to suddenly feel underdressed. "Your question presupposes that life has a purpose. I'm not sure it does."

"Perhaps you're right," Lauren said, "but it's hard to imagine that we're the result of some cosmic accident. I think most people believe there's a reason we are the way we are."

Ward nodded thoughtfully. "Maybe." He then wondered something that gave him pause. *A conversation dealing with existence. Was this her subtle way of introducing the notion she might not be alive much longer?* She had made it clear she would be the one to tell her son when the time came. Ward had happily agreed since he still had his doubts. And that Holy Spirit business—how was he supposed to deal with that?

Another thought struck him. Of all the topics she might have chosen and all the questions she could have asked, why that particular one? There were so many issues of greater importance. Debating the purpose of life seemed detached from reality. He was beginning to suspect his daughter might be mentally unbalanced.

"It's something I've been thinking about," Lauren volunteered as if reading his mind. "For a long time actually."

"And what are your conclusions? Want to share your insights?"

"Not yet. I'm sure you're aware it's not a trivial question. Give the matter some thought. Work out your own philosophy. Maybe we'll talk after the sermon, or perhaps tomorrow, or whenever. By the way, son, did you remember to invite Trent to church?"

"I did."

"And…? What did he say?" Lauren downshifted as they closed on a stop sign, grinding the gears a little. "Sorry."

"I'm pretty sure he won't be coming."

"You two have anything planned for this afternoon?"

"Nope."

Ward could tell his grandson was holding back. Perhaps he could get the lad to open up later—or perhaps not.

As he pondered how to gain the trust of a resentful thirteen-year-old, he stared off into the distance. Then two blocks ahead, he recognized what he assumed must be the Rockridge Gospel Fellowship. A gold cross glittered atop its squat steeple. Quarried stone covered the church's outside walls to the level of the windows. From there, wood siding, painted white, extended upward to the shingled roof. The stones caught the morning light and threw it back in shades ranging from dark honey to coffee bean brown to slate gray. The double doors at the front of the sanctuary stood open. They looked to have been sculpted out of aged mahogany. The tops of the doors were arched, like the entrance to a cathedral. Individual panels depicted biblical scenes.

Ward was impressed. Someone with serious wood-carving skills had devoted considerable time and effort to their creation. The ornate doors seemed radically out of place for a humble sanctuary stuck out in the boondocks.

Lauren parked the truck and escorted her family inside. A number of people greeted her by name. She responded in kind, often adding a personal salutation or word of encouragement. Fewer spoke to Mathias. Fewer still acknowledged Ward, who found it interesting that only twice had his daughter introduced him as her father—but perhaps that was because there was little time to gab. The choir was on its feet.

The Reslins chose a pew toward the rear of the church but remained standing. Lauren and Mathias retrieved hymnals from the rack attached to the back of the pew in front of them. Ward clasped his hands behind his back.

Wearing a white robe with purple trim, the pastor smiled down at his congregation from the dais. Behind him, a simple altar draped with white linen bore an empty cross. Bouquets of flowers in standing baskets were positioned to either side. A row of tall windows, also with arched tops, extended along the exterior wall to the east. The window's glass was stained a rich golden yellow. The light streaming in gave the appearance that the church's interior had been filled with honey. The mood inside the sanctuary was both serene and uplifting. Ward felt moved as he recalled his years as a vagrant. No wonder people sought spiritual refuge in such poignant settings.

***

After church let out, Ward stood facing the refreshment table, an empty paper plate in one hand, a cup of strong coffee in the other. He sipped the coffee while deciding which delicacies to sample. The ladies' auxiliary had set out banana nut bread, pound cake, cookies, and a platter of Danish pastries cut into bite-sized squares. Lauren had insisted that they mingle with other members of the church community.

Feeling awkward and unsociable, Ward had objected but once again had been overruled, which he later decided wasn't entirely bad. Homeless people, as a rule, generally don't snack on banana nut bread or oatmeal raisin cookies. Neither do minimum-wage grocery clerks.

A small lawn bordered the church. A covered walkway extended along one of its sides. On the opposite side of the lawn, a low brick fence paralleled the sidewalk and the street beyond. The refreshment table had been set up in the corner of the lawn nearest the church. Ward selected four items. He would have taken more, except he planned on going back for seconds. Stuffing a morsel of Danish into his mouth, he turned around just in time to bump into the pastor, the Rev. Thaddeus McAllister.

"Excuse me," Ward mumbled.

Lauren stepped forward to stand at the pastor's side. She gave her father a warning look as she said, "This is someone I'd like you to meet."

Ward tried desperately to swallow while his daughter conducted the introductions. When the pastor extended his hand, Ward realized his fingers were sticky. Hastily, he wiped them clean on his pant leg. "Pleased to meet you," he said after taking a sip of coffee. He coughed when the hot liquid trickled down his windpipe.

"Likewise." Rev. McAllister fashioned a beneficent smile. "You can call me Thaddeus or Thad. Most people do." The pastor's hazel eyes measured Ward in the way a carpenter might evaluate a length of wood that needs trimming. The man had an oblong face with ears that rode unnaturally low on the sides of his head. His large incisors tended to poke out from beneath his upper lip. When he sniffed, his nose crinkled. Altogether, he reminded Ward of a bunny rabbit, except his demeanor was more outgoing.

"Welcome to our humble tabernacle." He gave Ward's hand another hearty shake before letting go.

"It was a fine sermon," Ward declared, mainly for his daughter's benefit. Had a pop quiz been handed out, he definitely would have flunked. He tried to resurrect a few specifics in case the reverend asked what parts he had liked best. He found it difficult to recall even one.

It occurred to Ward to wonder if his daughter might have told the pastor about her premonition. Had she confided her belief that she was doomed? He was, after all, her spiritual guide.

"Are you a man of faith?" Thaddeus said.

"Faith in what?" Ward replied innocently.

The pastor gave a burbling laugh. Lauren looked away, embarrassed.

Ward chuckled too, mostly to hide his confusion. Judging by his daughter's response, he had committed a serious faux pas. Problem was, he wasn't exactly sure how.

"We can work on that." Thaddeus's eyes narrowed shrewdly. "Will you be in town long?"

"I don't know," Ward answered truthfully.

Lauren shot her father a determined look, leaving no doubt as to her position on the matter. In return, Ward shrugged. It was his way of conveying that honesty was the best policy.

"Well," Thaddeus said, "if you're still in the neighborhood, we'll expect to see you next Sunday. In the meantime, if you have questions or feel the need to talk, I'm available." The clergyman opened the front of his robe to fish a business card out of his shirt pocket. He handed it to Ward. "Give me a call."

"Perhaps I will." Ward wondered if he had just been invited to discuss his daughter's condition in private.

The ride home unfolded in much the same fashion as the ride into town, except that Lauren had stumbled and nearly fallen while getting into the truck. For a time, she had gripped the door handle tightly, as if unable to regain her balance.

***

A horsefly the size of a bumblebee buzzed around Ward's head. He repeatedly swatted it away but missed each time. When it landed on his bald spot, he tried again, but the insect was simply too fast. He wound up slapping himself on the back of the head like a parent disciplining a misbehaving child. A dozen paces ahead, his grandson laughed.

For more than an hour, they had trekked the meandering path that paralleled Tanner's Creek. To Ward, the surrounding underbrush looked exactly the same as where they had started. He had the odd impression they were tramping in place rather than walking in circles.

Ward harbored no illusions as to how he had come to his current predicament. Mathias may have extended the invitation, but the idea to send the two males out on a hike had been Lauren's from the beginning—a chance for her father to get to know his grandson. So far, her plans didn't seem to be working out very well.

"Come on, it's only a little farther." Mathias disappeared into a thicket.

"That's what you said twenty minutes ago." Ward redoubled his efforts to keep up. The cooling trend promised by the brief rainstorm two nights before had failed to materialize, and the heat wave had settled in again.

At a place where the trail crossed Tanner's Creek, Ward inadvertently stepped in a patch of mud. When he lifted his leg, the suction nearly tore his shoe off his foot. *Splendid*, he thought. *How would it look losing one of the new tennies my daughter paid for because I was out of money?* She had also purchased a pair of denim jeans, two work shirts, and a baseball cap. Putting on the cap with its imprinted logo, Ward had felt like a walking advertisement for the Seattle Seahawks. During their shopping expedition, he had discovered he truly disliked having someone else pay for his clothes, especially when they insisted on counting the cost down to the last penny.

Upon gaining the stream's far bank, he called ahead, "Hold up. I need a second to rest." He braced a shoulder against the gnarled trunk of a tall larch.

From farther up the trail, Mathias reappeared as if out of thin air. He retraced his steps to where Ward was catching his breath.

"You sure this trek is worth it?" Ward said.

"That depends." Mathias picked up a smooth stone and fit it into the leather pocket of his slingshot. Drawing back until the elastic straps stretched all the way to his ear, he sailed the stone toward a moss-covered rock. It struck the rock dead center.

"On what?"

"If you like being out-of-doors."

"Ah, communing with nature—becoming one with the sylvan habitat."

"What?"

"Getting to know the forest."

"Whatever."

"You enjoy this, right?"

"Yeah."

"Does your mother?"

"She used to till a couple months ago."

"What changed?"

"I don't know. She just stopped coming with me."

Ward looked down at his shoes caked in mud. Then he noticed that Mathias's shoes were clean.

"Try stepping from rock to rock," the boy suggested as if having eavesdropped on his grandfather's thoughts. "You'll get the hang of it."

"If I live that long." Ward hooked his thumbs under the straps of his backpack and hefted it up to relieve the strain on his shoulders.

"You ready?" Mathias said.

"I suppose. Lead on." As Ward fell in behind his grandson, his eyes scanned the woods ahead. "Are you sure there're no bears around here?"

"The way you're wheezing, there won't be a bear within five miles."

They walked in silence for a time. Peering ahead, he thought he could see a clearing in the distance. He wholeheartedly hoped it was their destination. Then Ward said casually, "So, you want to tell me what's up between you and Trent?"

Mathias spun around. On his face, a look of dismay mingled with hostility. "How do you know about that?"

"A lucky guess. I watched how you answered your mother when she asked if he'd be coming to church. Seems to me you two had a dustup."

"A what?"

"A falling out, a disagreement. Am I right?"

"It ain't none of your business."

"It isn't any of my business."

"Exactly."

"You want to talk about it?"

"No." Mathias turned away and started down the path at a faster pace.

To the best of his ability, Ward hustled to keep up. His grandson had spunk, that was certain. And he seemed to have inherited his mother's strong-willed nature as well.

A minute later, Ward discovered he had been right about their destination. After dipping beneath an outcropping, the path opened up into a grassy meadow fifty yards across. Surprisingly, a few wildflowers still bloomed in shady places. The creek meandered along the meadow's edge. A faint breeze slid off Starfall Mountain in the distance to wash over the clearing, lowering the temperature several degrees. It was a lovely spot, one that Ward could have appreciated much more intensely had he arrived by car.

"Follow me," Mathias said. "There's a spot over here where we can set up." Lauren had packed picnic lunches for both of them. The boy led his grandfather to a place beside the creek where the vegetation had been cleared away.

Ward felt a sense of relief when he saw that the stream's banks were sandy loam rather than mud. Someone had carried rocks into the stream to retard the water's flow, creating a pool large enough to bathe in. He shed his backpack and sat down on a log at the stream's edge.

"Swish 'em around in the water," Mathias suggested.

"What?"

"Your shoes. Soak 'em in the stream. It'll take the mud off. Don't worry, they'll dry."

"You're not poking fun at a city slicker, are you?"

"No. We do it all the time."

Ward did as his grandson had suggested. To his surprise, in short order, his new cross trainers soon looked reasonably presentable.

"See," Mathias said. "Just be glad it wasn't that sticky gray clay you find up around Flint. That stuff is like glue. Mom tried using it to make her pottery. It was a disaster."

"Sounds vile."

"It is."

"So, in a couple weeks you'll be entering high school?" Ward said after racking his brain for things to talk about. "Are you excited?"

"How excited should I be?" Mathias began unpacking his lunch, bringing a swift end to their chat.

Ward decided he was too tired to eat. Instead, he pulled an aluminum bottle out his own pack and unscrewed the cap. After taking a long drink of water, he replaced the cap and returned the bottle to his pack, lamenting that it wasn't 80 proof whiskey. Shifting sideways on the log, he braced his back against the trunk of a pine tree. He leaned back and closed his eyes.

"You don't want to do that," Mathias said in an offhand tone of voice.

"Do what?" Ward kept his eyes closed.

"Cozy up to that tree."

"Why not?"

"Pitch. If it gets on your shirt, you may never get it out."

Ward's eyes snapped open. When he sat forward, he felt the tree tug against the fabric of his shirt. Too late. *Damn*, he thought. *So many things I don't know*. He felt completely out of his element, like the earthworms after the rainstorm a couple days before. Having crawled out of the ground to keep from drowning, when the sun had come out, they had shriveled up and died.

"Don't worry," Mathias said. "I have some pitch remover at home. It should do the job." He didn't sound convincing.

"Thank you."

Mathias drew back his slingshot and skipped a stone across the surface of the creek.

Ward rummaged around in his backpack till he found the granola bar Lauren had included in his lunch. He peeled back the wrapper and took a bite. "You don't want me here, do you?"

"I ain't got no say in the matter." The boy skipped another stone.

"I don't have any say—"

"Exactly."

"If it were up to you?"

"Sir, I'll be honest. I don't know you. And from what I've heard, I'm not sure I want to."

"What have you heard?"

"That you cheated on my grandmother. When she found out, you walked out on her. That's why she died."

The boy's frankness startled Ward. His immediate impulse was to hit back. Instead, he bit his tongue. When could his grandson have overheard such talk? The only occasion that came to mind was the previous night when he and Lauren had spoken again, believing the boy was asleep. Ward tried to recollect what else had been said. Giving the matter some thought, he felt fairly confident that Lauren's health issues had never become part of their discussion. In the future, he would have to be more careful.

"It's true I cheated on my wife. I'll regret that for the rest of my life. But she didn't die because of me. Yes, she was deeply hurt. Yes, that part was my fault. But people who commit suicide choose to do so. No one forces them. They have the same opportunity to pull themselves together as everyone else. I was devastated when Lily died, but I didn't kill her." The night before, he had told his daughter pretty much the same thing. Her reaction had mirrored the contempt he now recognized in his grandson's eyes.

Ward turned away. If this was how a man builds a relationship with his kin, he wasn't sure he wanted any part of it. What he really wanted was a drink—a whole lot of them.

"Let me know when it's time to go back." Ward sat on the log and hunched forward with his elbows on his knees. For a while, he simply stared at the flowing water.

***

With a start, Mathias caught himself gazing out through the classroom window. He shifted his attention back to the teacher standing beside her desk and wondered how much he had missed. Sondra Dale preferred the title information technologist rather than computer geek. After welcoming her students to their first day of high school, she had written her name on the blackboard. Four days later, it was still there. She had also written the name of the course, Computer Science 1—as if her students, being newbies, might have trouble figuring out where they were.

In their first year, freshmen were allowed two electives. Mathias had chosen computer science because computers were cool. He had then chosen physical education so he could be out of doors, not because of any special athletic prowess.

This was Mathias's fourth class of the morning, and he was bored. As usual, he had picked a workstation near the middle of the room. Front rows were for brownnosers, back rows for goof-offs and dropouts. In grade school, he had learned that if you sit in the middle, you could seem interested, but not overly eager.

The lunch bell sounded. Students began rising from their chairs. About to join them, Mathias abruptly realized that his teacher had written their homework assignment on the blackboard. He plopped back into his seat and hastily scribbled down the chapters he was to read.

As Mathias stood to leave, his thoughts again gravitated to his grandfather. It was their relationship he had been reflecting upon while staring out the window. In the two weeks since hiking along Tanner's Creek, he and his grandfather had fallen into a routine—a state of mutual tolerance. In a way, they seemed like a pair of gears so misaligned, their cogs meshed only once per revolution.

"Mathias," Ms. Dale said as he was about to exit the classroom, "do you have a moment? I'd like to speak with you." The expression on her face remained unreadable. She leaned over her workstation keyboard and typed in a command. Throughout the room, a dozen flat-panel monitors went dark.

"About what?" Mathias returned to stand in front of his teacher's desk. What had he done this time to get himself into trouble?

As the prettiest teacher at Rockridge High School, Ms. Dale took extra care to keep her good looks from interfering with her teaching responsibilities. She straightened up and smiled. Stepping to the door, she closed it after the last student had departed. She then returned to her desk. "Are you settling in?"

"How do you mean?"

"Are you getting the hang of being a freshman? High school can be daunting."

"It's different, but I'm okay."

"You don't enjoy school, do you?"

"Sometimes I do." Acutely self-conscious, Mathias looked awayhim. Only four days, and he was already being singled out. Maybe he should sit more toward the back of the room where he would seem even less conspicuous.

"I think it's because you're bored. That's my opinion." Ms. Dale retrieved a manila folder from the corner of her desk. It alarmed Mathias to read his name on the tab.

"I've reviewed your file," Miss Dale said, "and I've looked at your scholastic aptitude tests. I've also spoken with your grade school teachers—"

"You talked to Mr. Harrow?"

"I did. And Mr. James. I must say, you made quite an impression. They informed me that you can do exceptional work when you choose. I've watched you these first few days. You spend half your time daydreaming. I think that's because the work is too easy for you. I could be wrong. The school year has only just started. What do you think? Be completely open. This won't impact your grade in the slightest."

Great, Mathias thought. *She's about to double my homework because she thinks I'm bored.* He recalled the other assignments he had been given that morning. He had chapters to read in Algebra 1, English 1, and biology.

Ms. Dale lifted the top sheet off a small stack of papers. "This is the open book test you turned in yesterday. I graded it last night."

A knot of anxiety formed in the pit of Mathias's stomach. "Did I mess up?"

"Quite the contrary." Ms. Dale moved around behind her desk. "Do you have a computer at home?"

"No, but I have a smart phone. I can do calculations and stuff."

"Do you have Internet access?"

Mathias shook his head, embarrassed that his family couldn't afford the monthly fees.

"That's what I thought." Ms. Dale held up the sheet of paper. "At the beginning of each new school year, I test my students to find out how familiar they are with computers. It was only your second day, yet without a computer, you got twenty-nine out of thirty correct. How did you do that?"

"I didn't cheat," Mathias blurted defensively.

"I know you didn't. No other student even came close. There was no one you could've copied from. So how'd you do it?"

"The questions were about configuring a computer the first time you turn it on. The same stuff is described in the examples in the book. I studied how they were done and thought it through."

"In other words, you saw the answers in your head."

"I guess."

"That's what I suspected." Ms. Dale set the manila folder down and returned the homework assignment to the stack on her desk. "I have a proposition for you." She bent down, opened the desk's bottom drawer, and took out a flat box, ten inches wide and fourteen inches long. She handed the box to Mathias. "The district launched a new program last year. It's intended to encourage gifted students. I asked permission to get you this. It's a laptop, a fairly nice one I might add. We've also arranged for the phone company to provide you with Internet service at home. The district will cover whatever costs are involved."

Mathias went to hand the package back. "We don't take charity."

"It's not charity. Think of it as a stipend of sorts, payment for the work you'll be doing in this class."

"Did you talk to my mom about this?"

"I called her this morning. She's in full agreement. She wanted to be here to see your reaction, but she isn't feeling well."

"She has a cold," Mathias declared truthfully. When he'd asked about her low-grade fever, that was the explanation she had given. He regarded the box. "You're telling me I can use this at home?"

"It's portable, so you can use it anywhere you'd like, subject to several conditions. You'll have to bring it back periodically so I can do system maintenance—scan for viruses, check the hard drive for bad sectors. As we go forward, I'll teach you how to care for it yourself. And you can't be looking at porn. I'll know if you do."

Mathias's cheeks flushed a bright red.

"I'm kidding." Ms. Dale smiled. "I know a boy your age would never think of doing something like that. Here's the deal. This computer is yours to keep, permanently, provided your final grade in this class is A- or better. If you earn a B+ or anything less, you'll have to give it back at the end of the year." She stuck out her hand. "Agreed?"

Mathias hesitated, but then nodded. "Agreed." Ms. Dale's skin felt soft and smooth.

"Good. It's probably best if you don't tell the other students. They might be envious."

After leaving the computer science lab, Mathias hurried to his locker to store his gift before heading to lunch. He felt a sense of joy on two accounts. One was because he knew a world of discovery awaited him now that he had his own computer. The other was because no one had ever called him gifted before. What he might have found intriguing, had he thought about it, was that he was more concerned with how his grandfather would interpret his good fortune rather than how his mother would respond.

By the time Mathias entered the school cafeteria, the serving line had thinned. Only a few members of the kitchen staff, all wearing starched pale green uniforms, remained. The school dietitian on the opposite side of the sneeze guard ladled sliced peaches, peas, and something akin to beef stew onto his plate. He added a slab of wheat bread and a pint of milk. Threading his way between clusters of noisy students, he headed for a table in the corner where he had noticed his classmate, Rich Havers, sitting alone.

On the first day of school, Mathias had made the mistake of choosing a table near the center of the room. A cadre of seniors had surrounded him. Their belligerent taunts had made it clear he had invaded their territory. By tradition, underclassmen were to keep to the periphery.

"Hey," Rich said as Mathias set his tray down, "what do you think?"

"About?" Mathias sat down on the opposing bench seat and slid his legs under the table.

"You know—high school, higher education, our opportunity to become the pillars of tomorrow?"

Mathias rolled his eyes at the reference to the principal's welcoming speech. He sampled his beef stew. It wasn't half bad. "So far, so good."

"You're taking computer sci, right?" Rich said.

"Yeah. Why?" Mathias eyed his classmate with suspicion. Had he been eavesdropping outside the computer lab?

"What do you think of Ms. Dale?" Rich flashed a licentious grin, which on a kid his age gave the impression he was suffering from gas pains.

"She's nice."

"Nice? Is that the best you can do? I think she's hot."

Mathias shrugged. About to take a bite of bread, he stopped with his hand halfway to his mouth, a faraway look in his eyes.

"Something wrong?" Rich said.

"I was just thinking…"

"About Ms. Dale?"

"About my grandfather. I thought he'd be gone by now, but he keeps trying to fit in."

"What's he like?"

"He's old and pretty much useless around the house. It's like he never learned how to do what needs doing. Probably because when he was our age, I'll bet he paid someone to do his chores. He's even a bigger klutz in the woods. A couple weeks ago, we hiked Tanner's Creek. On the way home, I decided to have some fun. I ducked behind a big spruce and stayed out of sight. Before you could blink, he was wandering around, totally lost. All he had to do was follow the damn creek. It was sad—truly sad."

"Old people are weird."

"Tell me about it. It was frustrating, always waiting for him to catch up, but the day wasn't a complete loss. I thought up another rule: 'It's hard to get where you want to go if you don't know where you are.'"

Rich laughed. "Good one. How many does this make?"

"It doesn't have a number yet. Mom hasn't made it official."

"Why not?"

"She'd probably ask how it came to me, and I'd have to confess ditching Ward."

"Excellent point." Rich popped a peach into his mouth. "What's your next class?"

"Human geography—like I'm ever going to visit India or China or Great Britain. Why do I need to learn about people I'll never meet?"

"You're right." Rich slapped the table for emphasis. "For me, it's the same with algebra. Someday I'm going to take over the farm. Why do I care if X plus the square root of Y equals the diameter of a horse's ass? By the way, what about you? What are you gonna be when you grow up?"

"A computer programmer," Mathias declared without hesitation, surprising even himself.

"Is that what you told Ms. Dale? I suspect you just want to hang out in the computer lab."

"I didn't tell her nothing." Mathias looked around to see if any nearby students were aware of the color rising in his cheeks.

"Of course you didn't." Rich hooked a thumb at the wall clock. "Time to go." He stood and gathered up his tray.

"Already?" Mathias said with dismay as he regarded his lunch. He had eaten less than half. He thought about scarfing down what remained, but it seemed more important not to be late.

After sliding his tray into the collection cart, Mathias paused to look out across the room. In a far corner, he noticed Trent Blaine seated at a table with other underclassmen. The two boys made eye contact. Trent raised his fist and extended his middle finger.

Mathias fashioned a broad smile in return. Apparently, mending their friendship wasn't going to be as easy as he had hoped.

***

Ward entered the kitchen just as Mathias downed the last of his pancakes. Lauren had fixed her son's breakfast and was washing the skillet in the sink. The clock above the stove read 7:00 a.m. Outside, the light of a new day was chasing away the darkness.

Three weeks had gone by since Ward's arrival in Rockridge. He recalled waking up on his first morning. Dawn had broken a bit earlier then; the days were growing shorter and the mornings cooler. The heat wave had finally dissipated. In the backyard, trees were turning different colors. He had read about the progression of the seasons and how the earth donned a new garment every couple months, but he had never witnessed the change firsthand. Had it really been only three weeks?

"Morning all." Ward headed straight for the coffeepot.

"Morning." Lauren's voice sounded husky as she looked up from washing dishes.

"Gotta go." Mathias gathered up his knapsack and started to leave the room.

"Say good morning to your grandfather," Lauren commanded.

"Morning," Mathias muttered but kept his eyes averted.

Ward nodded in return.

"And bring me your breakfast plate so I can wash it," Lauren added.

"I'll miss my bus," Mathias protested as if picturing a five-mile hike into town.

"That's not my fault," Lauren declared curtly. "You should learn to get up earlier."

With a sigh, Mathias grabbed his plate off the table, set it on the counter beside the sink, and darted out of the room.

As Ward sampled his first sip of coffee, he thought about pouring himself a bowl of cereal but decided he wasn't hungry. He stepped around the table to sit in the chair that faced into the kitchen. In anticipation of the day's chores, he had dressed in a work shirt and denim jeans. "It's like that backpack is part of his anatomy. You know, I still can't believe the school just handed him a laptop."

Lauren nodded. "I told you he was bright. That's why they let him start high school a year early."

"He may be smart. That doesn't make him intuitive. When do you imagine he'll start warming up to me?"

"What are your plans for this morning?" Lauren replied, changing the subject. They'd had the same conversation the day before and the day before that. Each time, her counsel had remained the same: be patient and communicate in ways the boy can understand.

"I thought I'd try my hand at splitting firewood, though I'm not sure how much I can do. It would help if I were in better shape. But I did manage to bring down that dead tree yesterday." Ward smiled with pride. Using a chainsaw for the first time, he had felled a tilted snag that loggers refer to as widow-makers. To a city boy, collecting firewood on a sunny day in September had seemed mad, like buying flood insurance in the middle of a drought.

"Before you start, I could use your help in the studio." After drying the iron skillet, Lauren oiled it with a smear of bacon grease so it wouldn't rust. She returned it to its place in the cupboard beside the stove. When she turned around, the mask she had worn for her son's benefit had fallen away. The breath caught in Ward's chest when he noted the distress in his daughter's eyes.

Rather than ask if she was all right, he said simply, "Sure. How can I help?" A number of telltale signs had appeared during the previous week. At the time, he had successfully ignored them, but denying their significance was becoming harder and harder.

"I need to teach you how to wedge clay."

"Wedge it where?"

Lauren chuckled as she sat down at the table. "Basically, wedging is compressing clay against a hard surface. It pushes the air bubbles out. I no longer have the strength, and I need to get a new order out the door."

"What you need is rest."

"I can't."

"Why not? You're your own boss."

"There are bills to pay." Lauren looked to be on the verge of tears. "The mortgage is due at the end of the week. The balloon payment on the truck loan will come due next month. There are utility bills and grocery bills. The invoice for our homeowner's insurance arrived in yesterday's mail. Not to mention buying the stuff I need to make pottery—I stiff the vendors, and they stop shipping my supplies." Lauren closed her eyes as if reasserting her self-control. "Sorry. I shouldn't do that. Worrying is a sin."

"Excuse me?" Ward looked at his daughter with a puzzled frown.

"Worrying demonstrates a lack of faith. We are to be anxious for nothing." Lauren studied her father's expression. "There are things I need to tell you. It might as well be now. I apologize in advance for dumping this on you, but you need to know. We're nearly out of money. When Jake died, he left a small insurance policy. It wasn't much, but it's kept us afloat these past five years. Now it's almost gone. Up till about a month ago, I was able to supplement my pottery income by waitressing nights and weekends at the Leaky Canoe, but the stress got to be too much. I couldn't keep up. I had to quit. Recently, my productivity in the studio has fallen off. My output is half what it used to be."

Ward's fingers gripped his coffee mug. "I hear you. It's hard being stone-cold broke, but you get through it."

"You survived by living on the street and eating garbage. You think that's what I want for my son? I've always imagined that someday he would inherit this property. I never thought the bank might repossess it. I'm at my wits' end. What am I supposed to do? I try to keep my faith. I know that's what God expects of me." Lauren covered her mouth with her hand.

For a moment, Ward suspected his daughter might be experiencing another nosebleed. Then he saw the tears. "Maybe God isn't in this."

"What do you mean? Of course He is."

"Then why are you sick? I've heard your prayers. You plead with Him to deliver you from whatever this might be."

"What I pray for is that He will deliver me through the sickness. God promises to walk beside us through the storm, not make the storm go away. He's more interested in our character than our comfort. It's my responsibility to learn the lessons He's trying to teach. What I need is wisdom and understanding, a clear vision of the path I'm supposed to follow."

Ward cocked his head. "Wasn't it the Holy Spirit that predicted you were going to die? That's what you told me."

"That's correct."

"And for reasons I can't pretend to comprehend, you believe it's true?"

"Yes."

"So why ask God to walk beside you through the storm? Pardon me for being blunt, but if the Holy Spirit is right and you're not coming out on the other side, what's the point of having an escort?"

"Death isn't the final curtain. It's the beginning of eternity. I'm not afraid to die. Of course, I'm concerned—deeply concerned about the people I'll leave behind. But I'm even more concerned about what my maker will say when I stand before Him. The words I dearly hope to hear are 'Well done, good and faithful servant.' The key word is *faithful*. Faith is a believer's primary responsibility, no matter how severe the tribulation. Our troubles are really opportunities. Which reminds me, do you remember the first Sunday you were here and the question I asked you?" Lauren formed a faint smile.

"You mean, 'What's the purpose of life?'"

"Good. You were paying attention. Did you think about it?"

"Occasionally, mostly while mending garden fences and felling trees. To be honest, I haven't come up with an answer. What's your opinion? Obviously, you have one."

"I'm not going to tell you what I think. You need to figure it out on your own."

"Why?"

"Because what you decide will determine everything that follows. If you come to believe that life has a purpose, your only rational option is to do your best to fulfill that purpose. I'll give you a hint. The answer has to do with relationships."

"You call that a hint?"

Lauren grimaced and clutched her abdomen.

"What's wrong?" Ward said with alarm.

"Nothing. Just cramps. It'll pass. I've had them before. They come and they go."

"Enough of this." Ward started to rise from his chair. "I'm going to call the doctor."

"You will not. I just got through telling you we're broke. I'm not about to run up another debt we can't pay."

With reluctance, Ward slowly sank back into his chair and helplessly watched his daughter massage her abdomen.

A minute later, the pain evident on Lauren's face abated. She sat up straighter. "See. All better."

"How long have you had these attacks?"

"A while. Nothing to worry about."

"You need medical care. Why are you being so stubborn?"

"And why can't you hear me when I tell you we don't have the money?"

"Have you told Mathias? What would he say about your refusing to be seen?"

"I'll tell him when the time is right. And if you say anything to him first, I swear, you'll enter eternity before I do."

Father and daughter glowered at each other in silence. Then Lauren stood up and reached for her father's mug. "Want a refill? There's more I need to tell you."

"Really? In that case, make it a double."

Lauren placed the steaming mug in front of her father. "I've been struggling with how to tell you this since before you got here. Believe me, this isn't easy." She sat back down. "When I ran away from home, I despised you, just as I'm sure you were sick and tired of me. Over the years, I've tried to put you out of my mind but couldn't. My bitterness was too strong. I was glad you stayed away. Once, in a moment of weakness, I actually hoped you were dead. But then I came across a verse in the NIV Bible, Matthew 6:15: 'But if you do not forgive others their sins, your Father will not forgive your sins.' That verse literally pierced my soul.

"It's the reason I wrote you that letter. That verse changed my entire way of thinking. What I'm trying to say is I forgive you, totally, from the bottom of my heart. I forgive you for everything. And I'm asking if you can find it in your heart to forgive me. I was a terrible daughter, and I'm sorry."

As his daughter's words sank in, Ward looked up in amazement. He suddenly understood why he had come. He had just been handed the gift he never could have asked for, the gift he had no idea he desperately needed—redemption.

On the verge of crying, he stood and stepped around the table. Gently taking hold of his daughter's arms, he lifted her out of her chair and wrapped her in a loving embrace. "Of course I forgive you." His tears began to flow. "I forgave you thirteen and a half years ago. I just didn't know it until now."

***

Two days later, Lauren again stood near the kitchen window, staring out at the forest.

Mathias's breakfast was waiting for him when he shuffled in to the room, his eyes crusted with sleep. He looked at the table and saw bacon, eggs, toast with jam, banana slices, and a glass of orange juice. "Wow, what's the occasion?"

His mother failed to respond.

"Mom? You all right?"

"What?" Lauren turned around. "Sorry, I was someplace else. What did you ask?"

"Why this fine breakfast? What's the special occasion?"

"I felt like fixing you something nice. That's all. If you aren't hungry, I can take it away."

"No, no. I think I can handle it." Mathias sat down at the table. "Where's Ward? Out messing up again?" The previous afternoon, his grandfather had set out to fix the leaky faucet beside the house. All that had been needed was to replace a washer that had begun to disintegrate. Instead, he had wound up driving to the hardware store to buy a whole new fixture. In his absence, a huge puddle had formed in the backyard. "I'll bet he's still asleep. Early to bed and late to rise, that's his motto."

"He's gone."

"Gone where? If he's headed into the woods, we may never see him again."

"No, I mean he's not here anymore. He up and left."

"You mean like *gone*, gone?'"

"That's what it looks like."

"You sure?"

"Pretty sure. I checked his room. His clothes and personal items are missing. So's that old suitcase of his."

"Did he say anything? Did he leave a note?"

"I haven't found one."

"Should we go look for him?"

Lauren shook her head. "He has free will like the rest of us. If he wants to be gone, so be it."

Mathias's brow furrowed as if wondering if he could be the reason his grandfather had departed so abruptly. "Why would he up and go?"

"I don't know. Eat your breakfast. It's getting cold."

The boy bit the end off a strip of bacon. "What are we going to do?"

Lauren gazed out the window again. "I don't know that either."

"Do you think he'll come back? I was just getting used to having the old guy around."

Lauren turned around to face her son. "Let's not worry about your grandfather right now. I'm sure he has his reasons. Whatever happens, it's in God's hands."

The hutch in the dining nook caught Lauren's notice. That was where she kept her finest pottery, the best of her creations—the pieces she had held back for herself. The collection was her legacy, a gift for her son. It said: "This is who I am. Remember me." But the set was incomplete. Items were missing, specific pieces yet to be crafted. She had envisioned making them as her skill increased. Now, it seemed that wasn't going to happen.

Lauren looked to her son and suddenly realized she would not be there to celebrate his life's milestones: his first date, his graduation from high school and then college, marriage, the birth of his first child.

Dying wasn't her greatest sadness. What troubled her most was losing the opportunity to love and care for her son.

CHAPTER 3

Ages before the dawn of man, a great avalanche rumbled down the slopes of Starfall Mountain, damming up the perpetual stream that fed Tanner's Creek. Hundreds of tons of rock and shale had blocked the outward flow, backing the stream up till water filled the bowl-shaped canyon through which it passed. The result was Thadberry Pond, a pretty little lake with a wide meadow nearby and a gently sloping shoreline.

Indigenous tribes had used the canyon as a staging area, a starting point for their eastward journeys across the Rocky Mountains. The broad meadow had proven to be a perfect campsite. Through the ages, all manner of artifacts had been left behind, lost and forgotten in the surrounding terrain, arrowheads being the most common. Missed shots, human carelessness, and wounded animals too fleet to be tracked had scattered innumerable treasures. That was why Mathias had come.

Earlier, as a surprise, Lauren had told him he could take the morning off. As a rule, work always came before play, even on Saturdays. Yet for some reason, his mother had decided that his chores could wait. Mathias had seen no reason to argue. She had also informed him that she was on her way to Flint, a sleepy little town twenty miles north the Rockridge, to deliver a consignment to Wildwood Treasures. Feeling guilty, Mathias had volunteered to accompany her, but she had insisted she could manage on her own.

Thadberry Pond lay two miles from the Reslin Ranch. For a hiker accustomed to the wilderness, the gently sloping approach presented no challenge whatsoever. The pond's ease of access was both a blessing and a curse. Mathias could easily reach the little lake without overexerting himself, but then so could everyone else. For that reason, the pond was habitually overfished, especially in late summer. The odds of catching anything worthwhile were so poor that he hadn't even bothered to bring a fishing pole.

Mathias inched his way along the pebbled shoreline, his eyes scanning a sea of multicolored rocks for telltale anomalies.

A week had passed since Ward's disappearance. There was still no word, no explanation. Mathias tried not to think about his grandfather's leaving or the feelings of abandonment his departure had aroused. Resentment would ruin his day if he allowed it. His mother's mood had been hard to read when he had again broached the subject. Rather than angry, she had seemed dispirited, maybe a little scared.

In frustration, Mathias kicked a stone into the water. A glint of light caught his eye. An object submerged a foot from the water's edge had caught the morning light. He stepped closer. Peering beneath the surface, he fixed his eyes on the shimmering item as he shifted rocks aside. His fingers closed on a metallic trinket almost completely buried in silt.

The item he recovered looked to be a finely crafted charm bracelet. Made of silver, the ornament was the kind a lady of means might wear. After rinsing it off in the lake, he inspected it up close. It seemed undamaged. There was no telling how long it had lain there. It would make a splendid gift for his mother. He pictured it on her arm.

Perhaps a day hiker had lost the bracelet while picnicking. Mathias climbed partway up the shore to look around. There was nobody in sight. *Could it have fallen out of a pirate's treasure chest?* he wondered. *Could there be more loot farther out?* He thought about stripping off his clothes and diving in.

Don't be stupid, he told himself. *Pirates hide their stuff in caves. They don't use lakes to stash their booty.* For a time, he inspected the bracelet, admiring its craftsmanship.

"That's mine," declared an adolescent voice behind him. "Hand it over."

Mathias spun around and found Trent Blaine striding in his direction. He appeared to be alone.

"Where did you come from?" Mathias said. "You following me?"

"What if I was?" Halting two feet away, Trent held out his hand. "Come on. Let's have it. It doesn't belong to you."

"Oh, like this belongs to you? You'd look real sweet with a sparkly doodad on your wrist."

"I'm not kidding. Give it here."

"How do I know it's yours?" Mathias remembered times when Trent had claimed things that weren't true just because it suited him.

"'Cause I said so."

"Fine. Describe the charms, and it's yours. You can't, can you?"

"Don't play games, Reslin. I mean it."

"Or what? What are you going to do?" Mathias suddenly realized he had probably miscalculated, having assumed his once-upon-a-time friend was bluffing, putting on a show just to be a creep. He also perceived that he couldn't afford to back down. Any show of weakness would encourage future aggressions. He prepared to defend himself.

"This is your last chance. I'm not going to tell you again. Give it to me. Now."

"If you want it, come get it." Mathias slipped the bracelet into the pocket of his blue jeans.

Trent lunged. Mathias had anticipated his charge. He eased sideways and lashed out with his fist, catching his opponent on the shoulder. Off balance, Trent pitched forward and wound up sprawled on his belly on the shoreline, scattering rocks and pebbles in his wake.

In an instant, he was on his feet again and charged a second time. Mathias sought to redirect his momentum as he had done before but failed. Trent wrapped an arm around his waist and tackled him to the ground. Rather than let himself be pinned, Mathias twisted sideways and thrust hard against the shore with his foot. The loose gravel gave way, robbing him of his power. However, the thrust was sufficient to break free of Trent's grip. He scrambled to his feet, as did his antagonist.

Rather than wait for Trent to make the next move, Mathias lowered his head and barreled forward. His shoulder impacted the center of Trent's chest so forcefully, he knocked the air out of his lungs. Driving with both legs, he pushed his rival backward and did not let up even when he had passed the water's edge.

Both boys wound up fully submerged. They quickly released their holds on one another and fought to gain the surface. For a time, they thrashed about until their feet found stable ground. Again able to stand, they rose to crouched positions and faced one another with pugnacious glowers.

Mathias hesitated to see what would happen next. Sensing that Trent would continue their skirmish, he tensed his muscles. When he pictured how ridiculous they both must look, two scrawny teenagers with water cascading off their bodies and their hair in their eyes, he chuckled and then began to laugh.

Taken aback, Trent seemed momentarily confused but then started laughing as well. The tension bled out of their confrontation. Soon, they were slogging their way toward the shoreline, the hostilities having been forgotten.

"You fight like a girl," Trent said.

"Perhaps." Mathias shook the water out of his hair, "But you fight like a four-year-old."

Without consulting each other, they both headed for the meadow to dry off.

"I'm surprised you're alone." Mathias looked around as they skirted a thicket at the edge of the clearing. "Where are Tweedledum and Tweedledee?"

"Who?"

"Your minions, Danny and Marcus—the Osborne twins. I've watched you guys in school. They follow you around like you're carrying a pocketful of dog treats."

"They just like hanging out. We're not tight or anything."

"Could have fooled me."

When they reached a sunny patch of grass near a jumble of rocks, they stopped. Trent fished in his shirt pocket and drew out a pack of cigarettes and a book of matches. Both were soaked. "See what you did?" He wadded them up and tossed them aside, obviously unconcerned that he was littering.

"When did you start smoking?" Mathias asked.

"It's been a while." Trent made a show of adolescent bravado. "By the way, those were my only smokes. You owe me a pack."

"I probably saved your life. You can thank me later." Mathias remembered Rule 14: Don't smoke unless you're on fire.

The two boys stripped out of their clothes, all except their undershorts. When Trent dropped his pants, Mathias noticed several strands of coarse black hair on his lower abdomen. His own belly was still smooth and hairless. They spread out their clothes on the rocks to dry.

Trent slipped his shoes on without his socks and headed for a grove of small trees fifteen yards away. There, he picked up a dead branch and tested it to see if it might make a suitable walking stick. Dissatisfied, he snapped the branch across his knee and cast the pieces away. He then returned to where Mathias had seated himself on a flat rock. He sat down nearby. A moment later, he seemed bored.

"So, how do you like speaking Spanish?" Trent said. "*Se habla Español.*" Spanish 1 was the only class the two freshmen shared.

"To be honest, I detest it. Probably because I suck at it. I'll be lucky if I pass."

With a flick of his finger, Trent knocked a beetle off his rock. "But you're good with computers—so I've been told."

"I guess." Mathias had been careful never to mention anything about the laptop, which had turned out to be a godsend. Even he had been amazed at how quickly he had mastered the operating system. Homework assignments that previously would have taken hours were being completed in a fraction of the time.

Trent winked. "Rich Havers told me you've got a thing for Ms. Dale."

Blabbermouth, Mathias thought. *He'll pay for that.* "She's no different than any other teacher."

"Right—and Coach Nelson is a couch potato." Terry Nelson was Rockridge High's physical education instructor and something of a fitness nut.

Mathias shrugged. "He might be, for all I know."

"I've also heard your grandfather is living with you and your mom?"

"Nice to know you've been keeping up with the latest gossip."

"Is it true?"

"Not anymore. He took off."

"I wish my old man would split." Trent's voice dripped venom. "I hate the bastard."

Trent's proclamation reminded Mathias of the marks he had seen on his friend's body. He said nothing for fear of provoking additional displays of hostility. He lay back on his rock and again tried not to think about his grandfather. Instead, he wound up wondering why his mother had insisted he take the morning off.

The sun warmed his body, but the October breeze promised colder days ahead. The trees surrounding the meadow were wearing their autumn foliage. He closed his eyes and might have drifted off for a time. When he opened his eyes, Trent was getting dressed. As he reached for his own pants to put them on, he was relieved to feel the bracelet still in his pocket. Its presence implied that he had won their contest of wills.

When the two boys finished dressing, they headed home at a leisurely pace, hostilities forgotten. As the meadow disappeared behind them, Mathias remembered that he had set out to look for arrowheads, just as he had set out to go fishing that day at Horse Collar Lake. The similarities stood as a sad commentary on the nature of his relationship with his companion.

As they walked along, Trent eyed his buddy with a look of speculation. "A guy with wicked computer skills like yours, there's no telling what he could do. Such a dude might be useful to have around."

Ahead, Mathias recognized the spot where the shortcut to Trent's house branched off from the main path. "What do you mean?"

"Nothing in particular. I was just mouthing off. See you Monday." Trent peeled off and headed for the shortcut.

Mathias continued on and soon got to thinking about his morning. Why had Trent come to Thadberry Pond? To Mathias, it seemed unlikely that Trent had actually been tailing him. He must have come for other reasons, but not to collect arrowheads. And why had he insisted that the bracelet was his as if he owned the thing? Had he been to the pond before and lost it or tossed it away? Was it stolen? Could that be why he had so anxiously demanded it back? Mathias decided to hold off on giving the trinket to his mother as a gift. He needed to know more about its history.

When he drew within sight of his house, he groaned as he remembered his chores. The screen door needed mending. There were leaves to rake and windows to wash, both inside and out.

***

Evening shadows were already settling in when Ward Stanford knocked on the Reslins' front door. He was tired, sore, and as wilted as yesterday's lunch. In addition to a thirty-eight-hour bus ride, he had walked five miles from town carrying his valise. No one had stopped to offer him a lift. He peered in through the narrow window beside the front door. The entryway and living room were dark. So was the kitchen beyond. Perhaps nobody was home.

Had he made a mistake by not calling ahead? He had wanted to arrive unannounced, the same way he had departed so that his leaving and his return would have a certain symmetry, like bookends on a shelf. A squeaky stair announced that someone was responding to his knock.

Mathias opened the front door. Ward figured that since it was a school night, his grandson had probably been doing homework in his room. The boy seemed tired as if sleep deprived.

"Oh!" Mathias exclaimed when he saw his grandfather. "We didn't expect to see you again."

"You don't sound pleased."

"I'm not."

"Mind if I ask the reason? I thought we were starting to like each other? I had the impression you wanted to be my friend." Ward formed a genial smile. It was not returned.

"Well, you're wrong. Friends don't up and leave without saying goodbye."

"I am sorry about that. It was necessary."

"Oh yeah? Why?" Mathias punched his fists to his hips. "You're not about to tell me, are you?"

"Not until after I speak with your mother. Is she home?"

"She's out in the studio."

"In that case, mind if I pass through, or should I circle around the side of the house?"

Mathias opened the door wide. He made a point of staring directly at his grandfather's battered suitcase. Yet when his grandfather set it down in the entryway, he made no move to retrieve it.

"You know the way." The boy turned and headed back upstairs.

"Mathias!" Ward said sharply.

"What?" His grandson stopped and turned around.

"Nothing." Ward spoke more softly. "It's just that—well, I am glad to see you. I missed you."

"Whatever." Mathias climbed the remaining stairs and slammed his bedroom door shut behind him.

Ward exited the kitchen and noiselessly closed the screen door. Quietly he trekked the flagstone path until he could peer through one of the studio's small windows. He wanted to surprise his daughter.

Lauren sat at the workstation where she painted her creations. Her head was bowed as if in prayer. A greenware vase sat on the table in front of her. Wider at the base, the vase's graceful upward sweep flared at the top. It was a work of art, even unfinished. He had no idea how she had formed the vessel on her potter's wheel. She had once encouraged him to try his hand at throwing clay. He had failed utterly, with nothing to show for his efforts except a misshapen lump of mud and spatters on his shirt. He opened the door and stepped inside.

Ward gasped when his daughter looked up. She seemed to have aged five years. Her haggard face hinted at hours laden with desperation and sorrow. Her once-lustrous blonde hair trailed to her shoulders in uncharacteristic disarray. The loose skin at her throat showed that she had shed fifteen pounds—possibly more.

"My god," Ward whispered.

"Don't take the Lord's name in vain," Lauren cautioned in a raspy voice. She coughed once, then formed a smile. "Welcome back. I knew you would return."

"Did you?"

"There was never any doubt."

"Shame your son lacked your certainty."

"Mathias has his issues, but then you might have informed us you were leaving. It would have made things easier for him."

"I wanted to surprise you."

"And so you have."

"My coming back isn't the surprise. It's what I brought with me."

***

Ward listened to the sounds of the forest—the wind whispering through the pines, birds twittering in counterpoint melodies, the distant babble of Tanner's Creek. Rather than ask the nature of his surprise immediately, Lauren had invited him to accompany her on a stroll in the woods. She had promised they would never lose sight of the house, so there was no need to fret about getting lost. He had countered by suggesting they remain in the studio where they could talk with the doors and windows shut, but she had objected, claiming that the studio was too dusty. In recent days, she had lacked the energy to clean it properly. Ward suspected her true motive was that she wanted to make absolutely certain their conversation could not be overheard.

A single star, bright against the gray dusk, twinkled down through the forest canopy. A light shone out of one window at the rear of the house. Ward monitored his grandson's silhouette but could not decipher his movements. He motioned toward the shadow. "You haven't told him, have you?"

"Not yet." Lauren had shed her durable apron in favor of a lightweight jacket. She drew the lapels closed, a modest defense against the chill in the air. "But I'm sure he suspects."

"You'll have to tell him soon." Ward refrained from pointing out that her infirmities were becoming impossible to ignore.

Lauren frowned and looked away. "Aren't the woods beautiful?"

"I suppose you might say they are." Ward apprehensively scanned the forest, reassuring himself that all was well.

"I love this time of day." Lauren reached out and lightly touched a pine bough. "When the light fades and the day's struggles are winding down. It feels so peaceful, as if creation is moving at a slower pace." She paused to yank a tuft of needles off the limb. After crushing a few needles between her thumb and index finger, she raised the fingers to her nose and drew in a slow breath. "And I love the smells of the forest. You know, it's the little things that give life meaning."

A leaf rustled. A ball of gray fur skittered up a nearby tree.

"Relax," Lauren said when her father startled. "It's only a gray squirrel scavenging pine nuts to store up for winter."

The squirrel effortlessly hopped from one tree to the next.

Lauren watched until the industrious rodent disappeared from view. "So, what's your surprise?"

About to brace a shoulder against the rough bark of a spruce, Ward recalled his grandson's warning and how hard it had been to remove the pitch from his shirt. He turned to face his daughter. "You're aware, I'm sure, that the mortgage company I owned went bankrupt?"

"That's what I heard—not when it happened, but later."

"The creditors took everything—the house, my cars, and all my investments. They wiped me out except for one thing. That's because they didn't know I had it, and I sure as hell wasn't about to tell them. It was one of my most valued possessions.

"In the late seventies, when the business started making some real money and the feds weren't as paranoid about endangered species and environmental concerns, I bought a carved ivory tusk. I came across the thing during a trip to China, and it was gorgeous. Each little car figurine was incredibly detailed. Back then, it was a heck of lot easier to smuggle that kind of stuff through customs. After I brought it into the country, I had to keep it hidden. I couldn't display it at home or at the office. That's why you never saw it. I figured one day it would be worth a great deal of money, and I was right.

"As the creditors were closing in, I crated the thing up and stashed it in an abandoned mine shaft out in the desert, one of those featureless holes in the ground you can never find unless you know where to look. I wasn't sure it would still be there. That's why I had to leave to retrieve it. Besides, it's not like you can sell ivory tusks online. There are laws against it. The feds would've been all over me. It's a shame I had to make a private sale. I got less than half what the ivory was worth, but it should be enough.

"What I'm saying is, I now have enough money to pay for your medical care."

A sad look spread across Lauren's face. She took hold of her father's hand. "Thank you for caring, but I can't take your money."

"Sure you can. The money is for you. That's why bought the tusk in the first place—for you."

"I appreciate your thoughtfulness, but—"

"Look, let me help. I need to make up for having been a lousy father."

Lauren drew in a deep breath as if preparing herself. "I've already been to see the doctor. I went Saturday morning while Mathias was off collecting arrowheads."

"You changed your mind. Why?"

"I got scared. I'm ashamed to admit it. I prayed that my faith would be stronger, but I needed to know. So I worked a deal with Doc Livingston. The vase you saw me painting is payment for my office visit."

"What did he say? Did he find out what's wrong?"

"He drew blood and took a urine sample. He wanted to do a chest X-ray, but we agreed it could wait. He thinks I probably have a tumor."

"A tumor? You mean—"

"Cancer. Yes. He didn't use that word, but I'm sure that's what he was thinking. He told me he would know more in a few days."

Ward swallowed dryly. Hearing his suspicions affirmed, even provisionally, sent a wave of anxiety coursing through him. He had envisioned paying for his daughter's full recovery. But with the diagnosis being cancer…

"Well, good," he said bravely. "Now we can get you started on treatment."

"Let's see what the tests show first. I have a follow-up appointment scheduled for two days." Lauren let go of her father's hand.

A crescent moon was emerging above the horizon. A shaft of light fell at her feet. She squatted down to study a pinecone. She often decorated her pottery with themes and images taken from nature.

"Life is renewal. The new replaces the old. That's how it is. That's how it will always be." When she straightened up, she gave out a small yelp of pain.

Ward reached out to comfort her. "We're not giving up. You're a fighter. You will beat this. I know you will. We'll do it together." To his amazement, his daughter did not shrink from his touch.

Lauren wrapped her arms around herself. "It's not up to me, nor is it up to you. Let's go in. I'm cold."

They left the woods and, without speaking further, walked toward the house.

***

The doctor's exam room smelled of antiseptics. A wall chart displayed the human body with its skin removed and each muscle labeled. On a side counter, a glass jar with a stainless steel lid held a tangled mass of cotton balls. Its twin contained a stack of gauze pads. Assorted medical instruments lay on a clean white mat—a rubber hammer like a miniature tomahawk, a tuning fork, and a special light for looking in ears.

Ward hated doctors' offices. He had ever since the age of six when he had fallen out of a tree and broken his arm. Supporting his L-shaped forearm, his mother had rushed him to the general practitioner's office. Rather than give a proper anesthetic, the busy doctor had reset the fracture with a vigorous yank. Ward had both felt and heard his bones crunch back into place.

Doc Livingston, whose full name was Eli Reginald Bartholomew Livingston, had served as Rockridge's only physician for as long as most folks could remember. His easygoing manner caused Ward to question his medical skills, though Lauren had insisted he was capable of delivering excellent care.

Lauren sat fully clothed on the exam table. Since this was a follow-up visit, there had been no need for her to don a gown. Ward sat in a metal-framed chair backed up against the far wall, as out of the way as he could manage. Lauren had emphatically stressed that he was to be an observer, not a participant.

Doc Livingston wheeled his stool closer to Lauren. His waist-length white jacket and gray gabardine slacks fit the image of a country doc.

It pleased Ward to note that the GP's shoes appeared to have been rigorously polished. *You can tell a lot about a man by his shoes*, he reminded himself.

When the doctor addressed his patient, his demeanor changed from affable to serious. "Your blood work has come back, Lauren. I'm afraid it isn't good news. I was certain you were anemic, but I didn't expect this." He indicated the lab report in his hand. "I'm surprised you can still get around. You're going to need a transfusion or two, but that's not the worst of it." He reached out and took hold of Lauren's hand. "There's really no easy way to put this, so I'll just say it. You have leukemia."

Ward's glimmer of hope faded as quickly as it had begun. Anemia could be treated, but leukemia—that was serious. When he studied his daughter's face, he detected no hint of emotion. Perhaps she had misunderstood her diagnosis.

Doc Livingston continued, "You have acute myeloid leukemia or AML. Technically it's the M0 variety, an undifferentiated acute myeloblastic leukemia, one of the most aggressive forms. There are different types of white blood cells. Undifferentiated cells are those that haven't matured yet.

"What all this means is that a single strain of white cells has begun replicating rapidly. These new immature cells are pushing the other cells out of your bone marrow. That's why you're anemic. They also interfere with your immune system, and that's why you've had your recent infections. This diagnosis also explains the fatigue, the low-grade fevers, and your loss of appetite. We're going to need to start you on chemotherapy immediately."

"Chemotherapy?" Ward said hopefully, disregarding his instructions. "So there is treatment for this. That's great."

His daughter shot him a warning look.

"There is," said Dr. Livingston. He let go of Lauren's hand. "We usually begin with three drugs: daunorubicin, vincristine, and cytarabine. They are all cancer-fighting agents."

"Cancer?" Ward exclaimed. "I thought you said she has leukemia?"

"She does. Leukemia is a type of blood cancer."

"Oh." Ward sank back in his chair. His daughter's scowl declared that she would not tolerate another interruption. Numbly, he listened while the doctor explained medical terms, such as *induction* and *consolidation*. Next followed a sequence of statistics he found hard to follow. Yet as he listened, the gist of the doctor's message became apparent. Bottom line, his daughter would need immediate treatment to survive. He was still processing the dreadful tidings when his daughter abruptly stepped down from the exam table.

"Thank you, Doctor," Lauren said. "I appreciate your candor."

"Where are you going?" Doc Livingston sputtered. "We have arrangements to make. I need to admit you to Cedarwood Memorial and arrange for an oncology consult. A condition this serious is a little out of my league."

"Again, I appreciate your candor," Lauren said, "but what I need now is to go home and rest."

"Lauren, perhaps you don't understand what I'm telling you."

"Oh, I understand. It's just that I don't believe chemotherapy is the way to go."

Doc Livingston tugged off his reading glasses and looked straight at his patient. "Let me make myself clear. I hate being this blunt, but without the proper care, you're going to die. We need to start this very day. You are not going to get better on your own."

"I know. Believe me, I do. And again, thank you for your concern, but taking a bunch of poisons isn't going to help. Come on, Dad."

Doc Livingston pressed his hands together in a pleading gesture. "Lauren, please. Going through chemotherapy, it's not as bad as you might've heard."

"It's not?" Lauren's voice rang with disbelief.

The doctor shrugged an acknowledgment. "Only occasionally."

"Right. How about this? Give me a day or two to consider my options. If I change my mind, I'll call you. Yes, I understand the risks. You've done your job, but this is my choice. Okay?"

"In my opinion," Doc Livingston said, putting on his most professional demeanor, "you're making a grave mistake. Every minute counts."

"I get that, loud and clear." Lauren turned to leave.

Ward took hold of his daughter's arm. "If this is about money—"

"Dad, don't. This is my decision. If you intend to argue, give me the keys and I'll drive myself home."

Ward relented and followed his daughter out into the parking lot. As they climbed in the truck, he said, "Are you convinced you are doing the right thing?"

Lauren nodded as she settled into the passenger seat. "I am."

Ward tugged on an earlobe. "Won't you even consider chemotherapy?"

"Barring a miracle, there's no way I'm going to survive this illness. So why prolong the inevitable?"

"Are you sure about that?"

"As sure as I can be."

Well, that means she's not 100 percent convinced, Ward thought. *Good. Perhaps tonight I can change her mind.* He fired up the truck and reluctantly drove toward home.

***

Lauren stood at the bottom of the stairs leading up to her son's bedroom. Her hand gripped the handrail, her foot on the first step, but she remained motionless, frozen in place. Two days had elapsed since Doc Livingston had confirmed what she had known in her heart, and now the moment she so desperately had wished to avoid was upon her. She could put it off no longer.

After dinner, Mathias had retired to his room to do his homework.

Ward had helped wash and put away the dinner dishes. He had then driven the truck into town to fetch a few groceries and household supplies. He would be gone at least an hour. Though he hadn't broached the subject before leaving, Lauren assumed he knew what she intended. The need to tell Mathias had weighed heavily on them both. Thankfully, Ward had refrained from taking the task on himself. It was her responsibility, her burden to bear. Now all she needed was to find the will to proceed.

How does a mother tell her son, barely a teenager, that for the rest of his life, she won't be there to love him, to watch over him, to make memories together?

"Heavenly Father," she prayed softly, "fill me with your Spirit. Allow me the strength to do what needs to be done. Give me the words that need to be said. In faith, I submit my will to yours. Be with my son this night and bring him comfort and peace. Amen."

One step at a time, she forced herself to climb the stairs.

A soft rap on Mathias's door brought a muffled reply that gave permission to enter. She opened the door and stepped inside. Her son sat at his desk. Textbooks lay open in front of him, but his fingers were tapping busily on the laptop's keyboard, his eyes focused on its luminous screen.

Lauren closed the door behind her.

The latch's sharp click caused Mathias to look around, a questioning expression on his face.

"Is this a bad time?" Lauren said gently. "I was hoping we could talk. I can come back later if you're busy."

"No, I'm good. Let me just…" Mathias shut down the programs he had been running and logged off his laptop. When he again regarded his mother, his apprehension had increased.

"May I?" Lauren eased into the room and sat down on the foot of her son's bed.

"Mom? What's going on? Is everything okay?"

"I wish it was. Actually, that's why I wanted to talk. There's something you need to know."

"It's not Ward, is it? If he's done something to trouble you—"

"I wish you would call him *Grandfather*. Refusing to address him properly doesn't change your biological relationship. Surely you must realize that. And no, what I'm about to tell you has nothing to do with him, at least not in any way you would imagine."

"Is it something I've done?"

"Not at all. You're a good son, and you're going to be a fine man. I doubt that any mom could be prouder of her boy than I am of you. And don't you ever think, even for one minute, that what I'm about to tell you is your fault. It's not."

"Mom?"

"I'm sorry. I'm not doing a good job of this. I had hoped it would be easier. Very well then. You've probably noticed I've had some health problems recently. For several months, I've been feeling tired and not myself."

"You've had a couple colds, one after the other. That would wear anyone down."

"The truth is it's a little more serious than a cold or two. I've been to see Doc Livingston. He ran a few tests. The results have come back. I'm afraid it's not good news. Son, I wish I could think of an easy way to tell you, but I can't. So I'll just say it. I have leukemia." Lauren drew in a deep breath and exhaled slowly. "I'm probably not going to be alive much longer."

"What?" Mathias exclaimed. Shock registered on his face. "Mom, don't kid around. It's not funny."

"You heard correctly. I have leukemia, a form called AML or acute myelogenous leukemia. It's an aggressive cancer of the bone marrow. The reality is that I'm dying. I don't know how much time is left to me, but it won't be long."

"I don't believe you!" Mathias hollered. "Why are you saying this?"

"Son, I am truly sorry. I wish it wasn't so, but I can't change the way things are. I wouldn't be telling you now, except you need to prepare yourself."

"The tests have to be wrong. Doc Livingston is a GP. What does he know? You're not…" Unable to speak the word, Mathias choked back a sob.

"Dying? Yes. I am. Even without the tests, my heart tells me it's true. I've known for a while now that my life is coming to an end. Soon I'll step into eternity. I won't be here to guide you, and that is why we need to talk. Come here." Lauren opened her arms wide.

Mathias left the desk and sat on the bed beside her. She pulled him close and drew his head to her shoulder. His young body, tense at first, seemed to melt into her arms as he breathed out sobs of anguish. "It isn't true," he whimpered.

She summoned every ounce of determination she could muster to keep her composure from slipping away. In that moment, her only desire was that in future years, her son would look back and understand that his mother had not been afraid, that she had faced death without flinching, and that her faith had carried her through a time of agony and despair.

"I don't know how long," Lauren admitted. She sat facing her son with one leg drawn up on his bed. His tears had diminished, but his brokenheartedness had intensified. She continued her efforts to bring what comfort she could by saying gently, "Many of the troubles that come our way have no explanation. I can't tell you why things work out the way they do, but I trust that there is a reason. Perhaps only by coping with uncertainty—when logic and reason offer no measure of solace—can we grow in our faith. Do you understand what I'm trying to tell you?"

Mathias nodded that he did, but his countenance suggested otherwise.

"Let me put it this way," Lauren offered. "You know that I love you?"

"Yes." Fresh tears welled up in Mathias's eyes.

"How do you know?"

"Because you're my mom. I just know."

"Even when I'm upset or when I punish you for being disobedient? Even then do you believe I love you?"

"Yes."

"And so it is with God. He loves us all the time, even when we rebel against Him."

"But why does He have to take you away?"

Lauren reached out to touch her son's cheek, wiping away a tear. "That's what I'm saying. He hasn't told us why. But because I know He loves us, I can trust that there is a reason and that the reason is good. Remember, you must never, ever blame God. Keep your faith. Keep it strong. Trust God's mercy and compassion. Follow Him and obey His commands. Promise me you will do this."

Again Mathias nodded, this time with greater certainty.

"Say it. Promise me and mean it in your heart. If you can do that, I'll know I haven't failed you."

"I promise."

"Do you mean that for yourself, not because I'm asking?"

"Yes."

"I know it won't be easy, but I expect you to keep your promise—for your sake, not mine. Now, there's something else we need to talk about. I've asked your grandfather to look after you when I'm gone. He's going to be your legal guardian."

"No way. He doesn't even like me, and I sure as… I'm not that fond of him either."

"I've watched him when he's around you. It's not that he doesn't like you, it's that he hasn't figured out how to relate. He had the same problem with me when I was a girl. Sadly, I chose to leave rather than stick around and build a connection. It's true that the man has his faults, but he is trying to change."

Mathias scowled. "He only stays with us because he gets free room and board."

"Maybe at first, but that's not why he came back. He came back for you."

"Me?" Mathias blurted out with astonishment.

"Indeed. When he first came to Montana, I told him of my premonition—that my life was drawing to a close. I also let him know it would be his responsibility to look after you. He could have stayed gone, left us to our fate. But he didn't. Instead, he's elected to become part of our family. And that's where you come in. You're going to have to help him."

"Help him? How?"

"First off, by being patient with him. He's city born and bred. You can't expect him to step into a rural lifestyle like ours and thrive. He's going to need time to adjust. Also, you'll have to work with him, not against him. If he rubs you the wrong way, talk it through. Don't just get mad and shut him out. Give him a chance to get to know you. Help him figure out how things work around here. Your grandfather is smart, and he has a lot more potential than even he realizes."

"I don't need him to look after me. I can take care of myself."

"Someday, that will be true. But until you turn eighteen, he's going to be your legal guardian. I've already drawn up the papers."

A look of resentment narrowed Mathias's eyes. Lauren recognized it immediately. The same expression had shown up right after his father's death as if Jake was somehow accountable for his son's grief.

"I know," Lauren said softly. "It feels like I'm abandoning you, and from a certain point of view, that may be true. But it's not because I want to. I would give anything to walk beside you on your journey into manhood. Sadly, though, that's not an option. So I have to make other provisions. I will not have you become a ward of the court—without family, without someone to care for you. It's not that your grandfather is the best choice, he's the only choice. And in this matter, you will respect my wishes."

"I'm sorry, Mom. I didn't mean… I know you wouldn't…"

Lauren drew her son close again. "It's all right. I understand what you're feeling. Believe me, if there were any other way, we wouldn't be having this conversation."

The sound of a truck engine drifted in from the driveway out front.

"Your grandfather must be home." She continued holding her son in a loving embrace as if terrified by the knowledge that she would soon have to let him go. "Tomorrow is Friday. What say that, just this once, we let you skip school? We should do something together."

"The two of us?"

"The three of us, if you're willing? Let's see how you feel in the morning."

***

Seated in the rocker in the corner of his daughter's room, Ward monitored the shallow ebb and flow of her breathing. The previous evening, Lauren had drifted off. At first, he had imagined that she had simply fallen asleep. Now, twenty hours later, it seemed likely that her torpor was due to something much more ominous. As he had in the middle of the night, he considered taking hold of her shoulders and shaking her to see if she would rouse.

But what would that accomplish? At least for the moment, she seemed at peace. Lauren had made her wishes clear. There was to be no heroic intervention, no futile prolongation of life, and it was now his responsibility to honor her wishes, regardless of how strongly he might disagree.

In the same way, Lauren had insisted that Mathias was to continue his schooling without interruption. That very morning, the boy had demanded that he be allowed to stay home. He had relented only after Ward had convinced him that his mother was merely sleeping and that his noisy presence might deprive her of much-needed rest. It had been a hard lie to tell, but often in times of crisis, there are no easy paths to follow.

Hazy midmorning sunlight spilled in through the bedroom window. Ward had watched the room brighten since the first glimmer of dawn. Outside, the air had taken on a foreboding chill. In town, the locals had told him that winter's bluster would soon shroud the landscape in ice and snow and that only a few days remained in which to prepare, though he had no idea what such preparations might entail.

Three weeks had passed since Lauren had shared her diagnosis with her son. At first, the telling had gone well, but then Mathias had grown increasingly rebellious. To Ward, it seemed the boy's stubborn refusal to accept the inevitable lay at the root of his increasing belligerence. The harder Lauren had fought to comfort her son, the farther he had pulled away and the more closed off and isolated he had become.

Ward had also tried to reach the boy, even to the point of resorting to bribery. He had offered to take his grandson shopping to buy him whatever treasure caught his fancy. Mathias had agreed to the outing, probably because he wasn't actually given a choice. Once there, however, he had shut down emotionally and had refused to participate. In retrospect, Ward had concluded that the entire enterprise had been a foolish notion; you can't ease a soul's agony by the acquisition of stuff. He later had tried other approaches. Those too had fallen short.

As Ward rocked slowly back and forth, he recalled Lauren's last visit with Doc Livingston. He especially remembered the doctor's look of helplessness because of his patient's persistent refusal to be treated for her leukemia. Eventually, the GP had given up and offered palliative care instead, including the use of narcotics for whatever pain might ensue. This therapy too had been emphatically refused. Lauren had staunchly declared she would meet her maker with a clear mind, unclouded by drugs. As Ward monitored his daughter's respirations, he wondered if her current condition meshed with what she had envisioned.

A stray memory dating back more than a decade surfaced in Ward's thoughts. He recalled a Saturday in Los Angeles toward the middle of the year. It had been in the afternoon, and the sun was settling toward the Pacific Ocean. The hum of the Mercedes's tires had resonated against the freeway's pavement.

***

Ward felt happy. He had just signed a crucial contract. The Respectable Mortgage Company was now the primary lender for a major housing project.

With his workweek drawing to a close, it was time to celebrate. And who better to celebrate with than his mistress, the woman he had been seeing for the past eighteen months.

As usual, she had listened attentively while he had described his victory and how he had triumphed over the competition by paying kickbacks to the developers. The woman had dutifully kept his glass filled with liquor and had welcomed his advances when the conversation had stalled. In bed, she had done her best to make him feel special. After all, her comfortable apartment, and indeed her entire lifestyle, depended upon his generosity.

Ward pictured himself sprawling on silken sheets, gazing out through penthouse windows. The sky was darkening. A storm was rolling in. Rain was imminent. In that moment, he also remembered his daughter's soccer match.

Leaping out of bed, he had thrown on his suit and drunkenly navigated the LA freeways at breakneck speeds, the alcohol he had consumed having achieved its full effect. A mile from his daughter's school, the rain had begun falling with a vengeance. The sedan's windshield wipers had barely kept up. Because of the torrent, he had narrowly missed sideswiping one car and rear-ending another.

By the time he had reached his destination, one figure was standing alone outside the school's main entrance. His daughter was still in her soccer uniform, her hair plastered to the sides of her head, drops of water cascading off her face and body. The rain mingled with the tears on both her cheeks.

"You promised you'd be here!" Lauren had screamed at the top of her lungs. "You promised you'd watch me play. Our team won, and you weren't here. I made a goal, and you didn't see me. You promised."

***

Rocking forward, Ward whispered through clenched teeth, "Never again." He looked at his daughter's motionless form. "On my life, I swear I will never again break any promise I've made to you."

Lauren's eyelids fluttered briefly. For a moment, her father hoped she might awaken, but they became still again. The faintest of smiles tugged at the corners of her lips, or at least that's what Ward imagined he had seen.

***

Mathias halted in the middle of what the mortician had referred to as the viewing room. Wooden pews bracketed him on either side. All were unoccupied. The low dais he faced was also deserted. His mother's memorial service would not begin for another hour. The funeral director had explained that this was to be a private time, just for family.

The very mention of the word *family* had made Mathias cringe. He had no family, not any longer.

The boy's only blood relative, the grandfather he had never known, stood at the foot of his mother's casket, head bowed out of respect. Blood was the only thing they shared. No bonds of love linked them one to another.

Ward motioned for his grandson to join him beside the casket. Mathias shook his head and stood locked in place, recalling the first time he had encountered the man—an aged scarecrow conversing on his front porch. Since that day, his grandfather had muscled up a little, and his shoulders didn't droop as severely, but even in a suit he still looked depleted—a warrior vanquished in countless battles lost.

Mathias looked around, having never been in a funeral parlor before. Plush drapes hid the walls, giving the impression he was inside a giant cloth box. Bouquets of flowers in ornate metal stands guarded the casket like floral sentries. More flowers graced the pews along the central aisle. The room smelled of lilac air freshener. From where he stood, Mathias could see only the upper part of his mother's body. Compelled by a sense of duty, he tried to take another step forward, but could not. His legs refused to respond. Soon, the mourners would arrive, and the memorial service would begin. Then he would be obliged to move, but for the moment, he felt frozen in place.

In a recent school assignment, he had come across the word *alabaster*. Unsure of its definition, he had looked it up online: "pale, translucent, smooth, finely textured." The word precisely described his mother's complexion as she lay in her casket. In death, she seemed even more beautiful than she had in life. *Why should that be?* Mathias wondered, not actually aware of having had the thought at all. In fact, over the last few days, many of his thoughts had hovered below the level of full consciousness.

Had the boy searched his feelings, the only emotion he might have recognized would have been rage—a deep, broiling hostility, an amorphous anger aimed at everyone and no one at the same time. The feeling had first taken root on the day his mother had visited his room to share her dreadful news. It had grown in intensity as her life had slipped away. With his mother's passing, his anger had become too hot even for tears, but then it had cooled into a glacial fury that now held him immobile. Had he been older and more mature in the ways of the world, he would have understood that he was experiencing the raw ferocity of unbearable grief. As it was, all he knew was that he needed to be somewhere else, anywhere else. He needed to be gone.

Beneath the rage, another concern had taken hold. A primal hunger, a need to understand had just arisen within him. In years to come, his quest for insight would mold his character in ways he could not now fathom. His brain was beginning its struggle with a single, one-word question: *Why?*

That morning, Ward had volunteered an unsolicited opinion. "I suspect you're asking yourself, 'Why did Mom have to die?'" His grandfather had then proposed an answer that was no answer at all. "There is no *why*. Sometimes, we don't get an explanation. Life is the way it is. That's all we can know."

Mathias had refused to even consider his grandfather's conjecture. Not for one moment did he accept the possibility that such a fundamental mystery could exist without a proper explanation. Although unable to express his feelings stranded there in the middle of the funeral parlor, his young heart told him that one day he would find the answer. One day, after he was long gone and far away.

CHAPTER 4

Two weeks after his mother's funeral, Mathias stood peering out of his bedroom window, his hands braced against the top of his desk. A blanket of low-lying clouds hid the morning sunrise. Shadows and outlines were all he could see in the backyard. The major landmarks, like the storage shed and his mother's pottery studio, were identifiable only because he knew every inch of the terrain by heart. His gaze tracked the rutted path that led to the river, and he pictured himself toting innumerable buckets of mud. Sadly, the yard no longer felt like home, nor did the house in which he had grown up. Running away wasn't going to be as traumatic as he had first believed.

He allowed his gaze to linger as he studied the grayness beyond the window one final time. Mathias then bent down to soundlessly slide open the bottom drawer of his desk. It was there he had sequestered items he considered essential for making good on his plan to run away. Before laying the items out on his bed, he paused to listen. The house was quiet except for its usual creaks and groans, plus a clatter of kitchen noises indicating his grandfather was fixing breakfast.

Reassured that he wouldn't be disturbed, Mathias emptied his school backpack of its textbooks, pencils, notebooks, and pens. He then refilled it with the survival items from the bottom drawer.

As he silently slid the bottom drawer closed, Mathias paused, restrained by a moment of indecision. He regarded the laptop on his desk, but then shook his head. "No," he whispered firmly to himself. He would leave the machine behind. Under some unlikely circumstance, the machine might prove useful, but it was simply too bulky to bring along.

As his final act, Mathias slipped a leather billfold into his hip pocket. Neatly sequestered inside was nearly $50, all that was left of the money he had earned doing tasks for neighbors. The sum wasn't much, but it would have to do. He chided himself for not having been more frugal.

With the survival items properly stowed, he reconsidered his plan of escape. He would have breakfast with his grandfather, mindful to give the impression that this was a normal school day. He knew that after the dishes had been washed and put away, his grandfather would retire to his room to finish dressing. That would be his cue. He would stuff the remaining spaces in his backpack with as much food as he could scrounge. Next, he would fill his plastic water bottle, the one item he absolutely could not afford to forget.

Then he would depart. In the days following his mother's passing, a ritual of sorts had evolved. Leaving the house together, Mathias would ride his bike to school while Ward would head for town to search for employment.

Except this day, Mathias had other intentions.

The family pickup pulled ahead as Mathias pedaled down the long gravel driveway. Rather than try to keep up, he held back till the truck disappeared. Ward had offered to toss his bicycle into the back of the truck and take him into town. Mathias had declined, claiming he needed the exercise. Truth was he had no intention of going anywhere near the high school. At the edge of town, he would head west, keeping to the back roads and alleys to avoid being noticed. No one would give a second thought to a student pedaling toward school. However, a kid headed in the opposite direction might attract attention.

At the end of the driveway, Mathias lingered for a last look back. A light drizzle had fallen during the night. In the cold morning air, tendrils of vapor trailed upward from the warming roof, giving the impression the house had caught fire. A momentary panic seized Mathias until he figured out what was going on.

Chuckling at his own gullibility, his lightheartedness evaporated like the mist when he perceived this might be the last time he would ever lay eyes upon the only home he had known. Steeling himself against a wave of loneliness, he mounted his bike and began pedaling toward town.

By pacing himself, Mathias made good time. Near midmorning, he reached the far western edge of Rockridge. From there, a two-lane country road would take him all the way to the Idaho panhandle and whatever lay beyond. He had memorized the route on a map, having never actually traveled that way in person. His spirits began to lift at the prospect of setting out on a new adventure.

Five miles farther on, his journey became more difficult as the road ascended into the western mountains. With resolve, Mathias pressed ahead. Fatigue, however, forced him to dismount to ascend the steepest hills.

An hour later, at a place less hemmed in by surrounding forest, he halted to catch his breath. Looking back, he shook his head in dismay. Not only had the inclines slowed his pace but so had repeatedly darting into the woods to hide from passing cars. He had traveled far less distance than he had envisioned.

Mathias tilted his head back to inspect the sky. The sun had disappeared behind a thick cloud bank. The world was growing darker. A frigid gust of wind evoked a shiver. As he mounted his bike and started off again, a snowflake touched his face, and then another and another. He zipped up the front of his medium-weight jacket. In no time at all, snow was falling briskly. Before heading out, he had forgotten to consult an online weather forecast. It would've told him that the first snowstorm of the season was predicted to degenerate into a full-blown blizzard.

The falling snow troubled Mathias. He had no clue how long the storm might continue. When he went to check the time, he discovered he had forgotten to bring his cell phone. He pictured it charging on his desk—right where he had left it the night before. He then remembered being distracted by worrying about whether or not to drag along the laptop. *Stupid*, he thought. *How incredibly, undeniably dumb.*

For a moment, he wrestled with the notion of turning around and pedaling home. The anger that roiled within him chased the thought from his head. Never would he admit defeat. With renewed determination, he turned his face toward the storm and continued on.

A short time later, above the howl of the wind, he imagined he heard the sound of a car approaching. In haste, he jerked the bicycle's handlebar, intending to leave the road as quickly as possible. Instead, his front tire slipped in new-fallen snow, sending him into a gully. About to crash, he lurched sideways to keep from being thrown headfirst into a pile of rocks. He might have regained control, except his rear wheel snagged on a jagged branch. Just before toppling over, he heard the metallic snap of his bicycle chain.

Mathias wound up on his back, his bike lying a short distance away.

Gingerly he moved arms and legs, flexed his spine, and tested other parts of his body. Thankfully, everything seemed intact and unbroken. The bicycle was a different story. Not only had the chain snapped, the rear wheel was mangled and completely unrideable.

After retrieving his backpack and putting on the gloves he had brought along, he slung his pack over his shoulder. Still unwilling to admit failure, he rejected any notion of turning around and making his way home. He decided that despite the risks, he would continue on foot, though it meant hauling the bicycle beside him with its wobbly rear wheel.

Half an hour later, it became apparent he had made a serious error of judgment. The storm was mutating from blizzard into what the locals referred to as a whiteout—when snow falls so fiercely that all visibility is lost.

Mathias raised an arm and found he couldn't identify his hand eighteen inches in front of his face. He had no way of knowing which direction he was facing. Then he remembered the compass in his backpack, but without recognizable landmarks, it would be impossible to plot a course. His only means of navigating was to gingerly test the terrain under his feet.

After ten minutes of stumbling forward with both arms outstretched in front of him, he had to stop. His feet were so numb it was impossible to tell if he was still on the road. The snow was now half a foot deep and rising rapidly.

A country witticism came to mind: if your feet are cold, put on a hat. In a chilly wind, the scalp loses a lot of heat. It was sound advice, except he had also forgotten to bring a hat. *How dumb can one kid be?* he wondered.

Fear bordering on panic began to rise up inside the boy. In the space of an hour, he had progressed from doggedly pedaling his bicycle to surviving a life-or-death scenario. He fought against the panic that threatened to overtake him.

Then Rule 17 came to mind: "If lost in the woods, don't run around and get more lost." He decided to build a snow cave.

By the time he finished heaping snow into a mound, tamping it down, and hollowing out the interior, his clothes were soaked and his fingers and toes were nearly frozen. With great difficulty, he gathered a few twigs and fallen limbs from the immediate vicinity. He would have searched more widely except he feared being unable to find the cave again.

After gathering enough wood to build a small fire, he crawled into the shelter. It was a tight fit; he would have to remain curled in a fetal position. With care so as not to jettison items into the snow, he fished around in the backpack, which he had positioned near the entrance. Eventually, he found his matches.

Working with numb fingers and shivering uncontrollably, he used up half his supply of matches before the small heap of twigs he had fashioned began to burn. When the blaze took hold, he felt a huge rush of relief. A minute later, as he was adding fuel, it became apparent he hadn't gathered enough kindling. He would have to venture out into the storm again, but for the moment, he could warm his hands. He stripped off his gloves and rubbed his palms together above the fire.

Unbidden, the question he had asked himself in the funeral parlor returned to trouble him: *Why? Why was this happening? What had he done to deserve this fate? Was God punishing him?*

To Mathias, the assumption that God had engineered his predicament—not to mention the unendurable loss of his mother—seemed entirely rational. His mother had believed in God and in His omnipotence. In her opinion, everything that transpired in the universe was a function of His will. If that was the case, wasn't God indeed responsible? Wasn't it His fault for allowing her to die?

A cloying fear fell upon Mathias. "God, forgive me," he whispered. "I didn't mean that. If You are there, please help me."

At that very instant, the cave's roof collapsed, burying Mathias under a foot of snow. His fire disappeared in a puff of steam. Thrashing about, he clawed his way out from beneath the frozen heap until his head and shoulders were free. In desperation, he groped around until his fingers discovered his backpack. Hauling it out, he brushed it off and wrapped his arms tightly around it. His gloves, however, were lost.

"Now what?" he cried aloud. His chattering teeth made staccato clicking sounds as he spoke.

Constructing another snow cave seemed out of the question. He dreaded the prospect of being buried again. Instead, he inched his way forward till he came up against the trunk of a tree. As he huddled in close beneath its drooping branches, he prayed they would shelter him from the wind. Sitting there, hugging his backpack with his knees drawn up to his chest, he remembered the supplies he had brought from home. He opened the pack's top flap and took out his water bottle. The liquid inside was slushy, but not completely frozen. He popped the cap and downed a swallow. The frigid water sent a chill coursing through his gut. "And yet another dumb move," he shrilled into the wind. "How about we warm it up first?"

He ferociously tore a thin branch off a tree limb and another as well. After scooping snow away from a patch of ground near the trunk, he fashioned a teepee-like structure out of pine needles and added thicker twigs on the outside. Cupping one hand to block the storm, he struck a match and lit the pine needles. The fire blazed for an instant, but then went out. He tried again with more pine needles and smaller twigs. The tinder caught, and soon he had a small fire burning brightly. After warming his hands a moment, he held the water bottle close to the fire. His plan seemed to be working. Then the fire hissed and abruptly went out. He had burned a hole through the plastic bottle. His water was now gone.

The numbness in his fingers and toes began creeping into his arms and legs. Remarkably, his shivering seemed less intense, which he remembered was a bad sign according to the survival manuals he had read. Suffering from hypothermia, his body was on the verge of giving up. Propped up in a seated position, he leaned back against the tree's trunk and tried to think. He could make his way to the road, but then he remembered the rule that had come to him while hiking the shores of Tanner's Creek with his grandfather. His mother had officially labeled it Rule 38: "It's hard to get where you want to go if you don't know where you are." He decided to stay put because he had no idea where he was.

He thought about starting another fire, but with the blizzard still raging, he feared wasting the last of his matches.

Mathias assumed it was probably getting on toward evening, though he really had no idea how much time had elapsed since the storm had begun. The impenetrable grayness that surrounded him gave no clue. In Montana, storms wax and wane. He could think of no reason why this one should behave any differently. Perhaps if he waited long enough, the whiteout would cease, and he could make his way to the road. He closed his eyes and listened to the sound of the wind.

***

Sometime later, Mathias awakened with a start. He had drifted off. There was no telling how long he had been asleep. He tried to move, but his limbs were blocks of ice. Seized by the irrational notion that he was already a corpse, he forced his joints to respond to his will—first his shoulders, then his elbows, then his wrists, and finally his fingers. Next, he worked his way down his legs. Satisfied that he wasn't dead, he looked around.

To his amazement, the storm had abated.

Still sheltered by the tree, he tried to judge his location. As best he could tell, he had penetrated the forest by a distance of only twenty feet. He was closer to the road than he had imagined. Looking up through the tree's branches, he saw a patch of black sky dotted by countless stars. Snow more than eighteen inches deep had accumulated beyond the tree's circumference.

Mathias decided that the smartest thing to do would be to make his way to the road. But when he tried to crawl out from beneath the tree, he found he couldn't move. His body was still too stiff. He had forced his joints to flex a little, but there was no way he could walk or even crawl, not without warming up first. That meant using the last of his matches to start another fire.

With extreme difficulty, he retrieved the waterproof container from his backpack. When he checked inside, he was shocked. Only two matches remained. He would have to be exceedingly careful.

After again clearing a patch of ground near the trunk, he built another tepee out of needles and twigs. Several times he tore it down and started again, making certain the job was properly done. Finally satisfied that the fire should ignite, he took the first match and struck it. It flared and, because there was no breeze, continued burning until he dropped it, his ice-cold fingers having lost their sense of touch.

A panicked desperation descended upon Mathias. He needed a fire, and he needed it now. Without heat, his body would cease to function. He had one chance remaining.

With as much vigor as his chilled body would allow, he began pounding his hands against his thighs and slapping the front of his chest. He tried shaking his hands at the wrist and working his fingers. Gradually, he regained a minimal degree of control. When he felt he had limbered up as much as possible, he retrieved his last match and struck it. It too flared into brightness, and when he slowly lowered it to the pine needles, they began to burn.

With extremely great care, so as not to disturb his tenuous blaze, he added fuel—small twigs at first and then others that were larger. He could feel the heat of the fire on his face. A flicker of hope sparked within him. "Thank you," he whispered without appreciating to whom he was speaking.

Loosened by heat rising from the flames, a large glob of snow plopped down suddenly from a limb above his head and snuffed out the fire.

Mathias stared in disbelief, too shocked to react. His deliverance was now a sizzling pile of embers.

"So that's the way it is?" He closed his eyes and leaned back against the tree's rough bark. There was nothing more to be done. Maybe someone would chance upon his bike and search for his corpse.

What happens when we die? he wondered. "Guess I'm about to find out."

Mathias allowed his body to relax. There seemed little point in struggling with all his might to move only a few inches. A feeling of serenity came upon him. The more he relaxed, the stronger the sensation became. The anger that had fueled his foolish flight gradually dissipated. He was at peace and ready to embrace whatever fate awaited him. Soon, he would see his mother again.

***

The faint sound of a twig snapping drifted in from the direction of the road. The boy opened his eyes to peer beyond the forest. For a moment, he thought he saw movement. "Hello," he called out through frozen lips. His mind was too clouded by cold to be certain he was even awake.

"Mathias? Is that you?" said a familiar voice.

"What?"

"Mathias? Where are you?" the voice called out more loudly.

"Here!" Mathias screeched at the top of his lungs, his voice raspy from the cold. "I'm over here."

"Oh, thank god," the voice said.

Ward burrowed beneath the tree's branches and knelt over his grandson. "I had almost given up hope. I thought I'd lost you, but then I saw your signal or thought I did. I only caught sight of it out of the corner of my eye. When I looked straight at it, it was gone. I wasn't sure I had seen anything at all. Can you stand?"

"I don't think so."

"No problem. I'll carry you." Ward scooped his grandson into his arms. Trudging through knee-deep snow, he slowly slogged his way out of the forest. After struggling up the side of the ditch, he was panting for breath when he finally reached the road.

With difficulty, he managed to open the truck's passenger-side door while still carrying his grandson. He then settled the boy on the bench seat and swaddled him in several layers of blankets. The truck's engine was still running, so Ward reached across to crank the heater up to its maximum setting. Next, he refocused the heater's vents so they blew hot air directly on Mathias's frozen frame.

"Let's get you to the hospital as fast as we can." Ward made sure his grandson was safely tucked in and that his seat belt was securely latched.

"You came for me," Mathias said, his voice muffled with disbelief. "I thought you'd have given up by now."

"You're my grandson. I will never give up on you. Never."

Ward climbed in on the driver's side, shifted the truck into gear, and sped off as fast as road conditions would allow.

***

Five days later, Ward softly rapped a knuckle on the door to his grandson's bedroom. After a brief pause, he opened the door and stepped inside.

Fully clothed, Mathias lay propped up atop his bed, his bandaged left foot resting on a soft pillow. Frostbite had required the amputation of his fourth and fifth toes, which, remarkably, were the only digits he had lost. At first, his doctors had worried he would lose a couple fingers as well, but his circulation had unexpectedly improved, and he had been permitted to leave the hospital. Over the next forty-eight hours, his recovery at home had progressed smoothly—one of the blessings of youth, according to Doc Livingston.

"How was lunch?" Ward stepped forward to collect the tray balanced on Mathias's lap. Chips and a grilled cheese sandwich had seemed hardly sufficient for a growing boy, but that's what his grandson had requested.

"Good."

"Did you get enough? Can I get you something else?"

"I'm fine, Grandfather. It doesn't feel right being waited on like this."

Taken aback, Ward stared at Mathias. As best he could recall, that was the first time he had been addressed by his familial title rather than his given name. Something must have changed in the boy's way of thinking.

Ward grinned to himself. "While I was out this morning, I stopped by your school. Your teachers send their best wishes. They're all hoping you'll make a speedy recovery. I was able to pick up your homework assignments."

"Fantastic," Mathias replied, though he did not seem pleased.

"They're doing you a favor. If you fall too far behind, they'll make you repeat your freshman year."

"Can I ask you something?" Mathias said, changing the subject. His demeanor made it clear something important was on his mind.

"Sure." Ward set the food tray down on the study desk. He gestured toward the foot of the bed. "May I?"

Mathias nodded.

Careful not to jar his grandson's bandaged foot, Ward sat down. "What's on your mind?"

"How did you find me?"

"Luck, mostly, I guess. I just happened to be in the right place at the right time."

"*Providence* is what you said before, but there has to be more to it than that. I want to know. How did it happen?"

"The details?"

"Please."

"Well, where to begin? I guess when I came home for lunch. You know I'd been out looking for work. I was hungry, but I didn't feature spending money to eat in town. Coming home turned out to be a really good thing because I was here when the school called. They let me know you hadn't shown up for any of your classes. I was concerned, so I set out to look for you. I don't know your routines, so I spent the early part of the afternoon driving around, visiting places where I thought a boy your age might hang out. The more I looked, the more I worried because nobody had seen you.

"Just before the storm settled in, it occurred to me that you might actually have run off. That was when I got really frightened. I knew you were feeling—that you'd been through a pretty rough season. I called the police, but they told me it was too soon to file a missing person's report, that you were probably at a friend's house or chilling somewhere. What they said didn't feel right, so I sat down to puzzle out in which direction you might've gone. Honestly, I just had to guess. I don't know this area, but it seemed there were more points of interest to the west than to the east, so that's the direction I headed.

"The farther I traveled into the mountains, the worse the storm became. Three times, I got stuck and had to dig my way out. Let me tell you, that was nasty. At times, I couldn't see the road. The worst patch was right about where I found you. I suspect that was why you didn't hear the truck. Obviously, I passed right by you. It was slow going, but I made it all the way to the Idaho border before turning around. Thank goodness for four-wheel drive. I was on my way back when I caught a glimpse of your fire."

Mathias nodded thoughtfully. "That's what I wanted to ask about. How did that happen?"

"Not much to tell. I remember I was pointed downhill. The snow had stopped, so I could see better. I had the headlights on and was focusing on the road ahead so as not to get stuck again. That was when I saw a flash of light out of the corner of my eye. When I turned my head, it was gone. You know how if you press on your eyeball you see a flicker? I thought maybe that's what it was. I almost kept on going, but something told me to stop. It was a near thing. That's for sure."

"What made you stop?"

"I don't know. A feeling—maybe it was Providence. I'm not sure."

Mathias seemed troubled. "Grandfather, do you believe in God?"

"What? You think He had something to do with my finding you? That He's the reason I happened to be exactly in the right spot at exactly the right moment?"

"You just said it was Providence. If I understand the word, it means divine intervention."

"Hmmph. That is one meaning. I was thinking more along the lines of good fortune."

"So you don't believe God had anything to do with your rescuing me?"

"That's not what I said. Truth is, I honestly don't know. Why? What do you think?"

"I don't know either. That's why I was asking. A lot of what happened is fuzzy, especially right before you showed up, but I remember being mad at God, you know, for taking Mom… I had this feeling I was being punished, but I couldn't sort out what I had done wrong—other than make some really dumb mistakes." Mathias pursed his lips. "Maybe it's 'cause I was angry. Maybe He just wanted to teach me a lesson."

"Maybe, but then I might not be your best resource when it comes to interpreting God's intentions." Ward started to rise from the bed.

"It makes you uncomfortable, doesn't it, talking about God? Me too. I remember times when I really hoped Mom would change the subject…talk about anything but religion."

Ward sat back down. More than once he had fervently hoped his grandson would open up and they could have a genuine conversation. The mystery of God was not the topic he would have chosen, but it would suffice. The boy was right; the subject did make him uncomfortable. On the other hand, this was an opportunity too precious to waste.

Ward decided to jump right to the heart of the matter. "It's tough, losing someone you love. Missing her is hard. For me too. Lauren was my only child. I wish I'd been given more time to get to know her. I can only imagine how you feel."

Mathias tensed up as if assailed by unwelcome emotions.

Sensing that he had overestimated his grandson's readiness to confront his grief, Ward thought for a moment and decided to chance nudging their conversation to a more adult level. "It seems that in fact, you're asking two questions. First, was God punishing you, or by extension was He responsible for your predicament? Second, does God exist? Clearly, you need to answer the second question first because if God doesn't exist, your first question becomes moot."

"You're right," Mathias said with amazement. Eagerness replaced his look of sadness. "I need to figure out whether or not God is real."

Good luck with that, Ward thought. "Let me know what you decide." He stood up and retrieved the tray after making sure Mathias's crutches were within arm's reach of the bed. "I'll bring your homework up. Is there anything else you need?"

"Not really. I have my laptop. I'm going to see what I can find online. By the way, did the doctor mention when I get my stitches out?"

Ward glanced back from the doorway. "We see him tomorrow morning. I believe that's so he can change your dressings. When your stitches come out will depend upon how your wound is healing. He did indicate that you should be back in school by the first of next week."

"Splendid. I'll be able to use the library to do my research." This time, Mathias seemed genuinely pleased—not the sort of reaction Ward would have predicted. The sincerity in the boy's affect left little doubt he had already committed himself to his quest.

***

"Hey, Reslin," Tommy Jackson called out as he stood beside his school locker. "What happened to you?" Tommy, a beefy kid with broad shoulders, had a laid-back personality. Due to his size, the coaches had persuaded him to play center for the school football team. As a junior, he was two years ahead of Mathias, and though not a close friend—in a small community like Rockridge, everyone knows everyone—they had hung out on occasion.

"I had foot surgery." Mathias hobbled over, mindful of where he planted the tips of his crutches. Ten days had passed since his surgery, and his navigating skills had improved to the point that he was feeling less awkward, but the floors looked to have been freshly waxed.

"Oh yeah?" Tommy slammed the locker's metal door shut and spun the dial on his padlock.

A sharp tingling sensation raced along the bottom of Mathias's foot from instep to heel. He had forgotten about not putting too much weight on his injured limb. "Frostbite," he said. "They amputated my fourth and fifth toes."

Tommy's ears perked up. "No kidding? You messing with me?"

"No, man, I'm not." Mathias straightened his leg to show off the gauze bandage that encased his foot from toes to ankle. "It may not look like they're gone, but that's because of the padding."

Nearby students edged closer to listen. More kids joined them. Attracted by the commotion, a small crowd formed, blocking the hallway. Trent Blaine was among those at the periphery.

"How'd you get frostbite?" said a female voice behind Mathias.

"I got caught in that freak storm we had a week and a half ago." Mathias looked around to see who had spoken.

Before he could assign a face to the voice, another student spoke up. "What was it like?"

"Truly awful. I thought I was going to die. I didn't know I could be so cold."

A flurry of questions followed one on top of another. He tried answering each in turn but was often interrupted. Then someone asked, "What were you doing out-of-doors in a blizzard?"

"Riding my bike," Mathias answered without thinking.

"Seems like a dumb thing to do," said a male voice, "bike riding in a whiteout." Mathias suspected Trent had offered the comment. Several students snickered.

It dawned on Mathias that his reputation was on the verge of being trashed. What would people think if he admitted he'd been running away from home? And no way could he acknowledge the foolish mistakes he'd made. His lack of foresight would mark him as an idiot. Losing a couple toes to bad luck is one thing. Having your foot mutilated because you're brainless is quite another. He chose to lie. "If you must know, I have a cousin who lives twenty miles west of town. I'd spent the night and was heading home when the snowstorm took me by surprise. It came on so quickly, there was nothing I could do."

A wave of apprehension washed over Mathias. What if someone were to ask something like "Hey, I live out west of town. What's your cousin's name?" How would he respond? The problem with lying is that if you keep shoveling, sooner or later you're going to bury yourself. To his relief, he was saved by an unlikely turn of events.

Trent shoved his way to the center of the circle. With his voice dripping sarcasm, he said, "Well, lookee here, will ya? It's our own eight-toed sloth. What do y'all think? Is our football team ready to welcome its new place kicker?"

A handful of students chuckled, but most looked away in disgust.

"Reslin, you take care," said Tommy Jackson as he turned to leave. "Out of my way, dude." He elbowed Trent aside.

Other students followed his example, and the crowd thinned.

"That was real funny," Mathias said to Trent.

"I thought so." Trent touched his forehead in a middle-finger salute before sauntering off.

The day continued much as it had begun. Between classes and over the lunch hour, students pressed Mathias to hear the details of his ordeal. Gradually the telling became boring, then tedious. As a result, he stopped answering questions altogether. By the time the final school bell sounded, he was yesterday's news—just another student coping with the academic grind.

Mathias's brief notoriety had unexpected consequences. First off, only a few students had mentioned his mother's passing, for which he was intensely grateful. Second, distracted by his celebrity status, he had forgotten that he had intended to prove or disprove the existence of God. Not until his junior year would the challenge be remembered. Only then would he take up the quest that had captured his imagination during his winter travail.

***

Toward the middle of Mathias's third year in high school, Mr. Arlen Zucker scribbled a list of topics on the blackboard; then he turned to face his human biology class. "It's time to talk term papers."

A chorus of groans and muttered protests erupted throughout the classroom.

A short man with a receding hairline, Mr. Zucker's smile exposed the gap between his front teeth. "Here now. Surely you must have suspected this was coming. As you can see, I've posted seven topics. Choose one to be the subject of your essay. I won't require a minimum word count, but bear in mind that grades are assigned based upon scholastic thoroughness. The highest grades will go to those who teach me something I don't already know. All essays will be due five weeks from today. There will be no extensions. And remember, in my class, a term paper counts for half your final grade, so be diligent in your research. Any questions?"

Seated in the second row, Mathias reviewed the topics listed on the blackboard. Subjects like "The Circulatory System" and "How Nerves Communicate" both seemed incredibly droll. The assignment that caught his notice was "Insulin's Role in Controlling Blood Sugar." He remembered being curious as to how insulin causes glucose to move from the bloodstream into cells.

He opened his notebook and wrote the topic down as the header on a clean sheet of paper. His next class was study hall. The library's computers would enable him to begin his research immediately. Now a junior, he had learned that procrastination could destroy whatever hope you might have of getting into college.

When the bell rang, Mathias rose and headed for the library. In the two-and-a-half years since his winter ordeal, he had trained himself to walk without a limp, regardless of how his foot might be feeling. Although not as frequently as early on, there were still days when he thought he could feel his toes. This happened to be one of those days.

***

Ward Stanford sat at the kitchen table, thumbing through pages in an outdoor magazine. He glanced up when his grandson entered through the back door. "You're late." He set his magazine aside. "I was starting to worry."

"No need," Mathias said. "I can take care of myself."

"That may be," Ward responded with a touch of annoyance, "but you're fifteen, and I'm still your guardian. I worry when I don't know where you are."

"That's not my fault."

"Maybe not, but I'd appreciate it if you'd keep me informed. By the way, where have you been?"

"I stopped by the library. I'm researching a school assignment—must've lost track of time."

Ward seemed dubious. "Sure it wasn't a young lady?"

"No, Grandfather. I don't have a girlfriend. Why do you keep bringing it up?"

"Because someday you will."

"Not."

"We'll see. Anyhow, now that you're home, I can start dinner."

"I'll clean up. Then I want to show you something."

"First, allow me to share my good news." Ward stood and punched his fists to his hips like a heroic action figure. "I've been promoted. I am now the production supervisor for the Fairworth Lumber Mill. The boss credited my skill with numbers. Spreadsheets and flowcharts are how we balance resource acquisition against production demand. Starting tomorrow, yours truly is a member of management."

"Doesn't sound like a whole lot of fun, pushing numbers around."

"Hey, I thought you liked math? At least I won't be doing grunt work any longer."

"Must be tough getting old." Mathias stepped forward to plop his backpack down on the kitchen table.

"I'm only sixty." Ward eyed glanced at the bag. "Maybe if I had started out doing physical labor as a young man…"

"I'll move it in a second," Mathias responded. "There's something I want to show you. Does this mean you'll be getting a raise?"

"A modest one. We'll still have to pinch pennies, but we won't have to do without as often." Though they never acknowledged the subject openly, both understood that the money Ward had brought back from California was nearly gone.

Mathias bristled. "Like I've told you before, I'm fully capable of helping out. There is no reason I can't get a job. I can work after school and on weekends."

Ward shook his head. "You worry about your education. I'll worry about hearth and home. We'll be okay."

"You won't reconsider?"

"What did you want to show me?"

"This." Mathias unzipped the pack's side flap and took out the article he had copied. While in the library, he had come across an op-ed published in an obscure scientific journal. He handed the papers to his grandfather.

Ward sat down to study the material. "What am I looking at?"

Mathias sat down beside him. "You remember the conversation we had a couple years ago, about proving or disproving the existence of God?"

"Vaguely."

"In biology class, I'm supposed to write an essay describing how insulin controls blood sugar. I came across this paper while doing some research. It reminded me of that conversation. The author's position is that insulin metabolism disproves the theory of evolution. I was hoping you could help me with parts I don't understand."

Ward sighed. "Ah, lad, I'm no scientist. Show it to someone who knows what they're about." He held the paper out to hand it back.

"Fine, if it's too much bother, I'm sure somebody at school will give it a try." He reached out to accept the article.

Abruptly, Ward drew it away. "Hang on. Maybe we can figure this out together. So insulin controls blood sugar?"

"Correct. Insulin allows glucose, a type of sugar, to move into cells where it is converted to energy. Without insulin, cells burn fat and protein to do their work. This leads to a condition called ketoacidosis, which is fatal. In other words, a lack of insulin quickly results in death."

"I'm with you so far," Ward said proudly.

"Good. According to this article, insulin is a protein, and proteins are made up of amino acids. When insulin is produced, it starts out as preproinsulin, a chain of 110 amino acids linked together like a string of pearls. Before insulin can do its work, the preproinsulin molecule gets twisted, cross-linked, and reshaped."

"According to this," Ward pointed to a paragraph in the article, "the amino acid chain is reconfigured into a metabolically active molecule." He smiled, still feeling pleased with himself.

"Right. You know about genomics, don't you—the study of DNA, the stuff inside every cell that contains our genetic codes?"

"Sounds familiar."

"DNA serves as a template for making proteins. It's like building something based on an incredibly detailed set of instructions." Mathias tapped a section of the article. "Follow along. See if I get this right. Because of the way DNA encodes proteins, there's only one chance in 10^{150} that human preproinsulin—a molecule 110 amino acids long—will be formed as a result of random chance."

"Hold on. I'm lost." Ward studied the text until he found the section his grandson was quoting. "Give me a moment. This stuff is deep." He scanned a couple paragraphs and then said, "Okay, go ahead."

Mathias closed his eyes as if visualizing what he had read. "Suppose there are ten billion humans on each of ten billion worlds, and each human can produce one unique molecule per second, and suppose they do so for ten billion years. In all that time, all those people on all those worlds would produce only one quarter of the molecules necessary to be assured of exactly matching human preproinsulin. How'd I do?"

"Not bad. I thought you didn't like numbers?"

Mathias ignored the taunt. "What I found interesting is that insulin does its work by binding to specific receptor sites on the surface of specific cells, like fitting a key in a lock. Wrong key and the lock won't open. Wrong insulin molecule and glucose can't get inside the cell."

Ward scanned the text. "That's what it says. It also says that without insulin, the subject dies." He looked up. "If all ten billion people on each of the ten billion worlds are dead, how can they produce one molecule per second for ten billion years?"

Mathias grinned. "That is precisely the point. They can't. If they don't get it right the first time, they won't survive, and the odds against getting it right are one in 10^{150}. By the way, 10^{150} is an unimaginably huge number. It's estimated there are only 10^{80} atoms in the entire known universe."

Ward combed his fingers through his hair. "Where is this leading?"

"There's more."

Ward sighed. "Really?"

"To make insulin, you need functioning cells with intact cellular mechanics. The odds against evolving a functioning cell out of nothing are vastly greater than the odds of creating human preproinsulin. Also, for humans, the insulin-glucose relationship presupposes you already have all the other biological processes that support life, like the heart, lungs, kidneys, liver, etc. Without insulin, a being could not live long enough to form the necessary organ systems. And without the necessary organ systems, insulin can't do its job. It's a classic catch-22. To survive, a being must evolve everything all at once. Statistically, it's impossible. That means evolution can't be true."

Ward nodded. "If that's the case…"

"Evolution is a lie. There is no way that we humans evolved. And if we didn't evolve, we were created, and if we were created, there must be a creator. In my mind, that proves there is a God." Mathias sat back with a smug look on his face.

"I suspect a whole lot of people would disagree with you. They would discount your arguments and cite an abundance of evidence to the contrary."

"Probably, but then insulin isn't the only proof. For instance, where are the precursors? If every organism is doing its best to evolve into a new species, why aren't we toting around hundreds and thousands of proteins whose functions are yet to be defined?"

"Good point."

"Also, as the article points out, insulin is but one example. The same reasoning applies to the thyroid, adrenal, gonadal, exocrine, and vasoregulatory hormones. They are subject to the same probability analysis. What's the likelihood that all those biological processes evolved at exactly the same moment so life could exist?"

"I hear you, but there are those you're not going to convince."

Mathias grinned even more broadly. "I don't have to convince them. Right now the only opinion I'm concerned with is my own, and I now believe God is real."

Ward handed the reference article back to his grandson and stood up. "Great. Now that we've got that settled, what do you want for dinner? You can have a hot dog with pork and beans or pork and beans with your hot dog."

"Those are my options?" Mathias returned the paper to his knapsack and zipped it up.

"It's your fault. You've made my head hurt. Now I don't feel like fixing anything fancy."

"Then I guess I'll have a hot dog with pork and beans." Mathias hefted his backpack and carried it up to his room.

A huge smile lit up Ward's face after his grandson had departed. "Wow," he said softly to himself. "How about them apples?"

***

The next morning, Mathias met his grandfather at the foot of the stairs, both having just emerged from their respective rooms. Both were on their way to the kitchen. Rather than the denim trousers and a faded work shirt that Mathias was accustomed to seeing his grandfather wear, Ward had put on a pair of charcoal gray slacks, a dark blue dress shirt, a striped tie, and wingtip shoes.

Taken aback, Mathias paused to inspect Ward's attire. "Look at you, all fancied up."

"I told you, I'm now a member of management. I have to dress the part."

"It would appear you've succeeded, but you sure don't look comfortable."

"A small price to pay." Ward gestured toward the kitchen. "After you. What do you want for breakfast? I was thinking bacon and eggs."

"I'll pass."

"You sure?"

"Yeah. Maybe I'll have cereal if you don't mind. No offense, but we could use your eggs over easy as mud flaps for the truck." Mathias entered the kitchen and crossed to a cupboard, where he took down a bowl. From an upper shelf, he selected a brightly colored box of sugary wheat flakes marketed mainly to kids.

"Hey, if you don't like my cooking, you can always fend for yourself."

"Hence the cereal." Mathias grabbed a carton of milk out of the refrigerator and poured some on his breakfast. After fetching a spoon out of the silverware drawer, he sat down at the table.

Ward reached into a bottom drawer and selected one of Lauren's aprons, which he put on, tying the strings around his waist.

"Whoa," Mathias exclaimed.

"Better than splattering grease on my fancy duds."

"It's not that—flashback. I wasn't expecting…"

"Ah." Ward positioned a skillet on the stove and lay in several strips of bacon. "Sure you don't want some?"

"Maybe a couple while you're at it."

Ward grinned. "Thought so. You know," he said, turning around, waving the spatula in his hand, "I was thinking about that article you showed me yesterday. It occurred to me that those 10 billion people you mentioned wouldn't necessarily have to evolve insulin as we know it. Perhaps a different protein with a similar structure might work equally well?"

"Perhaps." Mathias swallowed a mouthful of cereal. "But a substitute protein doesn't change the odds. It only shifts the focus where the calculations are applied. Remember, insulin functions like a key in a lock. If you create a random molecule as the key, you have to evolve a specific receptor site as the lock. The odds against getting a correct fit would be virtually the same. Keep in mind that insulin starts out as a chain 110 amino acids long and that it gets twisted, cross-linked, and cleaved. Only proteins with a very specific configuration could undergo such remodeling."

"Meaning?"

"The vast majority of evolutionary attempts would fail out of hand because they wouldn't have the right structure, and any failure results in the organism's death."

"Enough. You've made your point." Ward flipped the bacon, careful not to splatter grease. "So now that you believe God is real, where does that leave you? Obviously, you must have thought about it." He refrained from looking directly at his grandson for fear of provoking a nebulous response, which is what he got anyway.

"It doesn't leave me anywhere."

"Bull. You know what I'm asking. If God created man, does that mean He created everything?"

"Of course. It would be absurd to assume He created man but the rest of the universe just happened."

"So if God created the universe and everything in it, then—"

"What do you want me to say?"

"I'm hoping you'll share your thoughts—truthfully. Tell me what's on your heart. You've been carrying around a heavy burden. It's time to let it go."

"What are you talking about?"

"For a long while now, something has been troubling you. Every time we get close to talking it through, you wall yourself off. Be honest. Tell me how you feel. I think it'll help if you open up."

"What do you want to hear? That God is responsible for my mother's death—my father's as well? That He could have saved them both but He didn't? That it's His fault they are gone? You're asking me if I blame God, aren't you? Will the truth is, yes, I do. He took my parents and left me alone."

"Not alone, exactly."

"You might be wearing my mother's apron, but you're not her, and you never will be. You know what, forget the bacon. I'm out of here." Mathias stood and retrieved his cereal bowl. After dumping what was left of his breakfast into the trash, he started to leave.

"Wait," his grandfather commanded.

Mathias halted and spun around. "I know you mean well, but I don't need you inside my head. How I deal with my grief is my business, not yours."

"Why are you so afraid to speak your mind?"

"I'm not afraid. I just choose to keep my thoughts to myself. Look, I have track practice after school. I won't be home till later. Don't worry about fixing dinner. I'll grab something in town." Mathias rushed out of the room before his grandfather could comment.

"That could've gone better," Ward said to an empty house. He shook his head. "It's going to take a miracle to set that boy free from so much anger."

CHAPTER 5

The narrow aisles of the Best Shot Sporting Goods store overflowed with equipment and supplies appropriate for life in the great outdoors. Mathias trailed behind Trent Blaine as they threaded their way past shelves loaded with fishing paraphernalia. Still in their junior year of high school, both boys were bored. For over an hour, they had wandered around with nothing to do on a Saturday afternoon. Small towns could be like that.

Several days had passed since Ward had pressed his grandson to open up about his feelings. The friction between them had lessened but not abated. Feeling ill at ease, Mathias had finished his chores early. He had then petitioned his grandfather to be allowed to head out on his own. Ward had wanted to talk, to make right the state of affairs between them, but Mathias had resisted. Instead, he had jumped on his bike and pedaled off in the direction of town.

On his way into Sterling's Foods to buy a candy bar for lunch, Mathias had literally bumped into Trent. They had soon discovered they were equally bedeviled by the tedium of rural life. Trent had suggested they hang out together. Mathias would have preferred spending time with someone less volatile, but no one else was around. It made him wonder if some community activity might be underway, one he knew nothing about.

Wandering through the camping gear section, Mathias picked up a collapsible water bottle. "Cool, huh?" After checking it out, he put it back.

"If you say so." Trent did not seem impressed. "Did you get your learner's permit?" He peeked over the top of a knife display to see what Charlie Sullivan, the store's owner, was up to and if he were watching.

"Grandfather says I'm too young. He thinks I need to turn sixteen first."

Trent scowled. "Montana law says you only have to be fifteen."

"He doesn't care. He claims it's for my own good."

"That's too bad. My dad is exactly the opposite. He'd be thrilled if I got my license."

"How come?"

"Then there wouldn't be anything to keep me from leaving home." Trent snaked his arm around to the back of the display case and snagged an expensive-looking folding knife, which he hurriedly stuffed into the pocket of his denim jeans.

"Are you crazy?" Mathias hissed. "What if he sees you?"

"He never has." Trent shot a wary glance in Mr. Sullivan's direction. "I doubt he can see anything past the end of his nose. Hey, I know what we can do. I can help you get your license. What you need are driving lessons." He turned and quickly threaded his way toward the exit.

"What are you talking about?"

"Follow me." Head down, Trent strolled out the front door.

Mathias fell in behind, fully expecting to hear an alarm sound at any moment. The store remained silent.

"Piece of cake," Trent declared smugly after they had moved more than a block away.

About to round a corner, Mathias looked back. "My bike," he said, having recalled he had parked in a community rack.

Trent grabbed his arm. "Leave it. It'll be safe. Where we're going isn't far. You can come back for it later."

*****

"See, just like I told you." Trent indicated a neon blue BMW 4-Series Coupe. "Isn't she a beauty?"

"It's rad, for sure." Mathias shifted his attention to several of the homes nearby. From what he could tell, Trent had guided him to an ordinary middle-class neighborhood. When he looked back at the residence where the BMW was parked, he saw that the house seemed deserted, even though there was an expensive car sitting in the driveway. "Who lives there?"

"Like I said, my uncle. He's out of town." Trent stepped off the curb to cross the street.

"Where are you going?" Mathias said, feeling a sense of uneasiness.

"Wait here. I know where he keeps the key. I'll be back in a minute."

"No, man. Hold up. This doesn't feel right."

"What's the matter, no guts? Look, you don't have to worry. My uncle is a cool guy. He's let me drive his car a bunch of times. We'll be fine." Trent sprinted away, then he circled around the side of the house. After scurrying up and over a six-foot fence, he disappeared into the backyard.

As Mathias watched him go, a troubling sense of apprehension took root in the pit of his stomach. On the verge of turning and walking away, something prevented him. Most likely, he was deterred from leaving by his need to rebel, to lash out against his unresolved anger. Or maybe he simply felt compelled to proclaim his own identity—to become the arbiter of his own fate—even if it meant breaking the rules. Whatever the reason, he chose to stay put.

A moment later, the front door opened and Trent emerged. He held up a set of keys and motioned for Mathias to join him.

"Are you sure about this?" Mathias called out as he crossed the street.

Trent tossed him the keys when he was near enough. "You drive. After all, you're the one who'll be testing for his permit."

"I can't."

"You've driven your grandfather's truck, right?"

"Only in our driveway and once in the supermarket parking lot when nobody was around. Both times, Grandfather was with me."

"Well, this time, I'll be with you. What's the difference? We gonna do this or not? Don't chicken out on me now."

Mathias inspected the fob in his hand and then looked at the car. With a shrug, he closed his fist over the fob and stepped forward. "Why not?"

After studying the fob again, he pressed the button to unlock the car, then he settled into the driver's seat. The first thing that caught his notice was how low to the ground he felt—almost as if he were sitting on the pavement. The second thing he noticed was the number of gauges arrayed on the dashboard. This vehicle was a far cry from the family pickup.

Trent hustled around to the passenger-side door and climbed in. With a wry grin, he reached over to pat Mathias on the shoulder. "This is going to be fun. Go ahead. Start her up."

Mathias did as instructed. When he pressed the keyless ignition, the engine roared to life with a deep, throaty growl.

"Oh yeah!" Trent exclaimed, excitement in his voice. "Where do you want to go?"

The two teenagers stared at one another. Neither had thought that far ahead.

"How about Lake Borman?" Mathias suggested. The lake, a picturesque body of water five miles out of town, was a lousy fishing site, and its shoreline was poorly suited for hiking. In all probability, there would be few, if any, visitors hanging around.

"Let's do it," Trent agreed.

Mathias slipped the car into gear. When he let out on the clutch and stepped on the gas, the car lurched forward. The front bumper struck the garage door with a loud *thunk*.

"Oops," Mathias muttered softly.

Trent tapped the top of the gearshift. "See. Reverse is all the way to the left, then forward. That's away from you. Got it?"

"Got it."

Trent's eyes nervously scanned the neighborhood. "Let's not dawdle, shall we?"

The car jerked repeatedly as Mathias backed out of the driveway. When he shifted into first gear, the transmission gave out a metallic grinding sound in protest. Happily, his driving smoothed out as he pulled away, except that the front half of the BMW wound up in the intersection at their first stop sign. After a bit, he seemed to get the hang of it.

"There is a rumor going around that you're in line for a scholarship," Trent mused. Mathias sensed a touch of envy. They cruised through the outskirts of Rockridge on their way out of town.

"What rumor?"

"People are saying the scholarship committee wants to give you money because you're a computer whiz?"

"I do like computers. As for being a whiz, I don't think so. Besides, I'm not sure I want to go to college. I'm only a junior. I haven't submitted even a single application."

"Hey, if they want to give you money, you'd be stupid not to apply."

"We'll see."

As they rounded a curve, an empty stretch of road opened up in front of them. Mathias stepped on the gas, and the BMW surged forward. An exhilarating rush washed through him. He gripped the steering wheel with both hands—so tightly his knuckles blanched. But then a growing sense of apprehension caused him to ease off on the accelerator.

"Why are you slowing down?" Trent said with an air of disapproval. "Punch it. Let's see what this baby will do."

Far ahead a figure materialized, someone hiking along the side of the road. Mathias slowed even more when he recognized Abraham Finkel. "That's Abe. What's he doing out here all alone, I wonder?"

"Try not to run him over," Trent suggested. "On second thought, why not? It's not like anybody's going to miss a fat—"

"Be nice. You two need to kiss and make up. Abe is an okay guy once you get to know him. Let's see where he's going. Maybe we can give him a lift."

"You've got to be kidding. What do you think we're doing here?"

"What's the problem? Your uncle lets you use his car, right? That's what you said." Mathias pulled onto the shoulder of the road and stopped a few feet ahead of where Abe was walking. He stuck his head out of the side window and looked back. "Hey, man, how's it going? You need a lift?"

"Mathias?" Abe quickened his pace and soon stood beside the car, looking down. "Nice ride. Is it yours?"

"I wish. Where you headed?"

"Lake Borman—to take pictures." Abe indicated the camera that hung by a strap around his neck.

"That's where we're going. Hop in." Mathias opened his door and tilted the back of his seat forward.

Abe lifted a foot to climb in, but then froze when he noted Trent glowering at him from the passenger seat.

"Don't worry," Mathias said. "He won't bite. I'll make sure of it."

Abe's look of uncertainty indicated he was not at all convinced. Even so, he settled into the back seat, and Mathias drove off. Trent, for his part, gritted his teeth and ignored their new companion.

With the windows down and the forest rushing by, Mathias felt a thrill of excitement. It seemed a perfect day until he heard the wail of a distant siren.

"Stop!" Trent shrilled when he too perceived the warning. "Stop the car. Pull over. I mean it. Pull over right now. Let me out."

It took a moment for Mathias to comprehend what was happening. The owner's neighbors must've called the police.

The problem with lying to yourself is that sooner or later, it becomes impossible to ignore the truth. In a rush, it dawned on Mathias that he was in serious trouble, and he became afraid. Overreacting, he slammed on the brakes, causing the car to skid so violently he nearly lost control. The BMW came to rest in a shallow gully beside the road.

Without a moment's hesitation, Trent jumped out and bolted for the trees a dozen yards away. "Run!" he yelled back over his shoulder. "Don't let them catch you."

Moving on autopilot, Mathias followed Trent's lead and set out at a dead run. He reached the edge of the forest just as the sheriff's cruiser skidded to a stop behind the BMW, its light bar flashing red and blue. The shrill of its siren followed Mathias into the trees. A short ways on, he looked back to see if he was being followed. To his amazement, no one was chasing him. What he saw instead was Abraham Finkel tilted up against the BMW with both palms pressed against the hood and a policeman patting down his pockets. Trent was nowhere to be seen.

By plodding through the woods along a route that paralleled the road, Mathias made his way back to town without being observed. It was slow going crawling over fallen trees, dodging snags and branches, and crossing duff-clogged terrain. By the time he retrieved his bicycle, he was tired, smeared with forest grime, and terrified of being caught. More than that, the truth of Trent's dishonesty had finally sunk in. They had stolen a car and nearly wrecked it. They had broken the law, meaning he was now a wanted felon. What really hurt was how easily Trent had deceived him. In all probability, there was no uncle. Most likely, the car's owner was no relation at all. The whole thing had been just another one of Trent's lies. What hurt even more was how easily he had bought into the deception.

As Mathias pedaled home, he teased apart the likely consequences of his criminal misconduct. With increasing shame, he pictured what lay ahead. Overcome by anxiety, he began to tremble so violently that he nearly crashed. A quarter-mile from his driveway, he stopped to shore up his nerve. It seemed certain the police would be waiting for him at home, ready to whisk him off to jail. For an instant, he considered turning around and heading out for parts unknown, but then remembered the last time he had run away and how that episode had ended. Feeling absolutely miserable, he prepared himself to face his fate.

As he bicycled down his driveway, Mathias saw that the open area that fronted the garage was deserted. No deputies were waiting. There were no lights flashing red and blue to greet him.

When he entered through the back door, his grandfather said without turning around, "Good. You're home. I was starting to worry." Looking up, he exclaimed, "What happened to you?"

"I went for a hike in the woods. It turned out to be more than I expected."

"Well, go clean up. Dinner will be ready in fifteen minutes. I hope you're hungry. We're having beef stew."

Oddly, the fact that the sheriff wasn't waiting to arrest him made Mathias feel worse, not better. He headed up the stairs to change clothes.

***

The next morning, being Sunday, Mathias found himself seated in church. He had pleaded to be left at home, but his grandfather had insisted. When pressed as to why, Ward had declared that there were issues that needed clearing up, and it wouldn't do to procrastinate any longer.

You have no idea, Mathias had admitted to himself in lieu of a reply.

As the sermon unfolded, he sensed that every word, every phrase was crafted to sear his conscience. What he found most troubling was that the image of Abraham Finkel being frisked wouldn't leave his mind.

Mathias felt certain Abe had been arrested. The fact that he himself was free meant his friend had refused to reveal who else had been in the car. He also knew that if Abe kept silent, he alone would be charged with the crime, which wasn't fair. The kid was innocent. He had done nothing wrong.

The guilt Mathias suffered for being a car thief was bad, but the notion that an innocent victim was about to shoulder the blame on his behalf was worse. By the end of the sermon, he knew he couldn't let things stand the way they were. Rule 15 had come to mind: "Take responsibility for the choices you make, especially the bad ones."

Mathias grasped his grandfather's arm as they exited the sanctuary together. "There's something I need to tell you, and you're not going to like it."

He guided Ward to a corner of the grassy lawn beside the church where they might speak in private. As forthrightly as possible, he laid out the entire scenario, just as it had happened. The only thing he omitted was Trent Blaine's involvement. Holding yourself accountable is one thing. Ratting out an accomplice is a different proposition, no matter how despicably they might have behaved.

Later that afternoon, Mathias repeated his confession at the Windpine County Sheriff's Office.

*****

A warm breeze drifted across the food bank's parking lot. A few puffy clouds hung low in the sky like vaporous balloons. Evening was coming on, and the air smelled of honeysuckle and pine. Ward stood with his backside propped against the grill of the family pickup. He had been waiting ten minutes for his grandson to emerge from the rickety building. Although a quarter past closing time, the place was still hopping with activity. Among the clients coming and going, Ward noted a disconcerting number of young families with one or more kids in tow.

As part of his punishment, the judge had sentenced Mathias to one hundred hours of community service. Volunteering at the county food bank had been deemed to be an appropriate means of fulfilling that requirement. Mathias had counted himself fortunate because of the judge's leniency until he had done the math. At a rate of eight hours every Saturday, it would take nearly thirteen weeks to serve his sentence, which meant he'd be spending every Saturday of his summer vacation handing out groceries to needy families.

The food bank's front door opened, and Mathias stepped out into the warm glow of late afternoon. Ward lifted his chin in acknowledgment when his grandson took note of him waiting across the parking lot. Mathias waved back. A man carrying a box of groceries offered Mathias a comment in passing. Mathias smiled and wished him well.

As his grandson crossed the dirt lot, Ward was amazed by how much the boy had matured. He pictured the scrawny kid who had seemed so withdrawn. He thought about how traumatized he had been by his mother's passing. He also remembered the promise he had made to his daughter and wondered if Lauren would be pleased with how things were working out. His relationship with the boy was improving—in fits and starts.

"So, how was your first day of community service?" Ward leveraged himself away from the pickup's grill and walked around to climb in on the driver side.

"Better than expected." Mathias hauled himself in on the passenger side. "And worse." He looked back at the run-down building. "I had no idea how many families live off charity. They can't all be destitute. It's sad too because the food bank is barely scraping by. Whatever cash they take in goes to buy supplies. There's no money left over to fix the place up."

"Times are tough. Money is scarce." Ward started the engine and headed home. "There aren't a lot of jobs out there."

"Tell me about it." Mathias turned his face away to look out the side window.

At sentencing, in addition to community service, the judge had imposed a fine of $1,500, even though the owner of the BMW had refused to press charges. His car had been recovered undamaged, and it was Mathias's first offense. One consideration that had given the judge pause was Mathias's refusal to name his accomplice. On the other hand, he had stepped forward to shoulder all responsibility, completely exonerating Abraham Finkel.

Rather than offer money as a quick fix, Ward had decreed that Mathias must earn what he needed to pay his debt. In the best of times, landing a job could be daunting, even more so for a fifteen-year-old high school student with no experience. Every day for a week, Mathias had crisscrossed Rockridge after school, submitting applications to businesses wherever he could.

"What do I do if nothing turns up?" Mathias returned his attention to his grandfather.

"Be patient. You're bright and physically able. Somebody's gonna hire you for something, even if it means cleaning restrooms or washing dishes."

"Or slopping hogs like the prodigal son?"

"Feeling sorry for yourself?"

"Not at all. I got off a lot easier than I deserve. I understand that, believe me."

"What do you feel—if you don't mind my asking?"

"What do you mean?"

"I mean how do you view this experience? How has it affected you? What lessons have you learned?" Ward turned off the main road to ease down their driveway. He stopped in front of the garage.

"I'll get it." Mathias jumped out of the truck to open the garage door.

Ward pulled in and parked. After shutting off the engine, he joined Mathias. "Look, this isn't about making you feel even guiltier than you already do. You know what you did was wrong. You told the judge you screwed up. Let's leave it at that. By the way, if you don't already know, I'm incredibly proud of you."

"What for? Being a car thief?"

"For having integrity, for taking responsibility for your actions. You made a mistake, but you set about to make it right. More than that, you refused to let an innocent kid take the blame. For that, you deserve credit."

"Is that really how you feel?"

"It truly is. Now come inside. There's a question I've been meaning to ask."

After closing up the garage, they entered the house together.

Ward pulled a pizza out of the freezer while Mathias adjusted dials on the stove to preheat the oven.

"You want a salad," Ward asked, "or something to go with your pizza? I can heat up a package of spicy chicken wings."

"Pizza will be plenty."

Ward cast a sidelong glance at his grandson. "No need to go hungry just 'cause other folks don't get enough to eat."

"Volunteering at a food bank makes you think. I never realized how tough some families have it. But really, I'm not that hungry."

"You sure?"

"Are we going to have dessert?"

"I think there might be some ice cream left."

"Then I'm good with just pizza."

Ward centered their dinner on the oven's middle rack and set the timer. With a sigh, he sat down at the table, catty-corner to his grandson.

"Tough day?" Mathias said.

"I never knew managing a homestead could be so much work. Listen, I've been thinking about your legal troubles and how smart it was for you to plead guilty. That was a wise thing to do."

"I was guilty."

"I know, but there are those who would've fought tooth and nail. Because you chose not to, they settled your case in near record time. One place you don't want to be is all tied up in the legal system. Lawyers can drag cases out forever. Believe me, I know."

"That's right. Mom mentioned that you were in prison once. What was it like?"

"It was awful—worse than terrible. Trust me. You never want to be there." Ward leaned forward and braced his elbows on the table. "Have you heard anything yet from whoever's in charge of handing out scholarships?"

Mathias shook his head. A worried frown clouded his face.

"I wouldn't fret," Ward offered reassuringly. "I doubt this business will hurt your chances."

"It has to," Mathias countered. "Even if I don't screw up again. I mean, everybody knows what happened or they'll find out. The court won't fully seal my record till I turn eighteen. After all, it was a second-degree felony."

"You may be only fifteen, but they could've prosecuted you as an adult."

"It's a blessing that they chose not to, whatever their reasons."

"Truly. If they had, you'd probably be in jail."

"Most likely, but I'll still be on probation even after I graduate. The scholarship committee is bound to hear about my legal troubles, if they haven't already."

"So what if they deny you a scholarship? You can go to college. You can get an education."

"And how am I supposed to afford college? I can't even pay my fine."

Ward thought for a moment and said, "We'll sell the farm."

"You'd do that?"

"I would."

Mathias contemplated his offer and then emphatically stated, "No. This is our home. Look, is this what you wanted to talk about?"

"Not really." Ward sipped his coffee and tipped back in his chair, raising the front legs off the floor. "I was thinking about that conversation we had a month or so ago."

"Which conversation?"

"The one where we decided God is real. You laid out your reasons for thinking He created the universe and everything in it. That is what you now believe, correct?"

"Yes."

"And as Creator, He's responsible for everything that happens in His creation? True?"

Mathias's eyes narrowed. "I don't remember saying that precisely."

"Perhaps I'm paraphrasing, but isn't that how you feel?"

After giving the matter some thought, Mathias nodded. "I suppose it is. Yes."

"Tell me, did God make you steal that BMW?"

"Make me steal it? What are you asking?"

"Did God compel you to start the engine, put the car in gear, and take it for a spin?"

"Don't be ridiculous. Why even bring it up? You're trying to rattle my cage."

"Not at all. And why is the question ridiculous?"

"Because God didn't steal that car. I did. God had nothing to do with it."

"You're saying you acted of your own free will?"

"That's exactly what I'm saying."

"But you just acknowledged that God, as Creator, is responsible for everything that happens in the universe. So isn't He responsible for the theft?"

A light went on behind Mathias's eyes.

Ward smiled.

***

Later that night, as Ward was about to fall asleep, a knock sounded on his door. Sitting up, he switched on the lamp beside the bed. "Come in."

The door opened. Mathias stepped into the bedroom. He seemed agitated. "All right, I'll accept that men can act of their own free will. But that changes nothing. God could've saved my parents."

"True." Ward shifted his legs to make room for his grandson. "Sit down. On average, how would most people judge stealing a car? Would they call it a good act or an evil act? And no, I'm not trying to make you feel bad."

"They'd say evil." Mathias sank down onto the mattress and angled his body to face his grandfather.

Ward nodded. "So we can agree that evil exists. God created the universe. Does that make Him responsible?"

"Not if men choose to do evil of their own free will."

"Choice—an interesting notion. Would you agree that for choice to be legitimate, you need at least two valid options? Otherwise, it's not choice. It's compulsion."

Mathias sat up straighter. "You're implying evil exists so people can make legitimate choices."

"Bingo."

"Why is this important?"

"In a world where evil exists, bad things are going to happen, and most of the time, God isn't going to interfere. If He keeps bad things from happening or lessens the damage evil causes, He diminishes the consequences of evil and shifts the balance that makes free will possible. Remember, both options have to be equally compelling. Diminish one, and the choice is no longer legitimate."

"In spite of all that," Mathias declared flatly, "God still could have saved my parents."

"Yes, He could have."

"Then why didn't He?" Mathias's voice rang with hostility.

"That, my young man, is a conversation for another day. It's late, and I'm tired. We can talk more on our way to church tomorrow."

Mathias rose from the bed. "You want to go to church again?"

"Yes."

"What's brought about this spiritual revival of yours?"

"You did. You set me to thinking about issues I've been ignoring. No, I take that back. Your mother did when she invited me up here, and I got to know her. I guess I'm still trying to figure out what made her special. Church seems like a good place to look. Anyway, go to sleep. We'll talk tomorrow."

"Yeah, like I'm going to be able to sleep." Mathias glanced back from the doorway. "Good night, Grandfather."

"Night, son."

As the door closed, Ward turned out the light. After fluffing his pillow, he rolled over on his side and shut his eyes. His last musing before drifting off was an image of Lauren smiling and steadfastly refusing to fret about her impending death.

***

Ward backed the pickup out of the garage and turned it around so it faced down the driveway. He waited while Mathias clambered in. Both had overslept, meaning they had missed breakfast.

"How are you this morning?" Ward said, switching on the radio. He tuned the dial to a Christian station.

Mathias knuckled an eye. "About like you'd expect. It wasn't till the wee hours that I fell asleep. And it's your fault, with all your theories tumbling around in my head."

"Let me remind you that you're the one who started these conversations way back when." Ward steered the pickup onto the road that led into town.

Mathias became serious. "I was lying there with my eyes closed, going over what you said about free will. I think I figured something out."

"Want to share?" Ward switched off the radio.

"Having free will means we get to choose what we believe and who we believe in. It lets us define our relationship with our Creator."

"Well done." Ward turned his head and rewarded his grandson with a proud smile.

Mathias's countenance remained serious. "Knowing that still doesn't answer my original question."

"Which is 'Why didn't God save my parents?'"

"That's the one."

Ward drove a ways before responding. "The honest answer is, I don't know. I doubt it's possible to fathom the mind of God. Things are the way they are. As to why?" Ward shrugged.

"I'd hoped for a bit more."

"Perhaps you're asking the wrong question."

"And what would the right question be?"

"Why does God allow us to choose not to believe in Him?"

"Well, maybe—hmm." Mathias mulled the matter over in his mind. "Interesting. Not as straightforward as it seems." He looked at his grandfather. "What do you say?"

"Oh, no. I'm working on my answer. You need to come up with your own." Ward turned left on Main Street and continued in the direction of the church.

Mathias sat back on the bench seat. His instincts hinted that it might take a while to figure out a response.

CHAPTER 6

The first day of the new school year was also Mathias's first day as a Rockridge High School senior. Dozens of bikes crowded the racks at the edge of the parking lot. He fit his ten-speed into an empty slot, confirming it would remain upright. He then used a cable lock to secure the rear wheel and frame to the rack. Straightening up, he noted that in previous years, he never would have worried about his bike being stolen, but times were changing. A recent string of thefts had suggested that he needed to be more prudent since the perpetrators were yet to be caught.

Mathias adjusted his backpack to a comfortable position as he looked up at the autumn sky. A wedge of Canadian geese sailed by overhead, honking as they flew. He envied the ease with which they pierced the air. In a couple months, the flocks would head south, traveling hundreds, if not thousands, of miles. *What would that be like*, he wondered, *spending winters in a place free of snow and ice?* He raised the collar of his woolen coat against the morning chill.

As Mathias headed for the main entrance, he noted that the parking lot was filling up. Other students were also arriving early, which wasn't surprising considering it was the beginning of a new semester.

Richard Havers steered his sleek sports car into the parking lot and beeped his horn as he cruised past Mathias. The car's pearl-red finish glittered in the morning light. Mathias waved back but continued walking. The polite thing would have been to wait and allow Richard to catch up, but a trace of resentment born of envy kept Mathias moving forward.

When he reached the sidewalk in front of the school, he paused to admire the central building's red brick edifice. The structure was old enough to qualify as an historic landmark but was still in good condition. The main building housed the administrative offices and a few classrooms. More modern facilities have been added as needed. The town's growing population guaranteed that the school's enrollment would increase every year.

As he faced the front of the school, Mathias silently repeated the promise he had made to himself after his run-in with the law. *I will stay out of trouble. I will get straight As. I will qualify for admission to college.* Spending his summer working odd jobs to pay off his fine had underscored the value of an education—especially one that would allow him to work with his brain rather than his brawn.

In small clusters, students chatted outside the double doors—friendships renewed, rivalries revived. The inevitable cliques were forming.

As Mathias climbed the front steps, bits of conversation reached his ears—narratives about vacation adventures, regrets that summer was ending, worries about the school year ahead. He even heard his own name mentioned, but could not determine the context in which it had been spoken.

Mathias made his way inside. A glut of bodies, all in motion, thronged the central corridor. The noise level resembled that of a small riot. Rather than add to the tumult, he threaded his way toward the administrative wing. From experience, he assumed that would be where he would be given his enrollment packet. Anxious to learn his class assignments, he pressed ahead despite the congestion. It seemed every member of the student body was focused on the same objective.

Not realizing he was speaking aloud, Mathias muttered, "Who'd believe so many souls could fit in such a small space?"

"Totally," said a soft voice close to his ear. A feminine hand gently took hold of his forearm. "Can you help me? I'm sort of lost, and you seem to know where you're going."

Mathias turned to see who had interrupted his forward momentum and found himself gazing into the oval face of a girl near his own age. Her sandy-blonde hair, swept back on the sides and held in place with barrettes, fell to the tops of her shoulder blades. Her eyes were light brown, the color of roasted chestnuts. Of medium height and medium build, she had an athletic figure. Her navy blue slacks complemented her fleece coat and mint green blouse. She smiled.

Hers was an open, candid smile, the kind that said, "I am who I am." Unable to help himself, Mathias broached a smile in return.

"Hi." The girl released Mathias's arm and stuck out her hand. "I'm Darcy, Darcy Thurston."

"Hi. I'm Mathias Reslin." When he accepted the handshake, he noted that her hand was free of calluses. It was not the hand of a farmworker or summer laborer.

"I apologize for intruding," Darcy said, "but I'm new here. I'm not sure what I'm supposed to do."

"No problem." Mathias drew himself fully upright. "I'm on my way to the administration wing. Usually, there's a table set up in front of the student affairs office. Your registration packet will have all the information you need. If you'd like, I can take you there."

"Cool." Again Darcy smiled, and Mathias responded in kind.

Eyeing the tumult in the hallway ahead, Mathias said with determination, "Follow me." For a moment, he thought about grasping Darcy's hand again to keep from getting separated, but embarrassment dissuaded him. Over his shoulder, he called back loudly enough to be heard, "So you're new to Rockridge? Where did you go to school before?"

"Los Angeles."

"No kidding? What part?"

"Westwood. Do you know LA?"

"Not really. Actually, I've never been there, but that's where my grandfather is from. He owned a mortgage company years ago."

"Do you remember where in LA?"

"Malibu, I think. Somewhere close to the ocean. He doesn't like to talk about it. So what did you do in Westwood besides go to school? I mean, I assume that's where your family lived?" Mathias realized he was being nosy. "Sorry—didn't mean to pry."

"Both my parents were professors at UCLA. My father taught comparative religion. My mother taught history in the humanities department."

Mathias rounded a corner and halted abruptly. The throng crowding around a folding table blocked their way. Trailing behind, Darcy nearly collided with his back.

"Looks like we're in the right place," Mathias said. "Now all we need to do is elbow our way in."

"I'll follow you."

Mathias glanced back. "Why Rockridge? The nearest four-year college is a hundred miles from here—unless your parents plan on teaching high school? Do they?"

Darcy chuckled. "Heavens no. That would be horrible—going to school where your parents were teachers. Actually, we moved up here to get away from the congestion. And the politics on campus. Academicians can be…tedious, narrow-minded. We wanted to simplify our lives, so we relocated. One day while surfing the Net, my father came across a real estate listing that sounded interesting. It described a gift shop for sale in a rural community with strong spiritual values. That seemed like just the ticket, so we bought it."

"You're talking about the Silver Rose?"

"That's right. I keep forgetting this is a small town. My parents now own the business. I'll be helping out when I can."

"I am well acquainted with the Silver Rose. My mother used to sell her pottery there on consignment. She really liked Mrs. Grimes. So did I. She was nice. I didn't realize she'd put the place up for sale."

"It wasn't on the market long, only a few days. Finding it the way we did was sort of a God thing. Does your mother still make pottery? We're looking for craftsmen to help fill our shelves."

"My mom passed away three years ago."

"Oh, I am truly sorry. I didn't know."

"That's okay. Hey, look," Mathias exclaimed, glad to change the subject. "There's an opening. Let's see if we can ease our way in."

Working as a team, they gained the table and grabbed the manila envelopes that bore their names.

As they walked away, Mathias suggested, "We have a little time before first period. How about I show you around? There are a few things you probably will want to know, like where the restrooms are and the fastest ways to get to your locker between classes—stuff like that. Shortcuts help when you're pressed for time."

"Sounds like useful information."

Distracted by Darcy's smile, Mathias bumped into an underclassman and nearly knocked him off his feet.

***

The clatter in the cafeteria rivaled the cacophony in the halls of the administration wing. Students scurried between tables as they sorted themselves into groups according to class standing and relative popularity. The rules were as they had been in previous years—seniors in the middle, freshmen at the periphery, others in between. Within a week, everyone would know their place. For the moment, the room was in chaos.

Mathias slid his tray along the serving line. To his surprise, he noticed Darcy Thurston sitting alone at a table in the corner. When his plate was full, he headed in her direction.

She glanced up as he crossed the room but then returned her attention to her meal.

"You shouldn't be sitting here," Mathias cautioned when he had drawn close enough that she could hear.

"Why not?" Darcy looked up again. This time she did not smile.

"Tradition."

"Tradition dictates where I can eat my lunch?"

"The center tables are for seniors. It's a status thing."

"And if I choose to stay where I am?"

"I doubt anyone will evict you, but it might affect your social standing. You don't want to be labeled an outsider."

"I am an outsider. More than one girl has already made that plain. If you weren't born in Rockridge…" Darcy gestured in a way that said, "Tough luck."

"What can I tell you—it's a small school. Status is everything. Look, I didn't mean to intrude. I just thought you might want to know about our local customs." Mathias turned to leave.

"Wait. You can join me if you want."

"Here?"

"There's plenty of room."

Mathias tilted his head as he looked down. "Sure, we could start a mini rebellion—students against social conformity."

"Or we could just have lunch."

"You're on." Mathias deposited his tray on the table and sat down across from Darcy. "How was your morning?"

"Overwhelming. Would you believe I already have homework assignments?"

"Let me guess, English IV and chemistry."

"Close. World literature and environmental sciences."

"You're on the college prep track," Mathias said. "Me too."

"One day I plan on being a teacher like my parents."

"I'm going to be a computer programmer—write software for my own company." Mathias set his fork down. "Do you realize that's three things we have in common?" He ticked items off on his fingers. "We both have a connection with Los Angeles. We're both linked to the Silver Rose, though in different ways. And we both plan on going to college."

Mathias sensed his new classmate was troubled, and he had an uneasy suspicion he knew why. That morning, he had encountered similar reactions in other students. He decided to take the initiative, though it meant eating humble pie. "There's something you probably should know about me. Last school year, I did a really dumb thing. I got into trouble with the law."

"I don't generally listen to gossip," Darcy admitted, "but I kind of overheard something to that effect. Want to tell me about it?"

"Not much to tell. I stole a car, a really nice car, actually. It was a bonehead thing to do. At first, I was afraid, and I ran away, but then turned myself in. At my arraignment, I pled guilty. The judge chose to be lenient. I've completed my community service, and I'm working on paying off my fine. I'll be on probation till I turn eighteen. If I keep my nose clean, they'll expunge my record when I become an adult." He sat back. "That's about it."

For the first time, Darcy smiled. "It means a lot that you'd admit your crime voluntarily. It tells me you're not hiding anything."

"Who's your friend?" Trent Blaine's voice was deeper than in previous years but still unmistakable.

The hackles went up on the back of Mathias's neck. He looked up as Trent stepped forward to lounge at the end of the table.

"What do you want?" Mathias said.

"Just to get reacquainted. I haven't seen you all summer." Trent stood taller than Mathias remembered. He had filled out in other ways as well. What surprised Mathias most was that Trent was growing a mustache. The scruffy growth gave the impression that a caterpillar had curled up and died beneath his nose.

"That's because I had to work. I'm paying off my fine, in case you hadn't heard."

"About that. I probably owe you an apology."

"Damn right you do."

"No need to get huffy. It all worked out. You're still here."

"So much for the apology…" Darcy murmured under her breath as she kept her eyes fixed on her plate.

"Excuse me?" Trent shifted his stance to glower at Darcy.

"Nothing," Darcy replied brightly, looking up. This time, her smile did not reach her eyes.

Trent's mood softened. "It seems Mathias here has forgotten his manners. I'm Trent, and you are?"

"Having lunch with my friend."

"No kidding. Don't you want to get acquainted?"

"If it's all the same," Darcy replied, "I'd rather finish my meal." She took a bite of her chicken potpie. Her eyebrows lifted in mock delight.

"Well, no one can say I didn't try. Guess I'll be going." Trent turned to leave.

"Thanks for stopping by." Mathias's voice radiated sarcasm. When Trent had strolled out of earshot, he added, "That problem I had with the legal system, he was involved."

"So I gathered."

"The authorities don't know that, by the way, so I'd appreciate it if you'd keep it to yourself."

"Honor among thieves? Sorry, bad habit—saying what comes to mind."

Mathias leaned forward and declared earnestly, "You'd best steer clear of that guy. He's bad news."

"You really don't like him, do you?"

"It's his fault I'm in the mess I'm in."

"Is it?" Darcy said with complete seriousness.

Mathias blushed. "No. You're right. I acted of my own free will."

"I think it's good that you understand that. Pardon my saying so, but you do realize that at some point, you're going to have to forgive him."

"Forgive him?" Mathias blurted out. "He's pond scum. I wouldn't trust him to turn in my homework assignments."

Darcy replied softly, "You don't have to trust someone to forgive them."

With his elbows on the table, Mathias laced his fingers together in front of him. "Why in the world would you say I have to forgive him?"

"Because the Bible tells us we must forgive. It's a commandment. If we don't forgive, we won't be forgiven."

"It says that? What else does it say?"

"Quite a lot. You should read it."

"Who says I haven't?"

Darcy grinned. "If you had, you would have known about forgiveness."

"I imagine you've read the Bible all the way through?"

"Several times."

"Hey, maybe you can explain something that's been bugging me. Months ago, Grandfather and I got into a theological discussion about free will. He asked me something I haven't been able to figure out. Why does God, who created everything, let men choose not to believe in Him?"

"That's an easy one. More than anything, God wants us to love Him, just as He loves us. For love to be genuine, it must be given freely. Without freedom of choice, there can be no true love. That's why we can either open our arms and embrace God or turn our backs on Him and walk away."

The bell announced that lunch period was over.

Mathias startled. He looked down. Stuffing a roll into his pocket for later, he stood and picked up his tray. "I'm going to have to think about that."

"We should talk more." Darcy followed Mathias as they crossed the room to the collection cart. She too slid her tray into one of the slots. "What's your next class?"

"Calculus."

"No kidding? That's where I'm headed." Darcy made a wry face.

Mathias grinned. "Hey, what do you know? One more thing in common."

They both chuckled.

As they exited the cafeteria and headed for their lockers, Darcy asked, "Do you like horses?"

"I've ridden, but not a lot."

"My parents bought a small ranch. We have four horses. When we ride together as a family, one horse keeps getting left behind. Maybe you'd like to join us this coming Saturday?"

"Saturday? Yeah, I think so, now that I'm done with community service. I guess that means you don't have siblings?"

"Nope. An only child. You?"

"The same. Well, what do you know?"

In unison the two classmates declared, "One more thing in common." They both laughed.

***

Swinging his axe in a smooth arc, Ward struck a chunk of larch squarely in the middle. The block of wood split neatly in half. With the ax-head buried in the chopping block, he let go of the handle and straightened up to ease the strain on his lower back and legs. His fourth Montana winter was a month away, six weeks at most. He had learned to appreciate the importance of being prepared.

Wiping his forehead with his shirtsleeve, he studied the two piles of wood nearby. The unsplit pile was shrinking and the split pile growing larger but at a disconcertingly slow pace. The problem wasn't technique. After three seasons, he had mastered the art of splitting firewood. Rather, what troubled him was that he seemed to be losing his stamina.

Life in the north woods can be physically challenging. He recalled how hard he had struggled that first year after Lauren's passing, shoveling snow, patching leaks in the roof, clearing weeds, and tending the garden in the spring. It had seemed there was always something that needed fixing. Then he had taken the job at the mill, stacking sheets of plywood, sorting lengths of lumber, keeping the saws running smoothly. Never in his wildest dreams had he imagined he would make a living doing manual labor.

Gradually, he had adapted. His endurance had increased, and his muscles had strengthened to a degree unknown before. Yet in recent months, something had changed. Thank goodness he had been promoted to management. Otherwise, he might not have been able to keep up.

Ward scowled. Perhaps he was expecting too much. A man in his sixties might normally become more easily fatigued. Diminished energy capacity was an expected consequence of increasing age. What worried him, though, was the possibility that his past life was finally catching up with him, that years of self-neglect and alcohol abuse were to account for his dwindling endurance. He recalled Lauren's struggle and how she had deteriorated in her final days. It terrified him to think that he too might suffer a loss of his physical abilities because of illness. How would he follow through on the promise he had made to watch over his grandson?

The sudden memory of his daughter renewed Ward's determination. Freeing the ax-head, he picked up an eighteen-inch length of larch and stood it upright on the chopping block. Gritting his teeth, he swung the axe in a mighty stroke. His aim was off slightly, and a splintered hunk of wood flew several feet away. As he went to retrieve it, he again thought about his promise and, more importantly, why he had made it.

He pictured his own teenage years, when his future had seemed so promising, so full of potential. He also remembered his misanthropic father and how he had walled himself off emotionally. Always critical, always finding fault—the man had been incapable of showing any signs of affection. Never once had he said to his son, "I love you." Ward might easily have blamed his dad, except he couldn't. He refused to hold his father accountable for the messes he alone had made. They had been his mistakes, his lost opportunities. He alone had made the appalling choices that had ruined his life. His father might have laid the foundation, but brick by brick, he had built the temple in which his failures were enshrined.

Filled with self-loathing, Ward once again resolved to atone for the error of his ways. He would keep his promise. He would never give up. No matter how hard the journey, he would see it through to the end.

He replaced the chunk of larch on the chopping block and swung the axe with as much force as he could muster.

The sound of a car coming down the driveway interrupted Ward's musings. He waited. A car door slammed, then the vehicle drove away. A moment later, his grandson came around the side of the house. He seemed to be walking slightly bowlegged.

"How were the horses? Did you have fun?" Ward buried the head of the axe in the chopping block again and punched his hands to his hips.

"It would've been more fun if I could have driven myself instead of having Dr. Thurston pick me up and bring me home."

"We've been over this," Ward cautioned.

"I know, but it's embarrassing. If I get a learner's permit, in six months I could test for a provisional license. I'm sixteen. I should be able to drive myself where I need to go. That way, nobody would have to worry about hauling me around."

Ward chuckled. "Instead, I'd have to worry about higher insurance premiums, paying for the extra gas, not to mention bickering over who'd get to use the truck."

"Like I've said before, that won't be a problem. My fine is nearly paid off. If I keep working after school, by the time I have my provisional license, I could afford my own ride, even if it's just a beater."

About to put his foot down, it occurred to Ward that maybe the time had come to ease off on the reins and let his grandson follow his own lead. "Tell you what, you help me get this place ready for winter, and I'll think about it."

"Really?"

"You can start by cleaning out the gutters and the downspouts. According to the *Farmer's Almanac*, the rainy season will be upon us any day now."

"Wouldn't you rather have me split wood?"

"I need the exercise. Go change your clothes."

Mathias disappeared into the house. Ward went back to swinging his axe.

Thirty minutes later, when Mathias still hadn't returned, Ward entered the house to see what was keeping him. He found his grandson in his room, seated at his desk, engrossed in reading lines of text displayed on his laptop's screen.

Ward knocked on the doorjamb and stepped inside. "I thought you wanted to help me winterize the house?"

"I do," Mathias responded without turning around. "Guess I got distracted—lost track of time. Sorry."

Leaning forward, Ward read what was written on the computer screen. "Is that the Old Testament?"

"Dr. Thurston gave me a list of ten prophecies. I'm looking them up to see what I can learn."

"Why?"

Mathias turned his head to gaze up at his grandfather. "He claims they vindicate his point of view."

"Regarding?"

"Eternity."

Ward cocked his head with a quizzical frown.

"We were having this discussion," Mathias explained, "about Scripture. You know he used to teach comparative religions? We'd finished riding horses, and he was bringing me home. We got to talking. He asked where I planned on spending my eternity. I told him I didn't believe in eternity, that I didn't see how anything can exist outside of time. After all, there's nothing there. He told me that biblical prophecies prove God is eternal, and I said I didn't see how that could be possible, so he wrote out this list." Mathias tapped a sheet of paper lying on his desk. "He told me to study these prophecies and figure out how it could happen that they all came true. That's what I was doing."

"That may be all well and good, but you can deal with this later. Right now, we need to get to work. There's not a lot of daylight left."

Mathias opened his mouth as if to protest, but then seemed to change his mind. He shut down the laptop and followed his grandfather down the stairs.

Ward led the way into the kitchen. "It amazes me, the things you can do with that machine. Computers were just starting to make their way into the workplace when I lost my mortgage company. A few earlier models had been around a while. They were more toys than tools. I never learned how to make the blasted things do what I wanted. All they ever did was crash."

Mathias declared, "I could teach you the basics. You can do a lot with a modern operating system. Did you know that in the near future, every electronic device will have its own brain? You'll be able to manage every appliance in your home through an integrated interface?"

"I have no idea what that means."

"It means everything will be linked together." Mathias followed his grandfather into the backyard. "You'll be able to communicate remotely with every device, every appliance. It'll be like living inside a giant network. I'm teaching myself Java. That's a computer programming language primarily used to interface divergent platforms."

"I assume there's money to be made in computer programming?" Ward headed back to the woodpile.

Mathias turned aside to fetch the ladder out of the toolshed. "Absolutely," he called back over his shoulder. "Especially if you write software for an entire industry to use—particularly if you own the code. That's what I plan on doing."

A thought popped into Ward's head. For a moment, he considered asking if word had come down concerning his grandson's scholarship. Time was running out, but then he decided not to initiate such a sensitive discussion. Instead, he said supportively, "I have no doubt you'll make it happen."

Ward set to work again chopping wood but then paused. He looked to where his grandson was climbing the ladder that he had propped against the edge of the roof. He called out, "This girl you went riding with—do you like her? What's her name?"

"Darcy. Yeah, she's nice."

"Nice?" Ward could tell by his grandson's body language that the word *nice* came nowhere near expressing his level of interest. "That means you'll be seeing more of each other?"

"I suppose." Mathias scooped a handful of leaves out of the gutter and tossed them on the ground to be raked up later.

"In that case, you and I should have a serious conversation. It's high time we discussed the intricacies of human relationships."

"You mean you want to talk about sex?"

"Mostly."

"Not a problem. What do you want to know?"

Ward laughed but then realized his grandson was serious. Then he reminded himself he was living in an age of information overload. In all probability, the boy knew more about the birds and the bees than he did. He tried imagining how such a conversation might unfold. The more explicit his mental images became, the more disconcerted he felt. At length, he chose to change the subject as gracefully as possible. "All I'm saying is, just remember I'm here for you. If anything is troubling you, all you have to do is ask."

"So when are you going to take me to the DMV to get my learner's permit?"

***

138

Near the middle of the following week, Ward sat in the living room easy chair reading a mystery novel—his favorite genre. He had put in a long day at the mill and was relaxing in front of a cozy fire. The evenings had turned cold enough to justify igniting a blaze in the fireplace. As in previous winters, watching flames dance above the lengths of wood he had personally split brought a measure of pride.

A cup of hot cocoa sat on the table at his elbow. He remembered a time when in its place, he would've chosen mulled wine or something more bracing. In fact, he had considered stopping at the liquor store on his way home from work. Although tempted, he had resisted by reminding himself that he had walked that road before, or rather had stumbled and lurched along in a state of inebriation.

"Mind if I interrupt for a minute?" Mathias called ahead as he descended the stairs.

Ward bookmarked his novel and set it aside next to his cocoa.

Mathias sank down on the couch. "I've been going over this list of biblical prophecies, and I want to see what you think. Is this a bad time?"

"Not at all. I like it when you ask my opinion. In this case, I'm not sure it'll be worth much. What have you learned?"

Mathias sat forward and held up the list. "These prophecies are from the Old Testament. The majority have to do with the coming Messiah, like how He was to be born in Bethlehem and how He would be crucified. They predict that the guards would cast dice for his garments and that they would pierce His side, but not break His bones. They tell how Judas would betray Him for thirty pieces of silver and how that blood money would be used to buy a burial plot for the poor. The prophecy given to Daniel more than five hundred years before Jesus was born describes the exact day the Messiah was to reveal Himself to Israel."

Ward nodded thoughtfully. "Speaking of prophecies, there's something I've always wondered about. The three wise men, the guys who traveled such a great distance to reach Bethlehem, how did they know when to set out and which way to go? I'm familiar with the star and how it led them, but looking up at the night sky, how did they understand what the star meant? See what I mean?"

"That's along the same lines as what I'm saying."

"Sounds like you believe these prophecies?"

"I'm pretty sure they've all come true. That's not the point."

"What is the point then?"

"Dr. Thurston challenged me to explain how these prophecies came to be fulfilled. Far as I can see, there are three possibilities: The prophet makes a lucky guess. The prophet somehow forges the future. Or the prophet actually knows what's going to happen."

"Sounds about right."

"Can you think of any other possible explanations?" Mathias asked hopefully.

"None come to mind." Ward crossed his legs and focused his attention on his grandson. It pleased him to watch Mathias use his brain to figure things out.

Mathias said, "As for lucky guesses, how can anyone predict what's going to happen hundreds of years in advance? Civilizations ebb and flow. Nation-states rise up and are overthrown. The odds against a prophet guessing correctly are astronomical. The option isn't worth considering."

"I agree. Most years I can't even guess which team will win the Super Bowl."

Mathias nodded. "Precisely. Regarding the second possibility, I suppose in some cases it's conceivable that the person who's being prophesied about knows the prophecy and causes it to come true." Mathias massaged his forehead. "Except how would that work when multiple people are involved or when a specific set of circumstances must come to fruition at exactly the right moment, like when Jesus rode into Jerusalem on a donkey and was declared Messiah by the crowds? Also, I doubt His guards knew they were supposed to gamble for His garments or hold back from breaking His legs. And how, as an infant, did He arrange to be born in Bethlehem?"

Ward shrugged. "Like I said, I'm not sure I can be much help."

"Here's something weird. I read a theory online that says if you speak a prophecy, you shape the future—that somehow what we say defines what will happen. The problem I have with that notion is, what happens if two or more prophets speak incompatible prophecies? One might say something like, 'It's going to be sunny in Rockridge tomorrow at noon.' The other might say, 'It's going to rain.' Their predictions can't both come true. Therefore, one of them will fail to cause the future. And so it goes.

"The only other explanation is that the prophet knows what's going to happen. But how can someone know what will happen centuries in advance? In physics, we learned that the second law of thermodynamics mandates that time flows in one direction only. A person from the future can't come back and tell someone what they've experienced. Knowing the future requires a vantage point outside of time. It implies being able to see the end from the beginning. By definition, residing outside of time means existing in eternity. Dr. Thurston was right."

Ward touched two fingers to his temple. "Have you considered the possibility that these prophecies were written after the fact, and they only make it seem like they foretold the future?"

"The prophecies I researched were originally written in Hebrew and then translated into Latin and Greek, sometimes hundreds of years before the events actually took place. Copies of the translations still exist. There's no way they were after the fact."

"Where are you going with all this?" Ward said.

"You mean how do I feel about it? I don't know. What do you think?"

"I've always believed God is eternal. As for what it's like to be where He is, I haven't a clue nor I suspect, do you? Seems to me that in this life, we're not meant to know."

"You're probably right." Mathias shook his head. "It's sad. For all of humanity's collective wisdom, we have so many questions for which we have no answers. Anyway, I thought you might like to know what I've been working on."

"Thanks for sharing. Once again, you've made my brain hurt." Ward picked up his book and opened it to the pages separated by the bookmark.

*****

The lilting melody of a classic Christmas carol drifted through the Thurstons's living room. Pine boughs and sprigs of holly decorated the broad oak mantle above the brick fireplace. Strategically placed wreaths with red ribbon bows and brightly colored ornaments created an elegant mood of warm holiday cheer.

Mathias stood beside the dessert table. Chocolate candies, Christmas cookies, tarts, and other confections lay spread out before him. A second buffet table offered meats, cheeses, and rolls for making miniature sandwiches; a tray of vegetables with assorted dips; finger sausages wrapped in bacon; a pot of Swedish meatballs; and a platter of deviled eggs.

After surveying the feast, Mathias decided he wasn't hungry. He had endured a miserable two days, and his lack of holiday spirit made it hard to celebrate. Most of the families the Thurstons had invited had already joined the party, though more were still arriving. Although spacious, the room was beginning to feel congested. The noise level was increasing. Nearly everyone seemed lighthearted, especially the students. The local schools had recently let out for a two-week holiday recess and would not reopen till next year. That alone should have lifted Mathias's spirits, but it didn't.

Younger children were being dispatched to the family room downstairs. There they could play video games, roughhouse, and listen to contemporary music. Mathias thought about joining them but then realized he would feel even more out of place. Instead, he turned his attention to where his grandfather stood beside the wide fireplace, gazing at the undulating flames. He too seemed subdued.

Mathias suspected that his grandfather's reticence arose from his tendency to remain aloof in social settings, not from a spirit of dejection. He remembered gatherings when he had watched his grandfather and was surprised by how distant he had seemed. What intrigued Mathias was how Ward had come to be that way. Perhaps he had learned to keep others at arm's length during his years in prison or while living on the streets as an outcast.

Mathias stepped forward to join him. "I'm glad you decided to come."

Ward folded his hands behind his back and continued staring at the fire. "The Thurstons seem like nice people. They have a beautiful home."

"But you'd rather be hunkered down in front of your own fire, reading?"

His grandfather shrugged.

Mathias gave a sweeping gesture with his hand. "I know most of the kids and a fair number of parents. I could introduce you to some people."

As if on cue, Abraham Finkel strolled over to join them. "Is this place cool or what?" To Mathias, it seemed clear that the boy was becoming a man. In the last year, his height had increased several inches, and he was losing his baby fat. His voice was deeper, and there was evidence he had begun shaving.

"They know how to throw a party," Mathias agreed. "Have you met my grandfather, Ward Stanford? Grandfather, this is Abraham Finkel."

Abraham self-consciously offered to shake hands. "Mr. Stanford, nice to meet you. Call me Abe. Everyone else does."

Ward returned the handshake. "Finkel, Finkel—how do I know that name?"

With chagrin, Mathias admitted, "Abe was the guy they originally charged with—you know."

"Oh, right." Ward nodded as if mentally connecting the dots. "So you're the one?"

"About that." Abe turned to Mathias; his mood became somber. "I wanted to thank you again for getting me off the hook. I know what it cost for you to step forward."

No, Mathias thought, *you really don't*. He refrained from voicing his feelings. Instead, he looked to his grandfather, who seemed on the verge of posing a question. Instinctively, he knew what the question would be. Whenever the subject had come up before, his grandfather had pressed him to learn the identity of the other boy, the one who had run away.

Mathias turned to face the floor-to-ceiling picture window on the opposite side of the room. Outside, a recent snowfall had transformed the Thurstons' backyard into a winter wonderland. Strings of miniature lights encircled a number of trees, infusing the surrounding snow with a multicolored glow. "It's pretty out there, don't you think—like something out of a Norman Rockwell painting." He deliberately gave his grandfather an interested look as if to solicit his opinion.

"Very nice," Ward said distractedly. Then he seemed to lose his train of thought. "What's even nicer is enjoying the great outdoors from in front of a cozy fire."

"I gather you don't like winter?" Abe said.

"Son, I'm from Southern California. What can I say?" Ward resumed his contemplation of the flames dancing above the logs in the fireplace.

Mathias turned toward Abraham. "Does being here make you uneasy?" He thrust his chin at the hand-carved cross on the mantle.

"You mean because I'm Jewish? Not really—maybe a little. So far, I've counted four Bibles and three crosses. When it comes to declaring their religion, the Thurstons don't leave any doubt as to where they stand. Besides, remember that your Jesus happened to be Jewish. He even celebrated Passover." A young woman wearing a pastel party dress caught Abraham's eye.

When Mathias looked to see who had attracted his friend's notice, he realized it was Darcy, but she looked different—more mature. She wore her blonde hair twisted into a French weave. Her flawlessly applied mascara, eye shadow, and lipstick added five years or more to her age. She was speaking with a woman Mathias recognized as the parent of an underclassman.

Once again, the feature that captured his attention was Darcy's smile. She seemed sincerely happy, as if no problem were large enough to trouble her mood. Her lightheartedness reminded Mathias of how miserable he felt. He averted his eyes.

Abraham elbowed Mathias in the ribs. "You should go talk to her. I'm pretty sure she likes you."

"Maybe later." Mathias joined his grandfather in studying the burning logs.

"Time to go," Abraham blurted out. He then hurried off as a figure approached from across the room.

Mathias looked up as Trent Blaine drew near.

"What's up?" Mathias said sullenly, then with alarm, he scanned the crowd to see if Baxter Blaine, Trent's father, had joined the party. The man was nowhere to be seen, which was fortunate indeed. Trouble usually followed in his wake.

Mathias remembered one night during his sophomore year. His class had gone roller-skating. Baxter had volunteered to chaperone. Rather than monitor the kids for whom he was responsible, he had gotten drunk and picked a fight with another dad.

The hostility in Mathias's voice must have alerted Ward, who looked up sharply and seemed instantly on guard.

"I see you brought your grandfather. Howdy, sir. I'm Trent. You may not remember me. We met a couple years back." Sticking out his hand, Trent winced when the handshake was returned.

Ward commented, "Ah, yes. You are in my grandson's class?" He gave Trent's hand a final squeeze.

"I am. I'm surprised we haven't bumped into each other more often." Trent grimaced as he glanced at Mathias.

"I don't get out much." Ward eased away from the fire. "Look, if you'll excuse me, I'm feeling a mite hungry. I think I'll grab something to eat." He sauntered off toward the buffet table.

"What's with him?" Trent said.

"He's an excellent judge of character." Mathias cocked his head. "What do you want?"

"To bury the hatchet."

"What makes you think I'm interested?"

"You and me, we've known each other too long to let past differences ruin our friendship. I know what I did was wrong. I tricked you into stealing that car, but keep in mind, I couldn't have done it if you hadn't been willing. Besides, I owe you for not ratting me out. I know you wanted to."

"I didn't keep silent on your account."

"Whatever your reason, I'm grateful. Perhaps you haven't noticed, but ever since that happened, I've been keeping my nose clean. I am trying to change."

Taken aback, Mathias eyed his classmate, who seemed sincere.

Trent rested a hand on Mathias's shoulder. "I was thinking you might want to go snowmobiling this weekend. Maybe if we hang out together, we can put the past behind us."

"I don't own a snowmobile," Mathias said. "Not anymore. I sold it."

"Not a problem. I know where there's one you can borrow."

Mathias stiffened.

"Hold on. I can tell what you're thinking. This is legit. Danny and Marcus Osborne are out of town for the holidays. They're off visiting relatives. They said I could borrow one of their machines while they're gone. I'm sure they won't mind if you use the other one. You can call their parents if you'd like. I'll give you their number. They'll confirm the offer."

"I don't—"

"Come on. You used to love snowmobiling. This last storm surely must've dumped some serious powder up around Sawbuck Ridge. Man, it'll be fun. Besides, you can't hold a grudge forever. I know you."

"I'll have to check with Grandfather first—see if he has anything planned."

"That's the spirit. Call me when you find out. If you choose not to go, there are others who will." Trent looked to where Darcy was engaged in conversation.

Mathias said defiantly, "Don't even think about it. She's not your type."

"I'm just fooling. I know you two are an item. Seriously, we'll have fun. I miss the good times we used to have."

"Yeah. Me too," Mathias admitted grudgingly.

"It's settled then?"

"Not until after I check with Grandfather."

Trent nodded and turned to move away. "Think I'll play some video games. Want to come?"

"I'll pass."

Mathias watched his ex-friend leave. *What brought that about?* he wondered as Trent disappeared down the stairs. *Could their relationship be restored? Was that possible?*

Soon his grandfather returned to stand by the fire. Mathias explained what had transpired, but in the telling, he deliberately left out certain historical details.

Ward cautioned, "A skunk doesn't change its stripes. From what I've heard, he's an unsavory sort."

"What exactly have you heard?"

"Only that folks tend not to hold him in high regard. That doesn't mean he shouldn't be given a second chance, I suppose. Guess you'll have to make up your own mind."

Mathias resolved to sleep on Trent's offer and delay his decision till morning.

***

"If I didn't know better," Darcy said as she tapped Mathias on the shoulder, "I'd think you were avoiding me." The holiday atmosphere in the room had muffled the sound of her approach.

In the process of ladling punch into his glass, Mathias startled and nearly made a mess. He turned with the ladle still in his hand. "Not at all. You were chatting with your guests. I was giving you space."

"That's your excuse?"

He held up the ladle. "Want some?"

"Sure." Darcy smiled warmly.

Mathias filled a punch glass and handed it over. He returned the ladle to the punch bowl. "You look beautiful. You're probably the prettiest girl here."

"Very well, you're forgiven. You know, I've been watching you. Why are you so down this evening?"

"I'm not down—just quiet."

"Seriously? I can tell when something is bothering you. Come with me. We need to talk." Darcy led Mathias by the hand to a love seat that had recently been vacated. They both sat down. She smoothed her dress to cover her knees.

"I've been watching you too," Mathias said, making an effort to exhibit an upbeat attitude. "You seem especially happy."

"I got my learner's permit."

"For real? Me too—but I thought you already had a learner's permit?"

"I did in California. I had to reapply now that we live in Montana."

"Oh."

Darcy exclaimed, "I've also been accepted to Montana State. It's not my first choice, but it means at least I'll be going to college somewhere."

"Congratulations. I never doubted that you'd get in."

"I'm hoping to hear from UCLA soon. That's really where I want to go."

"So you've said—because of their history department. Are you sure you want to teach college-level history?"

"Actually, I'm pretty sure I want to teach religious history, like my mom."

"Who would have ever suspected?" Mathias allowed his gaze to track the various religious icons scattered around the room.

"Tease me if you must, but it's not the boring subject you would imagine. Many of history's greatest events were sparked by theological concerns. What about you? Any word on your applications?"

Mathias's feigned smile faded. "MSU invited me as well."

"Fantastic. What about UCLA?"

"I'm still waiting, but whatever they decide, it won't matter."

"Why not?" Darcy took hold of Mathias's hand.

"A few days ago, I discovered that Ms. Dale chairs the scholarship committee. Yesterday, after computer lab, I flat out demanded to know what my chances were. At first, she didn't want to tell me, but

I kept pressing. Finally, she confided that the committee has made its decision. Apparently, my legal troubles were enough to disqualify me. I asked if there was anything I could do to change the committee's mind, but she said the competition was too intense. Apparently, none of the other applicants have a felony on the record. Looks like I won't be going to college."

"Is a local scholarship that important? What about nationwide? Aren't there other sources of funding?"

"Same rules apply—and the same competition."

Darcy's cheerfulness seemed to bleed away. "Student loans?"

"Ms. Dale suggested that. She said I could finance my education by taking out a student loan every year. The problem is that after graduation, I'd have a mountain of debt to repay before I could even think about starting my own company. I did the math. It would take a decade or longer to accumulate the capital I'd need."

"What do you intend to do?"

"I'm beginning to think I don't have to go to college to get an education. After graduation, I'll look for a job here locally. On nights and weekends, I'll study computer science, teach myself what I need to know about software development. It's not the easiest alternative, but it should be doable."

Darcy's looked away. "I kind of expected we'd be going off to college together."

"So did I, but it seems that won't be happening."

***

The following Saturday, Mathias headed off to go snowmobiling. A frigid wind lashed his nose and mouth, the only parts of his face unprotected by his maroon watch cap, earmuffs, goggles, and thick woolen scarf. The snowmobile's engine roared as he maneuvered between trees, following in Trent's wake. It seemed a perfect day for venturing into the backcountry. The icy blue sky overhead literally glittered with flecks of snow—the last vestiges of a storm that had passed through during the night. Sprays of powdery snow gushed outward from the snowmobile's tread.

Reminded of the adage "Trust, but verify," Mathias had, in fact, called the Osbornes to confirm that their snowmobiles were available. The twins had validated the offer, and although amazed that Trent and Mathias planned on spending time together, they had agreed to loan Mathias one of their machines.

As he zipped through the forest, Mathias could occasionally make out the crest of Starfall Mountain a quarter-mile ahead. Sawbuck Ridge ran along the top of a huge bowl-shaped cavity carved into the side of the mountain, a thirty-minute hike from Horse Collar Lake. The depression seemed to have been gouged out with a gigantic ice cream scoop. For snowmobilers, the broad slope was a favorite destination. The usual plan of attack was to race as far up the mountainside as possible without stalling, turn, and dash back down at breakneck speeds. The risk of triggering an avalanche was part of the fun.

No one, as far as Mathias knew, had ever made it all the way to the top of the ridge. The hillside was simply too steep. Still, that hadn't prevented hotshots from trying.

When they gained the foot of the mountain, Mathias was glad to see that they were the only ones in view. Other snowmobilers might show up later, but for the moment, the only thing that awaited them was a vast expanse of virgin snow.

"Let's do this!" Trent yelled above the roar of the engines. He twisted the snowmobile's throttle and took off up the side of the mountain at a furious pace. He made it halfway before turning. A rooster tail of snow followed him down the hillside.

Mathias crested his upward rush a few feet farther than Trent had achieved. Then he too turned and raced headlong down the mountain. The exhilaration was magnificent. As he approached the bottom of the incline, he realized he was traveling a mite too fast. The second trick to navigating Sawbuck Ridge was to keep from smashing into the trees at the base of the slope.

At the last instant, Mathias yanked his machine sharply to the right. With both hands tightly gripping the handlebars, he leaned as severely to the uphill side as he could without tipping over. It was a dangerous maneuver. The threat was that he would dump the machine on its side and skid into the trees, striking them broadside. Instead, the tread bit the snow and skittered like a skater stopping on ice. He came to rest a few feet from the trunk of a towering birch. When the powdery plumes settled, Mathias was laughing so hard he had to sit down on the machine's padded seat.

"That was intense." Trent glided to a stop nearby. "Care to go again?"

"Oh yeah." Mathias wiped away a layer of snow to clear his goggles and took off up the hill.

For the next two hours, the two young men ripped across the face of Sawbuck Ridge until thoroughly exhausted. After one last pass in opposite directions, they came together at the bottom of the hill.

Mathias shifted his snowmobile's transmission into neutral but left the motor running. Engines cool rapidly in frigid weather and can be difficult to restart. Being stranded in the backcountry can quickly become an exercise in survival, as he well knew. He dismounted and retrieved a thermos from the insulated chest attached to the back of his snowmobile. Leaving his gloves on, he unscrewed the lid and filled it with steaming coffee. After taking several cautious sips, he offered the cup to Trent, who accepted it gladly.

"Tell the truth," Mathias said. "Why did you invite me up here today? What's on your mind?"

Trent grinned. "You mean other than having ourselves some tremendous fun?"

"That's your only reason?" Mathias noted the minute shards of ice that encased his companion's eyebrows and mustache, making him look like a winter demon.

"You think I'm up to something?"

"Aren't you?" Mathias accepted the thermos lid back and refilled it. He downed several swallows and handed it over again.

"What you see is what you get." Trent's lips must have been numb with cold because when he sipped the coffee, a small amount dribbled onto his chin. When he used his scarf to wipe the liquid away, Mathias noticed a fresh bruise along the edge of his jaw.

"What happened to you?"

"Nothing." Trent ran a thumb self-consciously over his bruise.

"Your old man?"

"Yeah." Trent's jaw tightened, and his expression became hard as flint. "But he won't do it again—not ever. This time I hit him back, and when he came at me, I laid him out. I told him I wasn't a child any longer, and if he ever assaulted me again, I'd kill him." Trent finished off his coffee in a single swallow.

"Why didn't you call the police?"

"For the same reason you didn't rat me out." Trent handed the empty lid back to Mathias, who screwed it on the thermos and returned the thermos to its pouch.

"You need to get away from him," Mathias said with conviction.

"I plan on it, right after graduation—after I get a job and can afford my own place." Trent gunned his snowmobile's engine. "Come on, what say we make one more pass and head home? It's starting to cloud up."

Reminded of graduation, Mathias's mood changed instantly. A majority of his friends would be leaving, heading off to college, and so would Darcy. It seemed incredible that another human being could have become such a close friend. He would miss her severely. Of that he was certain. As to how severely, he would have to wait to find out. He climbed back on his machine and took off up the hill for a final run.

***

The Silver Rose smelled of sandalwood and burning pine logs when Mathias entered. He hurriedly closed the door behind him. Outside, fresh snow was falling. Although a gentle storm by most standards, the cold front was proving remarkably resilient. Snowfall had set in right after the first of the year and had continued virtually uninterrupted for a week. Twice in two days, Mathias had cranked up his snow thrower to clear the long driveway at home. Otherwise, making it from the house to the road would have been seriously difficult, despite having a four-wheel-drive truck. Even the snowplows were having trouble keeping up. More than a few of the residential streets in town were impassable.

A fire blazed in the potbelly stove in the corner. Mathias headed in that direction. In passing, he noted that besides Darcy's mother, the gift shop was deserted. *Winter can be rough on retailers; it keeps customers away.*

Miriam Thurston, Darcy's mom, stood behind the counter where an antique cash register sat next to a modern credit card terminal. She looked up when the bell above the door tinkled. "Hello, Mathias. How are you this chilly morning?" Throughout the Silver Rose, unique gifts, collectibles, and upscale keepsakes were tastefully displayed.

"I'm doing well. How are you, Mrs. Thurston?"

"Good, good. What brings you out on such a blustery day?" Miriam was an affable woman with a quiet demeanor. She looked as if she belonged in front of a classroom, teaching history to budding intellectuals. She wore her light brown hair layered to the nape of her neck.

"I was in town, running errands. Thought I'd stop in and say hi."

"I see." Mrs. Thurston eyed her visitor with a knowing look. "Well, feel free to browse. If you see anything you like, just holler."

"Thank you."

Standing beside the stove, Mathias began peeling off layers of clothing. He removed his gloves and watch cap, and then his heavy woolen coat and cable-knit sweater. He hung each item on a peg rack attached to the wall. Stepping closer to the stove, he began rubbing his hands together briskly.

After he had warmed up a bit, Mathias said, "Is your husband around? I was hoping I might ask him about something he mentioned the other day."

"I'm afraid he's not. He's at the post office mailing parcels—orders we took in via the Internet. He wanted to make sure they went out today."

"So your Internet business is picking up?"

"It's still fairly slow, but every little bit is appreciated. Thanks for helping us get online."

"You're welcome."

"Are you looking forward to graduating? Or is that a silly question?"

"I suppose. I mean I'll be glad to be done with high school."

"What are your plans? Oh, that's right. I remember. Darcy mentioned that you probably won't be attending college. I was sorry to hear that. It's so important to get a good education."

About to respond, Mathias fell silent when the bell above the door jingled. A young woman entered. She too was heavily bundled against the cold. Mathias smiled when he could tell it was Darcy.

"Oh, hi," Darcy said as she moved to stand beside him at the stove. "What are you doing here?"

"I was in the neighborhood…"

Darcy and her mother exchanged knowing glances. She too began shedding layers of winter garb.

"Sorry I'm late," Darcy said to her mother.

"No worries. How are the roads?"

"Pretty bad. At least the snow hasn't compacted to ice yet."

"It will," Mathias declared. "Of that you can be certain."

"Winter takes some getting used to," Miriam confirmed. She then looked at her daughter. "There's a consignment that just came in. Would you check it over, make sure nothing is broken? Perhaps Mathias will help. It's in the back room."

Darcy turned to Mathias. "Care to?"

"Lead the way."

Darcy and Mathias disappeared into the Silver Rose's constricted business office. To Mathias, the room felt smaller than his bedroom at home. A rolltop desk sat backed up against one wall. A floor-to-ceiling bookcase stood against the opposite wall. A variety of notebooks, ledgers, catalogs, and stacks of paper graced the bookcase's shelves. A well-worn executive chair on rollers served the desk. Beside the desk, an armless wooden chair faced into the room.

"How can I help?" Mathias offered.

"There's really not much room in here. If we bump into each other, we might break something. Go ahead and make yourself comfortable." Darcy indicated the chair beside the desk. She then retrieved a letter opener from the desk's top drawer and began slicing through the packing tape that sealed the first of three boxes.

Mathias sat down and watched her carefully extract several handblown glass items from the shipping confetti. After inspecting each in detail, she set them on the floor out of the way. After unpacking the first box, she carried the items two at a time out to her mother. She then set about to deal with the second box.

"Anything new from the scholarship committee?" Darcy said hopefully.

"Far as they're concerned, the matter is settled. What about you? Any word from UCLA?"

Darcy froze with a fragile-looking glass butterfly in her hands. "I've been accepted. The letter came yesterday." She didn't seem nearly as joyful as Mathias might have predicted.

"Great. Will you be living on campus?"

"I'll probably stay in one of the dorms, at least for the first semester. After that, we'll see."

Mathias knew he should feel happy for his friend. Her dream was coming true. What he really wanted to do was to grab one of the glass figurines and smash it against a wall.

As if sensing his conflicted state of mind, Darcy suggested, "You know if you apply for financial aid again next year, your records will be sealed. You might have better luck. You could still go to college. You'd only be a year behind."

"Right. Who knows what can happen in a year. Look, do you mind if we talk about something else?" The realization that he and Darcy would soon go their separate ways filled him with a sense of emptiness.

After hanging out a while longer, he bundled up in his winter garb again and then left the gift shop to head out into the storm.

CHAPTER 7

In early August, two months after graduation, Darcy sat alone in the farthest corner of the Leaky Canoe's dining room. The restaurant had outdone itself. A pristine white cloth covered the semiprivate table she had reserved. The silver utensils gleamed, and the water glasses sparkled. Linen napkins, neatly folded, had been carefully positioned at both place settings. A solitary dark red rose in a slender vase stood beside a freshly lit candle.

Normally the restaurant didn't take reservations, much less provide an elegant dining experience, but Darcy had pleaded that this was a very special occasion. While she waited for her guest, she again looked at the wrapped birthday present intentionally positioned on the table opposite where she sat. The present's gold foil wrapping and iridescent blue ribbon seemed appropriate for the mood she was trying to set. There was no doubt in her mind that Mathias would appreciate his gift.

Darcy checked her watch. She had arrived early. Despite striving to remain calm, she was becoming increasingly anxious with anticipation.

Soon, the dinner hour would begin, but only two other tables were occupied. At one sat a middle-aged couple. Their faces seemed familiar, but Darcy couldn't recall their names. She smiled and waved politely when they looked in her direction. An older gentleman, whom she failed to recognize, sat alone at the other table. Darcy and her family had been in town for less than a year, hardly enough time to get to know everyone. In any event, the man ate quietly and tended not to look up.

When the front door opened and Mathias appeared, Lindell, the restaurant's only waiter, promptly disappeared into the kitchen but soon returned with the cook and busboy in tow. The three men stood in a straight line and sprang to attention when Darcy stepped forward to join them. She gave a signal, and all four began singing "Happy Birthday." The middle-aged couple and even the older gentleman joined in. When the chorus finished, everyone applauded except for Mathias, who blushed a remarkable shade of crimson.

A flush of embarrassment colored Mathias's cheeks, but he was powerless to stop it. He was reminded of the time he entered the girls' bathroom by mistake. Upon realizing his blunder, he had emerged immediately just as the school's football team was passing by. It had taken months for the teasing to abate.

"You set me up," Mathias whispered to his date.

Darcy grinned. "Surprise."

Lindell accompanied Darcy and her guest to their table and then held Darcy's chair while she sat down.

Mathias took note of the dinner setting. "I didn't know the Leaky Canoe could set such an impressive table."

"Ms. Thurston provided the utensils," Lindell confided. "All we did was arrange them."

"Isn't that one of my mother's vases?" Mathias exclaimed, indicating the solitary flower. He shed his coat but jerked it away when Lindell reached for it to hang it up. Instead, he draped it over the back of his chair.

"I hope you don't mind," Darcy said. "My parents found it on a back shelf at the Silver Rose. I thought you might appreciate it. You can take it with you when you leave."

"Thank you. That's very thoughtful." Sitting down, he leaned forward and whispered across the table, "You do realize my birthday isn't for another week?"

"If I'd waited, you wouldn't have been surprised."

Momentarily distracted, Mathias stared at the vase. "She used to work here—my mother did—waiting tables."

"I didn't know that." Darcy reached out and gently trailed a finger down the curves of the vase. "She was very talented. I wish I'd known her." Softly, she added, "Judging by her son, she must've been an amazing woman."

The elegantly wrapped package on the table commanded Mathias's attention. "What's this?"

"It's for you. Open it." Darcy fidgeted in a way that indicated she was extremely anxious to see Mathias's reaction.

With intentional care, Mathias undid the taped wrapping paper on either end. With the flaps loosened, he carefully opened the rest of the packaging, mindful not to tear the metallic foil.

"Will you hurry up?" Darcy exclaimed, barely able to contain her enthusiasm.

When at last the logo on the side of the box became visible, Mathias gasped. His eyes went wide as he recognized a tablet computer. "Is this…?"

"The new 4-Gen wireless with the 3.6 GHz processor? Yes."

"And 128 gigs of memory," he said, reading the specs on the box. "Plus, it's got the 7.02 operating system. I can't believe it. How did…?"

"I ordered it online. Do you like it?"

"Like it? I love it." Mathias stood and stepped around the table to lift Darcy out of her chair. Forgetting his surroundings, he wrapped his arms around her and kissed her full on the mouth.

The three members of the restaurant's staff who had been watching from the kitchen applauded. Lindell flashed Darcy a hearty thumbs-up. Mathias blushed again and retreated to his side of the table.

Darcy sat down and demurely positioned her napkin on her lap. "I wanted to get you something nice. Then I remembered what you'd said at graduation, that having a tablet to use along with your laptop might improve your programming skills. I hope this one will serve you well."

"It certainly will. Thank you. But you know, as much as I appreciate this fantastic present, what I appreciate even more is spending this evening with you."

"Do you mean that?"

"I absolutely do, without reservation. I hate knowing that in a couple weeks you'll be leaving for Los Angeles. I only hope you'll remember me while you're hurrying between classes at UCLA."

"About that." Darcy steepled her fingers in front of her. "I've decided to wait a year. I called the dean of admissions and explained that I didn't feel ready. I asked if there would be a spot for me in next year's freshman class. He said yes."

"You're not leaving?"

"That's the bottom line."

"But all along you've talked about how much you want to be a teacher like your parents. I don't get it. Why wait?"

"You know, for such a highly intelligent individual, you can be incredibly dumb sometimes."

Mathias blinked. "Because of me? That's why you're staying? But that's not right. You can't abandon your dream simply because I can't follow mine."

"Don't tell me what I can and can't do. Besides, I'm not abandoning my dream. I'm postponing it for a year. If I choose to delay going to college, so be it. It's not your decision to make. Besides, I thought you'd be pleased."

"I am. Oh, believe me, I am. It's just that I worry about your future as well as mine. What will you do job-wise?"

"I'll work full-time at the gift shop. Now, are you ready to eat? I hope you're hungry." Darcy signaled Lindell, who disappeared into the kitchen to fetch their first course.

"Don't we get menus?"

"I've already ordered. It's a special treat for your birthday."

Mathias sat back, unsure how to contend with his emotions. The possibility of spending another year with Darcy seemed thrilling beyond measure, but for her to put her life on hold on his account seemed completely wrong. It made him feel selfish.

"How is your grandfather?" Darcy asked, apparently sensing that their conversation needed to proceed in a different direction.

"I'm starting to worry. It's like he has a little less endurance every day. He didn't want to, but I convinced him to see Dr. Livingston. We've scheduled an appointment for the middle of next week. I plan on making sure he goes."

"I hope he's all right."

Mathias nodded pensively. "So do I. I never thought I'd say this, but I think I'm coming to love the old geezer."

"He is not an old geezer. He's very nice—in his own way."

"You know what I mean. Besides, anyone over fifty is a geezer, no offense to your parents. By the way, how old are they?"

"My dad turns fifty this year. My mom is forty-seven. Which reminds me, they are thinking about starting a second business, more like a ministry, actually. They plan on leading weekend seminars."

"What kind of seminars?"

"They'll be lecturing on the historical differences between various religions. Apparently, the topic is generating a lot of interest nationwide. This Saturday, they're having a trial run. I was wondering if you might want to go. I assume you'll be free. It's next week you start at the mill. Isn't that right?"

Mathias nodded. "Will you be there at the seminar?"

Darcy indicated that she would.

"Then count me in."

"Good. I have a pamphlet in the car. Remind me after dinner, and I'll give it to you. It has all the details."

Lindell served two bowls of hearty tomato bisque.

"How do you feel about working at the mill?" Darcy pursed her lips and blew on a spoonful of soup to cool it.

Mathias did the same. "It's a job. At least I'll be able to keep an eye on Grandfather—Trent too, I imagine. You know it's still hard to accept that he's changed, even if he did help me get the job."

"Trent signed on at the mill right after graduation, didn't he?"

"He'll have two months' seniority on me. I'll never live it down. When he heard a position was opening up, he told me I should apply before word got out."

A quizzical look appeared in Darcy's eyes—part teasing, part serious. "Are you excited about becoming a mill worker?"

"I wouldn't say I'm excited, but the work will be steady, and it will pay better than the piecemeal jobs I've been scrounging since graduation. It's frustrating, banging on doors and making a pest of myself just to find work that lasts a day or two. I wish people with small projects had a way of communicating directly with people who were willing to work." Mathias sat bolt upright. The spark of an idea had ignited a firestorm inside his head. "A phone app. It's brilliant." He grew silent as gears meshed in his brain.

"I know that look." Darcy sighed. "Hey, Einstein, think you can put your bright idea on hold, at least till after dinner?"

Lindell removed the soup bowls and served plates laden with prime rib, crisp vegetables, and rice pilaf. Mathias barely noticed.

Later that night, he lay in bed and stared up at the darkened ceiling. In the wee hours of the morning, he had fleshed out the framework of his idea. His outline lay on his study desk. The details were sketchy, but the more he thought about the app, the more doable it seemed. However, undertaking such a project would demand intensive study, having never developed code for smartphones before.

Mathias's last conscious thought before eventually falling asleep was to again consider his incredibly good fortune. Three blessings in one night—how could anything top that?

***

The Four Feathers Motel boasted about having the largest conference hall in Rockridge. The room was, in fact, the only indoor space large enough to comfortably host public gatherings. It was where, on the third Thursday of each month, the Rockridge City Council dealt with civic matters.

Mathias sat in an aisle seat toward the back of the room. The folding chair next to him was empty. Darcy had stepped away to check on the caterers. The cost of admission included a modest buffet-style lunch. It was her duty to confirm that preparations were progressing as they should.

Miriam Thurston, Darcy's mother, stood at the podium, comparing the history of Christianity to other world religions. Over the preceding hour, Douglas Thurston, Darcy's father, had noted their theological differences. The Thurstons were experienced lecturers. Both had PhDs. Mathias had paid close attention, as had the rest of the sizable audience. Attendance was good. Even Rev. McAllister had shown up.

During the midmorning break, Darcy's parents had made a special effort to welcome Mathias to their seminar. At the end of the encounter, they had referenced their daughter's decision to postpone her first year of college. Darcy had interrupted before Mathias could voice an opinion. After reminding her parents that it was her decision, she had assured them there was no reason for concern; her future would unfold exactly as it was supposed to. To Mathias's amazement, her assertion had seemed to quell their misgivings.

Repeated references to Christianity sparked something inside Mathias. He sensed the presence of an urge, a longing beneath the surface of his thoughts. An uncomfortable sensation nagged at him like a forgotten memory hovering out of reach. The more he tried to ignore his feelings, the stronger they became.

160

When the morning's lectures ended, the audience dispersed for lunch. Mathias lingered behind. A meditation room had been set aside off the main hall. Feeling troubled, he headed in that direction. His intent was to clear his mind. Upon entering the room, he noted that he was alone. At the opposite end of the room stood a solitary gold cross centered on a table covered in white linen. He imagined the centerpiece had probably been borrowed from the Rockridge Gospel Fellowship. Soft music played in the background. He recognized the instrumental rendition of "The Old Rugged Cross," one of his mother's favorites. The ceiling lights were dimmed, adding an air of tranquility.

When Mathias perceived he had entered a chapel, he turned to leave, but a sense of curiosity restrained him. Rather than depart, he took a seat in the row nearest the altar, closed his eyes, and allowed the music to wash over him.

He kept his eyes closed even when the door behind him opened. The new arrival stepped forward and sat down one chair away, which slightly annoyed Mathias. There were plenty of chairs available. He cracked one eye open to peak at the interloper. Unexpectedly, he found Darcy's father regarding him with a gentle smile. He had shed his suit coat. It lay on his lap.

Dr. Thurston exemplified the prototype of a college professor. A full head of prematurely gray hair framed his clean-shaven face. High cheekbones and a narrow nose added a bookish look. He had the same soft brown eyes as his daughter and the same warm countenance.

"I hope you don't mind?" Dr. Thurston said. He then turned his attention to the cross.

"Not at all." Mathias closed his eyes again but found it difficult to resume his meditations.

Dr. Thurston spoke softly. "I remember you telling me that you believe in God?"

"Excuse me?" Mathias's eyes popped open.

"You believe in a supreme being, an all-powerful creator who formed the universe and everything that's in it. Is that right—that's what you believe?" Dr. Thurston continued gazing at the altar.

"I suppose." Mathias fidgeted, feeling ill at ease.

"Good."

"Dr. Thurston—"

"Douglas, please. Being called Doctor seems so formal. Best we leave that for the classroom, don't you think?"

"Okay."

"By the way, I'm sure you know God wasn't responsible."

"What?"

"He didn't kill your parents."

Mathias bristled. "It seems Darcy has a big mouth."

"Don't be harsh with her. I've watched the way she is when you're around. It's easy to see she cares. Surely you must know that."

"I do. I feel the same."

"Good." Douglas angled his body so he could lay an arm along the back of the chair that separated them. "Someday you're going to have to accept that God didn't end your parents' lives. He wasn't punishing you. They died as all people do. Every life has a beginning and an end. It's what we do with the years in between that matters."

"How can you be sure He wasn't responsible?" Mathias blurted out.

"Because God is love."

"Really? You presume to know how God feels?"

"I do—because He's demonstrated His love. He loves us so much that He offered His son as a willing sacrifice on our behalf so that we might be saved. I know you have an interest in the Bible, and from what I hear, you and Darcy have had some fairly pointed discussions. So have you and I, for that matter. But have you ever truly looked at Jesus Christ and what He accomplished?"

"I've read the Gospels."

"But do you understand the gift you're being offered? All men sin. We can't help it. It's who we are. And it's our sins that separate us from God. Make no mistake, every person will be judged. By dying on the cross, Jesus made it possible for God to forgive our sins. Christ died willingly as a ransom for our salvation. But the thing is, you must accept His gift. God won't force you to take it. You have to invite Jesus into your life. Confess you are a sinner and ask Him to place His spirit within you. Only then can you be saved."

"Something you said in your lecture troubles me. How do we know Jesus is the Son of God?"

"Because of His resurrection. By raising Jesus from the dead, God demonstrated that we too can have eternal life. The resurrection is the linchpin. Otherwise, Christianity is just another philosophical discipline among many."

Douglas leaned closer and laid a hand on Mathias's shoulder. "This isn't something you can reason out. If you're looking for absolute proof, you're not going to find it. God set it up that way. Salvation comes by faith, not by scientific investigation. Look deep into your heart. Ask yourself what you truly believe. Was Jesus a real human being? Did He walk the earth as we do? Do you believe that as God incarnate, He died on that cross and, on the third day rose again? Now is the time to choose. Do you believe that Jesus is inviting you to join Him in eternity?"

All of a sudden, Mathias realized what had been troubling him. He trembled slightly. He had been fighting against God for so long. It was time to put an end to his rebellion. A tear of joy rolled down his cheek, then another. "Yes, I do. I do believe."

"Will you invite Jesus into your life?"

"I will. Yes, I will. Absolutely."

"Then pray this prayer with me. It's called the sinner's prayer. Almighty God, I confess that I'm a sinner, and I ask for your forgiveness. I believe that your son died for my sins and that He rose from the dead. I accept His gift of salvation. I trust you and will follow you as my Lord. Come into my life, and guide me to do Your will. Amen."

As Mathias solemnly repeated the words, he felt a tingling spread throughout his body. It was followed by a wonderful sense of peace. The nagging disquiet that had distressed him was gone. Later, he would have difficulty describing his experience, except to say it was awesome.

***

The exhilaration that had consumed Mathias after his confession of faith lasted only a few days.

Late in the afternoon, on his second day at the mill, the operation manager's voice sounded over the yard's loudspeakers an hour before quitting time, urgently summoning Mathias to the office by name.

Briefly, Mathias felt relieved having been given an opportunity to take a break. Even for the middle of August, it was an unusually warm day, and he had been working nonstop for hours. When he entered through the front door of the administration building, he sensed something was seriously wrong.

Mr. Leonard Doyle, operations manager for the Fairworth Lumber Company, stood waiting. He seemed anxious. "He's back here. Follow me." He led the way toward a small space at the end of a tight corridor. "It's your grandfather. He's not doing well."

"What happened?" Mathias increased his pace to keep up.

"We're not sure. He had some kind of spell. He came out to tell us he wasn't feeling well, then he sort of blacked out for a moment. We have him lying down on a couch in the break room."

Mathias recognized his grandfather's voice even before he turned the corner and saw him struggling to sit up. "I'm fine," Ward was saying. "And I'd appreciate it if you'd stop holding me down. I need to get back to work."

"What you need is to cooperate," said Mildred, the office manager, who was obviously flustered. She backed off when she recognized Mathias. "Maybe you can talk some sense into this knothead. He won't listen to me."

"Lie down, Grandfather," Mathias commanded as he sat down on the edge of the sofa. He gently coaxed Ward into a supine position. "Tell me what happened."

"Nothing happened. I got up too fast, got a little dizzy. I'm fine, I tell you. Now let me up. I have a production schedule to finish."

Mathias looked up at Mr. Doyle. "How long was he out?"

"A good thirty seconds, maybe longer."

"Can you move everything?" Mathias asked his grandfather. "Do you hurt anywhere?"

"Only my pride." Ward flexed and extended his arms and legs several times. "See, everything works. Now can I get back to doing my job?"

Mathias again looked up at the operations manager. "What do you think?"

Mr. Doyle shook his head. "I'd feel better if Doc Livingston were to check him out, just to be sure."

"Nonsense," Ward said. "I'm good to go."

"It's not up to you, Grandfather. If the boss says you need to see a doctor, so be it. This time, you're not going to cancel your appointment." Mathias stood and faced Mr. Doyle. "I know it's not quitting time yet, but would it be okay if I took him home? It may not be safe for him to drive."

"I agree," Mr. Doyle said. "Better safe than sorry."

"This is ridiculous," Ward groused. "All I did was faint."

Mathias leaned over and looked his grandfather straight in the face. "Give me the keys to the truck."

Reluctantly, Ward fished them out of his pocket and handed them over.

***

Doc Livingston appeared in the doorway of his waiting room and motioned for Mathias to step forward. "You can come back now. I've completed my exam." The doctor led the way to the examination room.

Ward was buttoning up his shirt. He had already put on his pants. He had also put on his socks and shoes, but the laces were untied.

"How is he?" Mathias said to the doctor.

"His blood pressure is a little low. Otherwise, he seems reasonably fit for a man who hasn't taken care of himself." As he draped his stethoscope around his neck, Doc Livingston shot Ward a look of chastisement.

Ward ignored the reprimand and finished tucking in the tail of his shirt. He then bent down to tie his shoes. When he straightened up, he wobbled. With one hand, he braced himself against the exam table to keep from falling.

Doc Livingston scowled. "Is that what happened before?"

Ward squared his shoulders. "Pretty much, except I didn't catch myself in time."

"I think maybe we should run some tests." Doc Livingston reached for the clipboard lying on the built-in writing table. He checked off several small boxes on the top form, which he tore off and handed to Ward. "Give this to the receptionist out front. She'll call Cedarwood Memorial and schedule your appointments."

"I don't think so," Ward said.

"Excuse me?" Doc Livingston looked up in surprise.

Ward made a gesture of appeasement. "I'm fine. I keep saying it, but nobody's listening. It's a hot day, and maybe I'm a little dehydrated. We don't need to run a bunch of tests I can't afford. Let me go home and get a good night's sleep. Tomorrow, I'll be fit as a fiddle."

"Stubborn like his daughter," Doc Livingston muttered, shaking his head.

"Of course," Ward replied. "Who do you think taught her to dig her heels in? Are we done?"

Doc Livingston regarded his patient with concern. "Promise you'll call if anything changes."

"If I don't, someone's bound to do it for me." Ward playfully grabbed Mathias by the scruff of his neck. "What say, hotshot? Ready to go?"

"Okay, but I'm driving."

"Have it your way. You know, you really need your own transportation." Ward followed Mathias out of the exam room.

"I plan on it as soon as I get paid." Mathias looked back as the doctor joined them in the corridor. "Sorry, Doc. I'll keep an eye on him."

"That would be wise." Still shaking his head, Doc Livingston stood with his arms folded across his chest and watched them go.

***

After dinner, Mathias left the house to join his grandfather in the backyard. Ward stood gazing up at the night sky. During the ride home from the doctor's office, he had spoken hardly at all. A nocturnal breeze had partially quelled the heat of the day. A squirrel chittered as if bidding the forest good night. The soft burble of Tanner's Creek could be heard in the distance. A dim glow above the mountaintops showed where the moon would eventually rise.

The forest seemed serene until Mathias noted an owl perched on the upper branches of a spruce nearby. As if on cue, the bird cast off to glide effortlessly between tree trunks, a lethal predator on noiseless wings.

Mathias mimicked his grandfather's posture and clasped his hands behind his back. "Caught sight of any griz yet?"

Ward continued his inspection of the heavens. "I never imagined there were this many stars. Makes you feel kind of insignificant."

"Like sand on a seashore," Mathias said, paraphrasing Genesis 22:17, a verse he had read just that morning. A moment later, he said, "Want to tell me what's really on your mind?"

Ward hesitated, but then replied, "I was thinking about Rule 11."

Mathias rifled through his mental filing system. "Live the way you want to be remembered." It was a good rule, though a tad morose. "Why that one?"

"No particular reason."

"Bull. Is it because of what happened today? You're worried, aren't you? I can tell."

"You think I'm worried? Actually, I feel terrific. You have no cause for concern, and frankly, I'd rather not talk about it, if you don't mind."

"What do you want to talk about?"

Ward pointed up at the sky. "Did you see that? A shooting star. That's something you never see in Los Angeles. The city lights are too bright."

"There goes another one." Mathias traced his finger across the firmament.

For a time, both men refrained from speaking while they listened to the muted sounds of the forest.

At length, Mathias said, "Can I ask you something?"

"That depends."

"Do you believe in Jesus?" His grandfather's relationship with Christ was a topic Mathias would never have dreamed of questioning before.

"I knew you'd get around to asking after what happened to you. Let's just say I'm keeping an open mind and leave it at that."

"I was hoping you could help me figure out some things."

"Like what?"

"Like how I'm supposed to feel. Today when they told me you'd blacked out, and I then saw you on that couch, I got scared. I know I'm supposed to trust God, but—"

"Let me put your mind at ease, son. I'm fine. You do not need to worry about me."

"That's not the point. Well, it is actually, but it isn't. What I mean is, if God is in control of my life now, how come I was afraid?"

"It's in our nature—has to do with anticipating traumatic events. We can't help it."

"But I've read that fear is the antithesis of faith."

"You're asking the wrong guy. You need to talk with somebody who knows about these things." Rather than wait for his grandson to press the issue, Ward switched gears. "What are your plans for tonight? You working on your computer stuff?"

"I thought I might. Is there something you need?"

"Not me. I'm gonna read for a while then go to bed. It's you I was thinking about. Remember that tomorrow is a workday. Don't be staying up till the wee hours of the morning again."

"I'll try not to, but this app I plan on creating is kind of exciting. The more I get into it, the more promising it seems. I've even given it a title: OddJober. Catchy, huh?"

"That's well and good, but if you crap out at the mill because you've run out of gas, they'll hand you your pink slip." Ward turned to head inside. "You know what sounds good right now? A cup of hot cocoa and a great mystery novel. You coming?"

Mathias followed. As he entered the kitchen, he wondered about his grandfather's comment regarding pink slips and to which of them it might apply.

***

The Rockridge Gospel Fellowship seemed deserted when Mathias approached the side door, which was to be expected since the church was normally vacant at seven o'clock at night. This night, however, he had scheduled a meeting with Rev. McAllister. Reassuringly, the side door was unlocked, and the lights had been left on.

With circumspection, Mathias made his way to the central corridor and listened. A series of clanks and clatters emanated from the rear of the building. He headed in that direction. When he glanced into the men's restroom, he saw the Rev. Thaddeus McAllister lying on the floor, flat on his back, head and shoulders crammed into the narrow cabinet beneath the sink. It seemed a remarkably uncomfortable position. The pastor held a pipe wrench in one hand and a crescent wrench in the other.

Rev. McAllister reached up to adjust something out of Mathias's line of sight. He then rested the wrenches on his chest and waited. Apparently satisfied, he slid his head and shoulders out of the cabinet. When he saw Mathias, he startled. "Oh, you're here. What time is it?"

"Seven o'clock." Then Mathias volunteered, "Is there something you need help with?"

"I think I've got it fixed. We had a small leak, but it was just a loose fitting. All better now."

"How come you're the one repairing the plumbing?" Mathias asked.

"Ralph Stark—he's the guy who usually volunteers for these sorts of repairs—went to check on his mother in Flint. You'd be amazed at the variety of chores that fall on a pastor's shoulders. If you intend to shepherd a small parish, you pretty much have to be a jack-of-all-trades."

The reverend's comment reminded Mathias of the app he was creating, but he sensed it was neither the time nor the place to mention it.

Being a rather portly man, Rev. McAllister rose from the floor with difficulty, grunting as he stood up. After gathering up his tools, he washed his hands, then he squatted down to look under the sink one last time, making certain the leak was sealed. Apparently reassured, he straightened up and turned to Mathias. "Let's go to my office. We can talk there."

The reverend ushered Mathias into his inner sanctum. With a gesture, he indicated the two chairs that faced his desk. Mathias selected the one nearest the window. The reverend stepped around behind his desk and eased his bulk into a well-padded executive chair. It squeaked under his weight. It occurred to Mathias that the man probably spent a fair amount of time seated as he was, studying theology and preparing sermons.

Two months had elapsed since Ward's episode at work, but his grandfather's medical condition was not the issue that had triggered Mathias's recent distress. What bothered him was an absence of inner peace. His anxieties suggested that somehow his conversion had misfired—that something had gone wrong and his salvation wasn't assured.

"Thanks for agreeing to meet with me," Mathias said. "I'm sorry the hour is so late."

"You're a working man now. I totally understand. You would be surprised how little of the church's business gets conducted during normal business hours. Besides, if I hadn't been here to use the restroom,

I wouldn't have discovered the leak. Who knows how much damage could have been done. God works in mysterious ways." The reverend chuckled. "By the way, let me congratulate you again on your profession of faith. I must admit, I was a little surprised it took so long. Your mother, I'm sure, must have encouraged you in that direction, even from an early age." The reverend sniffed, and his nose crinkled.

"I think she felt it was best that I make up my own mind. Everyone must gather their own manna."

"Ah, yes. Your mother was wise beyond her years and truly devoted. I think about her often. She was a respected member of the flock. I still miss her, as I'm sure you do. By the way, someday in the near future, we need to get you baptized."

"That's kind of what I wanted to talk to you about."

"I'm listening. What's on your mind?" Rev. McAllister leaned back and laced his fingers behind his head.

Mathias inhaled slowly. "I'm not sure I can express what I'm feeling. A couple months ago, I stopped by the cemetery to visit my mother's grave. It was on a Sunday, right after church, not long after I'd accepted Jesus. As I looked down at her tombstone, I realized for the first time that she wasn't there. She was in heaven. It was an amazing feeling. There was a joy I can't explain. I also remember feeling kinda guilty because I wasn't as sad as I'd been when she died.

"But a few days later, my grandfather had his fainting spell. The doctor called it a syncopal episode. He said he couldn't find anything wrong but proposed doing a battery of tests. Grandfather would have none of it. He's probably okay, but I hate the thought of losing him. Then other problems started cropping up."

"What sort of problems? You're not in trouble again, are you?"

"No. No. I've been behaving myself."

"What problems then?"

"We're not keeping up with repairs on the ranch. Things around the house need fixing, but we're both too tired to do what needs to be done. For a while now, we've been falling behind."

"That happens when everyone in the family works. Anything else?"

"There is. I recently bought an old Jeep. It's a beater, but it runs. Except now I have to buy my own gas and pay for my own insurance.

Worse, I just bought a new set of tires. All the money I've earned since last summer is gone. I should be buying my own food and helping with the mortgage. It's not fair for Grandfather to support me now that I'm working, but I don't have any money. Don't get me wrong. I'm not whining. I get that our responsibilities increase as we grow older, and that's cool. The problem is I feel anxious all the time. I worry and fret about what's going to happen next. I worry a lot. It's like I don't have any faith at all. I keep wondering if…"

A gentle grin exposed Rev. McAllister's front incisors. "What, that you don't have the Holy Spirit? Let me guess. You're concerned that you might not be saved, that God hasn't forgiven you?"

"Something like that."

The reverend rocked forward. "You're not the first parishioner to feel this way. Let's put this puppy to bed once and for all. If you believe in your heart that Jesus is the son of God and you confess with your mouth that He is Lord, you're saved. Period. It's a done deal. Let me be as clear as I possibly can be. God has forgiven your sins."

"If I'm forgiven, why am I so anxious?"

"Because salvation isn't the end of the story."

"What is then?"

"God doesn't promise us an easy life. He only promises that He will be with us when times get tough. He's more interested in our character than our comfort."

"My mother used to say that."

"That's maybe where I got it. In the years ahead, you'll have to make choices that test your faith. You'll encounter situations that are impossible to overcome without relying on the Holy Spirit. This is okay because God is shaping you to become the man you are supposed to be. The anxiety you feel—think of it as an internal buzzer, a reminder to rely on God. He wants you to trust Him, especially when you can't find a way forward."

"I didn't used to have these feelings. It seems odd that I should suddenly start worrying."

"These emotions began when?"

"Right after Grandfather—oh. You don't imagine—could that have been the trigger?"

"You were devastated when you lost your mother. Perhaps when you realized you might lose your grandfather as well…"

"He is my only living relative. What do I do?"

"Tell God how you feel. Ask Him to take away your anxiety. Prayer is an amazingly powerful tool. Don't be afraid to use it. One thing, however, is that when you pray, don't forget to listen. It's a two-way conversation, you know."

"What if I continue to feel uptight?"

"At some point, you must *choose* to let go." The reverend placed special emphasis on the word *choose*. "You must be willing to trust God. Rely on His strength, not your own."

Mathias frowned. "Does it get any easier?"

The Rev. McAllister shook his head. "If you are truly following in Jesus's footsteps and obeying His commands, it only gets harder."

"Splendid."

After thanking the reverend for taking time to speak with him, Mathias departed. Most of his questions had been answered. In their place, he had gathered a whole batch of new concerns to deal with. Foremost among them was "How does a loving God benefit from making a follower's life harder rather than easier?" As he slid the key into the Jeep's ignition, he sensed he might already know the answer.

When Mathias turned the key, the engine chugged a couple times and then quit. The battery was dead. He regarded the now-dark church and wondered if Rev. McAllister might still be inside and if he owned a pair of jumper cables.

***

The Fairworth Lumber Mill hummed with the sounds of industrial equipment—the ringing whine of the buzz saws, the repeating *thunk* of the chop saw, the rumble of the forklift, the whirring of the wood chipper. In the timber business, noise equated to making money. Silence signaled a problem with production.

Mathias paused to look around. He had been working at the mill nearly six months. Winter was drawing to a close. The harshness of the season had left the citizens of Rockridge feeling edgy and eager for relief from icy roads and frigid gales. Most of the region's snow had melted, except in the deepest shadows perpetually hidden from the sun's rays. The soggy ground was slick in spots. Treacherous puddles of mud dotted the lumberyard. Patches of still-frozen earth leached heat out through the soles of Mathias's boots. Walking vexed him because his cold feet made it seem as if he could feel his missing fourth and fifth toes.

By the luck of the draw, he and Trent had been assigned the worst duty possible—cleanup. Their job that day was to gather up scraps of lumber, rejected timbers, broken boards, knotholes, scraps, and such and toss them into a wheelbarrow to be emptied into the wood chipper.

The chipper was a monster of a machine. Standing ten feet tall, its whirling teeth could chew a six-foot 4×4 into sawdust in less than nine seconds. Longer bits of scrap were fed in on a conveyor belt. Wheelbarrows were dumped into the upper hopper, which was reached by ascending a ramp often slippery with mud. The job was as dangerous as it was repugnant.

Trent pitched a scrap of wood into the wheelbarrow Mathias had stationed nearby. "We ought to be able to start fishing soon. What do you think—a couple more weeks?"

Mathias regarded the tops of the mountain that could be seen in the distance. "Maybe. There's a lot of snow up there. I'd give it a month, unless we get a warm rain." He added a handful of splintered fragments cast off by the chop saw.

"Remember when we were kids and we used to hike to Horse Collar Lake?" Trent straightened up and flexed his shoulders. Both yardmen were feeling the strain. Since lunch, they had worked four hours straight without a break. "Those were good days."

"Certainly better than today." Mathias topped off their load with a length of mangled board. "Is it my turn?"

"Yep, you're up."

Mathias hefted the wheelbarrow by its handles and steered it toward the wood chipper. "Say, you heard anything from your dad?"

"No, and I hope I never do."

"Strange he would just take off. Do you know where he is?"

"Haven't got a clue, nor do I care." Trent fell in beside Mathias and occasionally helped steady the wheelbarrow. "You coming over this weekend?" He had rented his own apartment shortly after his dad had forsaken him. "Basketball season is underway. I'm pretty sure there will be a game on."

"We'll see. I may be busy. I don't know yet."

"Your computer stuff?"

Mathias nodded as he guided the wheelbarrow up the ramp attached to the wood chipper. Upon reaching the top, he looked down at the whirling blades, aware that if he were to fall in, he would lose an arm, a leg, or worse. Terrified by the prospect, he backed up a step. Feeding the chipper was the only part of his job he truly hated.

"I wish you liked to hang out in bars!" Trent yelled up loudly enough to be heard above the roar of the machine. "It's a great place to meet girls."

"I already have a girlfriend!" Mathias yelled back. "I don't need another one."

"Right, I keep forgetting. You two getting it on?"

"Not the way you're thinking." Distracted and worn out at the end of a long day, Mathias dumped the entire load in all at once. The mass of scrap jammed the hopper. He instinctively spit out a curse, but then breathed a silent thank-you when he realized that his expletive had been swallowed up by the wail of the spinning blades. In an environment where cursing was a way of life, he had resolved to set a better example.

Company policy mandated that no machine was to be shut down except for repairs. He would have to free the blockage manually while the chipper was still running. "Toss me up that length of 2×4," he called down to Trent.

"Really?"

Mathias shrugged. After positioning the wheelbarrow out of the way, he accepted the length of board that Trent handed up to him. Turning around, he positioned himself with most of his weight on his back foot. Easing forward, he began gingerly jabbing at the blockage, then with more vigor. Suddenly, his front foot skidded and he pitched forward, but caught himself in the nick of time. An anxious shudder surged down his spine. With much greater care, he resumed his efforts. When the obstruction finally broke loose, the hopper emptied in a rush. A gush of shavings and sawdust spewed out of the chipper's chute.

As Mathias backed away from the hopper, he realized that despite the air's coolness, he was sweating. He offered a prayer of thanksgiving. Looking out across the lumberyard, he was surprised to see his grandfather advancing in his direction. Ward seemed troubled.

Mathias left Trent in charge of the wheelbarrow and set out to intercept his grandfather. "What's wrong?" he called ahead when he had drawn within earshot. Normally, Ward stayed in his cubbyhole in administration. They rarely encountered one another out in the open.

"It's no big deal," Ward said, "but do you think I could trouble you for a ride?" He seemed uncomfortable, maybe a little rattled.

The request concerned Mathias. His grandfather had driven himself to work that morning. He should have been able to get wherever he wanted to go. Sincerely hoping his grandfather's problem was nothing serious, Mathias teased, "Is that old truck acting up again?"

"No, the truck is fine. I was just wondering if I could hitch a ride."

"To someplace in particular?"

"Just home."

"You want me to take you home?"

"If it's not a bother."

When Mathias reached out to take hold of Ward's upper arm, he was astonished to discover the old man was trembling slightly. "Want to tell me what's up?"

"Relax, it's no big deal. I just don't feel like driving."

Mathias looked closer and noted apprehension in his grandfather's eyes. "You've had another spell."

"I'm fine."

"You used to be able to fool me. Not anymore. Now I can tell when you are trying to snow me. Tell me what's wrong?"

"Like I said, it's nothing serious. I just don't feel like driving."

"You said that already. It's not an explanation."

In response to his grandson's penetrating stare, Ward seemed to relent. "I don't trust myself behind the wheel."

"Why? Are you feeling lightheaded?"

"Not light-headed. More like foggy-brained. I can't seem to focus. I'm worried I might cause an accident."

"Did you black out?"

"No."

"Are you in pain?"

"No."

"Nauseous?"

"No, but I am a tad short of breath. I thought maybe it was because I'm feeling tense. I can't seem to finish the schedule I've been working on. I tried resting for a space. It didn't help."

Mathias consulted his smartphone—twenty minutes until quitting time.

As if monitoring his grandson's thoughts, Ward said, "No need to clock out early. Just come get me when your shift is over."

"Enough of this. We're taking you to the doctor," Mathias declared flatly.

"Not today. Besides, the last time I went, Doc couldn't find anything wrong."

"That's because you refused to have yourself tested."

"Look, all I need is rest. I'll feel better after a good night's sleep. If I'm still feeling peaked in the morning, I'll give Doc Livingston a call. I promise."

Mathias pondered a moment. Ward could be stubborn. Arguing might do more harm than good. The last thing he wanted was to fuel his grandfather's distress. "All right. Give me your keys."

"Why?"

"I'm going to ask Trent if he'll drive your truck to our house. If he's willing, I can bring him back here after we get you squared away."

Ward fished in his pocket and handed over the truck's keys. "I'll be in my office. Give me a shout when you're ready to leave."

"Sure you don't want to go now?"

"There are files on my desk I need to put away. I'll see you when your shift is over." Ward seemed to weave slightly as he walked back toward the main offices.

***

Mathias emerged from Ward's bedroom just as the front doorbell rang. He had offered to fix dinner, but his grandfather had turned him down, claiming a lack of appetite. Instead, he had insisted on being allowed to rest. Reluctantly, Mathias had agreed, hoping that a little peace and quiet might ease whatever was troubling the old man.

When Mathias opened the front door, Trent tossed him a set of keys. Mathias poked his head outside and saw that the truck was parked in front of the garage. "I appreciate your helping out," he said as he moved aside. "Come in."

Trent entered and looked around. "It's been a while. The place looks about the same."

"You know what they say, 'Why redecorate when you don't have to?'"

"Is that one of your rules?"

"No, I just made it up. Are you hungry? I offered to feed Grandfather, but he turned me down. I think I'll fix him something anyway. You're welcome to stay for dinner."

"I'll pass on dinner. I have errands to run, but I'll take a beer."

"There's no alcohol in the house, but I can brew a pot of coffee."

"That's right. I forgot. You guys are teetotalers." Trent followed his host into the kitchen. After shedding his coat, he draped it over the back of a chair and sat down. "I remember when we were little and I used to sleep over. Your mom would fix us breakfast. We'd sit around this table, eating pancakes and laughing." Lost in thought, Trent stared off into space.

Mathias glanced outside. It was still daylight. With the days growing longer, the shadows of evening were only just beginning to appear. When he looked at Trent, he suspected he knew what his guest was thinking. "You never hear from your mom, do you?"

"Not since I was two. When she took off, she never looked back. I can't say I blame her."

"You know what I miss?" Mathias said with an air of nostalgia. "Our soccer games. Do you remember when we'd play two-on-two? We'd run around and wear ourselves out, yelling and screaming like banshees."

"I remember you kept tripping over your own feet."

Mathias nodded as he took a chair at the table. He sat quietly for a moment, having been reminded of Rule 13: "Every man lives in the house he builds." For him, it had been one of the hardest rules to grasp. Basically, it meant that every individual must ultimately deal with the choices he or she makes. Looking across the table, he said, "What happened to us, do you think?"

"Life happened."

The percolator signaled that its brew cycle had finished. Mathias stood and filled two mugs with coffee.

Trent accepted his and looked up. "So your relationship with Darcy is heating up?"

"Like I said, not physically, but we're spending more time together." Mathias returned to his chair.

Trent seemed surprised. "What's the problem? If you like the girl?"

"I do like her. That's why we decided to wait."

"You're not gay, are you?"

Mathias's face reddened. "No way. In fact, I'm thinking about asking her to marry me." He pitched forward with alarm. "Don't you dare tell her. I want it to be a surprise."

"Don't worry. I won't say a thing."

"Swear it."

"I swear, but tell me, how do you expect to support a wife on a mill worker's salary?"

"I won't have to."

"Why? Is she going to support you?"

"Not if I have anything to say about it."

"You've landed a second job?"

"Even better." Excitedly, Mathias continued, "Remember that app I've been working on? I just finished debugging the code, line by line. All that's left is to package it and put it on the market."

"Refresh my memory. What does your app do?"

"It matches people who have odd jobs that need doing with people looking for work. It'll run on smartphones, tablets, and most other platforms."

"You can make money matching people?"

"Oh yeah. Want to see? Come with me, and I'll show you."

Mathias rose and led his guest upstairs to his bedroom. Sitting down at his desk, he switched on his laptop. A moment later, his app was up and running. "See these empty fields, like this banner across the bottom of the screen." He tapped the display with his fingertip. "They're reserved for advertisements. Advertisers pay a penny a hit. A hit is when a visitor lands on a webpage. In other words, every time a visitor comes to my webpage, the advertisers will pay me one penny each. They'll pay ten pennies if that visitor clicks on their ad."

"That's what you call making money?"

"There'll be at least four ads per page, and I assume the average visitor will hit on at least three pages. If one visitor in ten clicks on an ad, and I get 75,000 visitors per year, which is entirely doable, that's an annual income of $9,750 for simply having the program up and running. But that's not the cool part. I plan on selling memberships."

"I still don't understand. What is this program is supposed to do?"

"Sorry, I got ahead of myself. Let's say you have a fence that needs fixing. You use my app to list your job. You describe what the work entails, how long it's supposed to take, and what you're willing to pay, plus other details. Your geographic location is automatically recorded by GPS. Let's say someone searching for part-time work comes across your listing. From within the app, they can send you a text message describing their work experience, availability, whether or not they have their own tools, and other qualifications. At this point, neither party knows the other's identity. Negotiations continue until a deal is reached. When both parties are satisfied, their identities are revealed, and each receives a contract detailing the terms they've agreed to."

"You mentioned memberships?"

"That's where the fun begins. A user's first year will be free. After that, they can continue using the app at no cost, but if they choose to join, an annual membership will cost $12.75."

"Why should anyone join if they can use your app for free?"

"When you become a member, you can continue building your profile, which was started during your free year. This works for both listers and seekers. At the end of a project, the people you've done business with will be asked to rate your performance. In the future, others will be able to read your profile and will know if they can trust you or not. Users with the highest ratings will have a competitive advantage when it comes to striking a deal. Also, members can arrange to have notifications sent out whenever a new project is listed or when a seeker with the right qualifications becomes available to work."

Trent stroked his chin. "How much do you expect to make on memberships?"

Mathias grinned broadly. "If only ten thousand people sign up nationwide, that's $127,500 annually."

Trent whistled. "Now that's what I call making money." He noticed the scratchpad lying on the desk beside the laptop. A name had been jotted down and underlined several times. Beneath it was a phone number. Around everything, a box had been drawn with stars penciled in at the corners. He read the name aloud, "TruFusion Software? Who are they?"

"It's a company out of Austin, Texas. They've expressed an interest in buying my code, but I've decided to host the servers and manage the database myself. It'll be more profitable over time."

"They made you an offer?"

"Yeah, a quarter mil. Can you believe it?"

"A quarter of a million dollars?" Trent gasped. "And you turned them down?"

"If this works out the way I believe it will, in a couple years, I'll be making twice that much."

"I had no idea."

The front doorbell rang. Mathias left his laptop running and headed downstairs to see who might be calling. Since he wasn't expecting visitors and thinking that he would return soon, he motioned for Trent to remain in the bedroom.

Leonard Doyle, Fairworth's operations manager, stood on the Reslins' front porch. He wore a heavy dress coat over his charcoal-gray suit. The collar of his white shirt was buttoned, and the knot of his striped tie was snug against his throat. His wingtips looked to have been vigorously polished. Mathias immediately sensed something was wrong.

"Is your grandfather at home?" Mr. Doyle said.

"He's resting. Can I help you?"

"It's important that I speak with him. Do you think you could see if he's available?"

"Sure. Please come in." Mathias ushered the operations manager into the living room and invited him to have a seat on the couch. "Can I get you something?"

"No, thank you." Mr. Doyle sat with his back straight and his hands on his knees. He hadn't bothered taking off his top coat.

Mathias disappeared into his grandfather's bedroom but then promptly returned. Mr. Doyle looked up at his approach.

"I'm afraid he's asleep," Mathias announced. "I'd rather not wake him. Perhaps you might want to tell me what's going on?"

Mr. Doyle seemed edgy. "It's a rather sensitive matter, I'm afraid. It might be best if I spoke with your grandfather directly."

"We don't keep secrets in this house. He won't mind if you tell me what this is about."

"Very well, if you insist. I've discussed this at length with the head of our personnel department. I've also talked with other members of our administrative staff. You must be aware that your grandfather has—well, his job performance hasn't been exactly stellar recently."

Rather than sit down, Mathias remained standing in the center of the room. "He's had some problems with his health, but I doubt you could name a more dedicated employee."

"I don't dispute that in the least, and don't get me wrong. I like your grandfather. I wasn't sure about him when he first came to work at the mill, but he kind of grows on you."

"Indeed, he does."

"Ironically, that's why this is so difficult. If I had a choice, I'd make an allowance in his case, but I don't. It's time to face the fact that he simply isn't capable of doing his job. He needs medical help."

"He and I have discussed this already," Mathias protested. "We'll be calling the doctor in the morning."

"I am so glad to hear that. I worry about him. Regrettably, that doesn't change a thing. Until we can be sure he's well enough to do his job, we need to make other arrangements."

"Other arrangements? You're firing him."

"Not in the full sense of the word. If and when his health improves, we will seriously consider taking him back. Until then, let's call this an extended leave of absence—without pay." Mr. Doyle stood up.

"You can't do that. It isn't right to fire a man just because he sick."

"We have no choice. Your grandfather's job is crucial to the smooth functioning of the mill. We depend upon him to keep our production up. Mathias, please understand. This decision doesn't affect our relationship with you in the least. You're a good worker, and we're glad to have you."

"Nice to know, since it looks like I'm now the sole breadwinner for this family."

Mr. Doyle shook his head with what appeared to be heartfelt regret. "I am sorry. Really, I am. I loathe having to lay employees off, especially the ones I regard as friends."

Laid off, Mathias said to himself. *How could it be? What are we going to do?*

The operations manager showed himself out, leaving Mathias to wonder how he would break the news to his grandfather. He plopped down on the couch and buried his face in his hands.

Ten minutes later, the bedroom door upstairs opened and Trent emerged.

"You heard?" Mathias said, having forgotten about his guest.

Trent nodded as he joined Mathias in the living room. "It's a rotten deal any way you slice it."

"I suppose I should have seen it coming. Look, why don't I take you back to your car? You have errands to run, right?"

"A few. Will your grandfather be all right while we're gone?"

"What worries me is how he'll be after I tell him the news."

About to step down from the front porch, Mathias turned back. "My computer—I left it running."

Trent stopped him. "Not to worry. I shut it down for you." When Mathias's brow furrowed, Trent added, "Relax. I didn't just hit the power switch. I exited your app first. I may not have taken CompSci, but I do know a little about computers. Hey, I thought I was doing you a favor. When I heard what was going on, I figured you'd have other things on your mind."

"Thanks," Mathias said with uncertainty. He turned and headed toward the Jeep.

CHAPTER 8

The corridors of Cedarwood Memorial Hospital bustled with activity as staff members efficiently went about their business. Some wore white coats. Others wore scrubs. Mathias rode the elevator to the fourth floor of the medical wing. This was his third visit since his grandfather's admission. It was also the day his grandfather was to be discharged.

The regional hospital was located in Grayline, thirty-four miles east of Rockridge. After getting off work, Mathias had covered the distance in remarkably good time. He had pushed the Jeep's engine to speeds it could barely tolerate because he had hoped to speak with the hospitalist before taking his grandfather home. On his two previous visits, he had learned that if you weren't there when the doctor made her rounds, it could be difficult to track her down later.

Exiting the elevator, Mathias targeted room 427 toward the middle of the corridor ahead. He hurried in that direction. When he had covered half the distance, he breathed a sigh of relief. A small woman was just emerging from his grandfather's room. She wore a white lab coat with a stethoscope in the side pocket. She fit the nurses' description of his grandfather's attending physician.

"Dr. Everett?" Mathias said as he drew near.

"Yes?" The woman wore her silver hair woven into a long braid and wrapped around the crown of her skull. Her glasses had thin gold rims and tended to slide down the bridge of her nose. Occasionally, she shoved them back into place with an index finger. Her most obvious trait, however, was her diminutive size. Mathias estimated she was less than five feet tall and had to weigh less than a hundred pounds. She also seemed to be moderately frustrated.

Mathias smiled politely. "Excuse me. I'm Mathias Reslin, Ward Stanford's grandson. I understand he's to be discharged today?"

"I was just giving him his final instructions. You're the one who cares for him at home?"

"Yep, that's my job."

"Well, I suspect you've got your work cut out for you. What I mean is, he hasn't been the easiest patient to treat. He can be—"

"Muleheaded?"

"I was going to say stubborn, but your phrase will do. Are there other members of your family, anyone else who needs to hear where we stand?"

"It's just him and me."

"Okay. Why don't we find someplace quiet where we can talk? Let's see if the lounge is available."

The narrow lounge reeked with a pungent smell as if the housekeepers had polished every surface with disinfectant. Mathias chose a chrome chair upholstered in synthetic leather, catty-corner to the doctor. As he sat down, he gave her his full attention.

Dr. Everett's feet barely reached the floor. She rested an elbow on the armrest. "We've finished our workup. How much has Dr. Livingston told you about your grandfather's condition?"

"The last time we spoke was when Grandfather was admitted. He told me then that there seemed to be a problem with his heart."

"I'm afraid Doc Livingston was correct. It's a condition we call cardiomyopathy. Basically, it's a weakness of the heart muscle, usually the result of another condition such as malnutrition or alcoholism. It can also be caused by infection, though in your grandfather's case, I doubt that's likely. Rarely, the damage is due to an intrinsic muscle disorder, but there is no evidence that's the problem here. Sometimes, we can't find a cause."

"It can be treated, can't it?"

"Yes, but oftentimes the treatment is only partially effective. In many cases, the heart grows progressively weaker despite our best efforts. I suspect your grandfather will fall into that category. He's already well along in the course of his disease."

"But he's going to be okay?"

"Mr. Reslin, certainly we'll do all we can, but I don't want to leave you with a false sense of hope. I'm afraid his disability is going to get worse—to the point he'll eventually be bedridden."

Jolted by what he was hearing, Mathias rocked back in his chair.

Dr. Everett shoved her glasses up the bridge of her nose. "There is another treatment option, one with a high level of risk. It's medically challenging and expensive."

"What treatment?"

"A heart transplant."

"My grandfather needs a new heart?" Mathias exclaimed. The magnitude of his grandfather's illness had abruptly become apparent.

"In time, I believe he will if he's to survive."

"How long does he have?"

"That's hard to say, not without knowing how he'll respond to therapy. I hate guessing, but if I must, I'd say nine months to a year. You must realize that's a very rough estimate. There's no way to know for sure."

Mathias remained silent, stunned by the terrible news. At length, he turned his face toward the doctor again. "Getting a new heart, can you explain what's involved?"

Dr. Everett laid out the mechanics of the procedure, then she shared that Ward's age was a factor, mentioning that every year only three to four hundred people over the age of sixty qualify for a transplant. Next, she described the process by which donors and recipients were matched and how, after surgery, patients had to take immunosuppressive drugs to prevent rejection. Finally, she reviewed the costs involved.

Mathias recoiled when he heard that the procedure could cost upward of three-quarters of a million dollars and that Medicare would cover only part of the expense, assuming his grandfather could qualify for disability. The bottom line was there might be more than $100,000 in bills to pay.

"That's a lot of money!" Mathias exclaimed with trepidation. "Grandfather doesn't even have insurance now that he's been laid off from the mill."

With undeniable sympathy, Dr. Everett said, "I understand. The good news is that if he has a transplant and it's successful, his remaining years could be virtually symptom-free. Look, I know I've given you a lot to think about, but no decision has to be made today. Let me take you to your grandfather's room, and we will get him ready to go home."

As they left the lounge together, the hospitalist halted for a moment. "Dr. Livingston will be supervising your grandfather's outpatient care again." She fished a business card out of her breast pocket and handed it to Mathias. "I know you'll have questions. If Eli can't answer them, give me a call."

When Mathias entered his grandfather's room, Ward was seated on the bed, fully dressed and waiting to leave.

***

The following Saturday, Mathias entered the Leaky Canoe shortly after seven in the evening. Darcy had already arrived. Mathias had offered to stay home, but Ward had flat-out insisted there was no reason for him to alter his routine. Dining out once a week had become something of a ritual, one Mathias eagerly anticipated. As a rule, date night offered a reprieve from the hassles of the daily grind, for a few hours at least. This night was different. His troubles had insisted on tagging along and refused to be ignored.

"How is he?" Darcy asked.

Mathias shrugged. Before sitting down, he shed his coat and hung it on the back of his chair. "To look at him, you wouldn't know anything was amiss. I left him bundled up in his easy chair with his nose in a mystery novel."

For this evening, Darcy had selected a table by the window. Mathias watched a young couple stroll down Third Street arm in arm. It was too dark to tell who they were. He unfolded his napkin and laid it on his lap. "How are things with you?" He could tell by the way she fidgeted with the saltshaker, turning it round and round, she was excited.

"I have news," she declared.

"Good news, I hope. Right about now, I certainly could use some."

"Probably good. We'll have to wait and see."

On the verge of continuing, Darcy was interrupted when Lindell stepped forward to take their orders. She selected the brook trout with almonds. Mathias chose to keep it simple. He picked the braised chicken with butterfly pasta, the least expensive dinner on the menu.

As Lindell moved away, Darcy leaned forward and spoke directly to Mathias. In a soft voice, so as not to be overheard, she announced, "My parents are thinking about hosting their seminars full-time."

"Really?"

"They haven't made their final decision, so keep this under your hat. It would mean they'd be traveling a lot. They could be away up to forty weekends a year. They believe there's enough interest to keep them busy. As word has gotten out, they've even had to turn down bookings."

"I'm not surprised. They have a way of making Christian history interesting without being preachy. What about the Silver Rose? Who's going to mind the store?"

"They asked me if I'd like to take over the business full-time."

"What about your education, your dream of being a teacher? In four months, you'll be heading off to college." Then Mathias looked up with a start. Her parents would never have asked her to run the store if they knew she'd be leaving. That meant she'd already made her decision. "You're not going to college. Darcy?"

"Not this year. Seems to me I can do more good by staying here."

Mathias sensed it wasn't her parents who she was thinking about. She confirmed his suspicions when she said, "Tell me about your grandfather's condition. What needs to be done?"

Mathias repeated what Dr. Everett had told him, then he enumerated the choices that lay ahead, ticking them off one at a time.

When their food arrived, neither one had much of an appetite.

"A heart transplant," said Darcy. "That's heavy-duty. How does Ward feel about surgery?"

"I was surprised. I thought he'd refuse to even consider it, but he says he'll go through with the operation because he has a promise to keep. When I asked what the promise might be, he refused to tell me."

"A promise? What's that all about, I wonder?"

Mathias gestured that he had no idea.

"You said Medicare covers most of the expense. What about the costs they don't cover? Can he afford a major operation like that?"

"Actually, I too have news to share. I was saving this as a surprise, but now might be a good time." Mathias described the app he had created and how it functioned. When he detailed its capabilities and expected usefulness, Darcy listened intently. Her eyes widened when he alluded to its monetary value. She gasped when he mentioned that TruFusion had submitted a tender offer to purchase his code for a quarter-million dollars.

"That's what they're willing to pay you?"

"That's what their letter of intent says."

"You've kept this news secret. When were you planning on telling me?"

"When the app was up and running. My original thought was to host the servers and manage the database myself, but that now seems untenable. It would take too long to generate a revenue stream. We'll need money sooner rather than later. The problem is if I sell the app, of course, it'll no longer belong to me. I'll have to sign over all rights to any future income. That's going to be a lot of lost revenue."

"I see. What are you going to do?"

"I don't have a choice. I'll never put money ahead of my grandfather's life."

"Have you prayed about this?"

"Without ceasing." A pensive expression spread across Mathias's face. "You know, I had this thought. Maybe God allowed me to develop my app so I'd be in a position to help grandfather when the time came."

"It does seem more than a coincidence. Do you remember that first day of our senior year, when I stopped you in the corridor and asked for your help? I knew then there was something special about you. I am so proud of you."

Mathias shook his head. "Despite the fact I totally screwed up?"

"You didn't screw up, not by any stretch of the imagination."

"Darcy, I love you."

The radiant smile that appeared on Darcy's face took Mathias's breath away. She reached out and took his hand. "You have no idea how I've longed to hear those words. I love you too."

***

The next day, upon returning home from church, Mathias found that his grandfather was still wearing his bathrobe and pajamas. Bundled up in his easy chair, a shawl draped his shoulders and a lap blanket covered his legs. Before leaving, Mathias had checked on his grandfather and found him still asleep. Rather than wake him, he had decided to let him rest.

"I didn't feel like making the effort," Ward protested when he noted Mathias eyeing his pajamas. His voice seemed to have lost some of its natural resonance.

"Are you okay?"

"I'm fine. Sorry about the mess."

Mathias glanced around. Seeing nothing amiss, he passed through the living room to peek into the kitchen. There he noted the dishes in the sink and the spilled cereal on the countertop. The cereal box lay on its side.

"I must be getting lazy in my old age," Ward called out sheepishly.

"No problem. I'll take care of it." After cleaning up, Mathias returned to the living room and sat down on the couch.

Ward said, "I hate having you wait on me—makes me feel like an invalid."

"We're going to fix that, remember? Tomorrow, we will submit your application for disability. After it's approved, we'll put your name on the list."

"If I'd known I'd wind up like this, I'd have taken better care of myself. Or come to think of it, maybe I'd have partied harder and saved myself the bother." The lap blanket slipped aside when Ward repositioned his feet on the ottoman.

Mathias noted that his grandfather's ankles were more swollen than they had been. "Are you remembering to take your diuretic?"

"Yep. Makes me pee like a racehorse. By the way, how was the sermon?"

"Good. It was about our heavenly rewards and the prizes we receive for serving faithfully." Mathias pursed his lips. "Grandfather?"

"What?"

"I know we've been over this, but the way things stand, we really need to talk about your salvation."

"Why, 'cause I might not be around much longer?"

"To be blunt, yes. None of us knows how long we have. You need to make a decision. Look, I've given a lot of thought to why people choose not to believe. How you mentally process an issue has a lot to do with how you feel about it. The way I see it, there are four approaches people take when figuring out what life is all about."

"What do you mean four approaches?" Ward seemed suddenly interested.

"Four ways to interpret reality. Say you're reading colored lines on a map. If you believe the blue lines are roads rather than rivers, you'll wind up in an entirely different place than if you interpret them correctly."

"These four approaches, what are they?"

"Simplistic, intellectual, scientific, and spiritual."

"If you say so."

"Think about it. The simplistic approach sees the world as having no meaning whatsoever. There's no need to consider how we got here or where we're headed. For people who think like this, life has no purpose.

"The intellectual approach sees everything as relational. There are no absolutes, no supreme will that decides what's right and what's wrong. Reason alone is the arbiter of choice.

"The scientific approach relies on observations. It methodically studies the natural world. Only what can be tested and verified is true. No allowances are made for phenomena that can't be explained.

"The spiritual approach, on the other hand, is rooted in faith. It accepts that there are dimensions beyond the ones we experience, and true reality exceeds our comprehension."

"So how do you decide which is best?"

Mathias nodded. "By thinking it through. Virtually no one accepts that life exists without purpose and that we're a by-product of some cosmic accident. As we have discussed before, reality is simply too complex to have evolved by chance. So we can dismiss the simplistic approach out of hand.

"The intellectual approach fails because man's reasoning is inherently flawed. Relationships are chaotic. No one has perfect cognition. Equally rational minds construct moral codes that are fundamentally incompatible. This leads to conflict and chaos, which pretty much explains why the world functions as it does.

"The scientific approach falls short because of our limited perceptual abilities. Our senses deceive us. We can't trust them. We think we understand reality and then discover the world is round, not flat. We first believe the universe revolves around the Earth. Then we learn we're nothing but a minuscule speck of dust in a vast cosmos. We must always wonder which of our scientific truths will prove false in the future."

"What about the spiritual way of thinking?"

"That's what's fascinating. By their very nature, spiritual issues can neither be proven nor disproven. There's no way to know if what you believe is really true. That's why it's called faith."

"I assume you favor this approach?"

"You have four options, three of which can be shown to be invalid. One can't be tested. Which would you choose?"

"What you're really saying is I should accept Jesus because I can't disprove He was the Messiah?"

"What I'm saying is, don't let flawed ideologies prevent you from living by faith."

"Son, it might interest you to know that I'm already saved. I accepted Jesus when your mother was still alive. It was right after I returned from California."

"What?" Mathias exclaimed, his eyes going wide with astonishment.

Ward grinned. "She shared the gospel with me, and God touched my heart. To my amazement, I discovered I couldn't refuse Him. She baptized me herself in Tanner's Creek."

Mathias glowered at his grandfather. "All this time, you led me to believe your soul was at risk of eternal damnation. Why?"

Patiently, Ward repliedpatiently, "It was your mother's idea—for the most part. She knew you could never be forced to accept the Scriptures. You had to find your own way, as you have. But as a new believer, you'd have a problem. You are too stubborn to listen to anything I have to say, and with no one else to guide you, how were you supposed to mature in the Word? Your mom figured that the harder you tried to puzzle out theological issues, the stronger your own faith would become. It seems she was right. Look at you now."

Mathias sank back into the couch's soft cushions and tried to assimilate what he was hearing. At length, he sat forward and said, "Congratulations. This is really good news."

"Don't be upset. Our intent was not to deceive you. Besides, think of all the amazing conversations we've had."

"I'll give you that. Some were truly incredible."

Ward coughed, a moist, crackling sound. When he had caught his breath, he said, "Your earlier comments about purpose reminded me of a question your mother once asked. She said I'd have to find my own answer, and I think I have, though it's taken a while. Now I'm going to ask you. Don't answer hastily. I want you to apply some of your considerable brainpower, find your own truth. Ready?"

"I suppose."

"What is the purpose of life?"

Mathias brightened. "I remember when she asked you that question. It was not long after you'd first arrived. We were in the truck on our way to church. I remember feeling really glad it was you she was testing, not me."

"It's impressive that you would remember. Have you thought about it? What have you come up with?"

"To be honest, I really haven't brought it to mind. You think it's important?"

"Oh, yes."

"Okay, then I'll let you know what I decide."

"Good. Now I need to rest. I'm tired." Ward adjusted the blanket on his lap and closed his eyes.

Mathias stood up. "I'm going to fix something to eat. You want anything?"

"No, thank you."

Mathias stepped into the kitchen to fetch himself some lunch.

***

Mathias headed to his bedroom after eating lunch. A litany of coarse snores followed him as he tiptoed through the living room and up the stairs. From the top landing, he looked down, making sure his grandfather was still asleep. He then disappeared into his bedroom. The time had come to prepare his software application to sell to TruFusion Software. He sat down at his desk. It was the first time he had fired up his laptop since Mr. Doyle had laid his grandfather off from the mill.

After calling up the program he used for code development, he clicked on the icon to open his source code. Nothing happened. He tried again with the same result, and then a third time.

Concerned, he made certain the integrated development environment he used as a platform for working in Java was functioning properly. When he tested it, all subroutines responded appropriately. The interface functioned as it should. He wrote a snippet of code, and it compiled as expected.

Mathias tried opening his app again without success.

Becoming increasingly anxious, he turned to his file management utility and navigated to the folder where his source code files were stored. Everything seemed in order when he listed the files.

Puzzled and more than a little apprehensive, he sat back and tried to imagine what could be wrong. Perhaps his aging laptop had failed to boot properly. He shut the computer down, waited a full minute, and then turned it back on again. When he reloaded his IDE and called up the application, he got the same results as before.

He wondered if perhaps the hard drive had suffered a sector failure, but a disk check found no evidence of file-system corruption.

Beginning to panic, Mathias took a deep breath and considered what to do next. If his code files were indeed corrupted and would not load, his only option would be to reinstall the files from backup. He opened his top desk drawer and reached in to retrieve the thumb drive he used to routinely save his work.

The thumb drive wasn't there.

Anxiously, Mathias rifled through the desk's other drawers, thinking he might have carelessly misplaced the eraser-sized device. He searched diligently, but the thumb drive was nowhere to be found. Next, he got down on hands and knees, hoping that his backup storage might have fallen on the floor. A thorough search came up empty. He then looked in his dresser, under his bed, in his closet, and anywhere else he could think to check. He even dug through the pockets of his dirty clothes. The thumb drive was simply missing.

Hoping against hope, he returned to his computer. Once again, he repeated the steps he had first taken, but it was no use. The app refused to run.

Perhaps his grandfather might know where his thumb drive could be.

Mathias rushed downstairs and, without thinking, jostled his grandfather's shoulder.

Ward startled and abruptly came awake. "What—what's wrong?" A coughing fit seized him.

Mathias ignored his grandfather's distress. "Have you seen my thumb drive?" He lifted his hand and held his thumb and index finger approximately three inches apart. "It's made of black plastic, about the size of a stick of gum, but thicker. It has a silver doohickey on one end."

"I know what thumb drives are," Ward sputtered. "I'm not a complete dunce. No, I haven't seen it. You say it's missing?"

"If it wasn't missing, I wouldn't be looking for it."

"Where did you last see it?"

Mathias paused to think. His forehead wrinkled when he remembered it was the night that Mr. Doyle had paid them a visit. He recalled he had been upstairs showing Trent how the app functioned. Perhaps he had inadvertently brought it downstairs when he had answered the door.

In desperation, Mathias spent the next four hours searching the house from top to bottom with no luck. With every passing minute, his anxiety became more and more intense.

"Do you have a hard copy printout?" Ward suggested hopefully as his grandson continued his hunt.

"My printer ran out of ink months ago. Printer cartridges are expensive. I was waiting until my app was ready to be published to buy a replacement."

Toward the onset of evening and with nowhere else to look, Mathias was finally forced to admit that as impossible as it seemed, his app was gone.

"What will you do?" Ward said with the truth staring his grandson in the face.

"I've been working on that app since my birthday last year. I suppose I'll have to start again. This time, it shouldn't take as long. I already have a handle on the logic flow. Most of the subroutines are still fresh in my mind. It's really just a matter of sitting down and grinding out the code. What's horrible is that I'll have to call TruFusion and ask for an extension. Their letter of intent has a cut-off date."

"What if they don't grant you one?" Ward too was beginning to sound worried.

"I don't know. I guess I'll have to trust that God has a plan."

"Amen." Ward drew the shawl tight around his shoulders as if a chill had passed through his body.

*****

At a recklessly high rate of speed, Mathias barreled along the Fairworth Lumber Mill's access road. He swerved into the employee parking lot and skidded to a stop inches away from the chain-link fence that enclosed the yard. Several workers glanced up in surprise. In anger, he surged out of his Jeep and slammed the door. Without hesitating in the slightest, he charged through the main gate, leaving it open behind him. The shift he had been scheduled to work had started hours before. He didn't care that he was late, and he didn't even bother to clock in. A dozen pairs of eyes followed him as he strode toward the chop saw, where Trent Blaine was processing lumber.

Mathias kept his eyes fixed on his destination, his jaw set and his hands balled into fists. "I know what you did!" he bellowed from halfway across the yard, not caring who was listening. "I also know how you did it."

Trent backed away from the saw. A look of apprehension spread across his face.

Mathias halted two feet from where Trent stood, just out of arm's reach. "You stole my app, and you sold it to TruFusion."

"What?" Obviously flustered, Trent backed up a pace. His arms reflexively came up in a defensive posture.

"When you were alone in my room, the night Grandfather got sacked, that's when you did it."

"Did what?"

"You stole the code files for my OddJober application. You also stole the thumb drive I use to store my backups."

"Man, you need to get a grip."

"I called TruFusion to see if they'd extend their tender offer. They told me they were no longer interested. Early this morning, I learned why. Their website lists my app as available for download. They've released it to the public."

"How do you know it's yours?"

"Because the interface is identical to the one I wrote, right down to the placement of the dialogue boxes and advertisement banners. The headers are the same, and the logic flow is unmistakable. It's my app. There's no question about it. Another funny thing, when I searched for their letter of intent, it too was missing. I wonder how that could have happened."

"You're accusing me?"

"You're damn right I am. You're the only one who could have stolen it, and I know how you did it. You copied random system files into my coding directory, making sure the copied files were near the same size as the originals. You then deleted the code files and renamed the copies, making it appear that the code files were intact. But you forgot something. The copied files had the wrong date stamps. That's how I figured out my code files had been replaced."

"I think you're giving me way too much credit."

"I don't think so. You told me you know about computers. Obviously, you knew enough to commit your theft."

"Keep this up, and I'll sue you for slander."

"Go ahead. If this goes to court, I'll subpoena TruFusion's execs. Under oath, they'll be forced to testify how much money they paid you. By the way, how much did you get? Never mind. Whatever it was, you owe me at least that much. Because of you, I'm going to have to sell Reslin Ranch to pay for Grandfather's transplant."

"You're selling the ranch? I'm sorry to hear that."

"No, you're not. You don't give a damn." Mathias stepped forward and shoved Trent so that he stumbled backward and nearly fell. Several of the yard workers had gathered around, attracted by the commotion.

Mathias took another step forward. "Not only are you a thief, you're a liar."

Trent recovered and braced himself in case another assault was forthcoming. "You're making a lot of wild accusations here. Prove it was me. Prove I did what you say."

"You know I can't, not without my backups, the ones you stole."

"Then get out of my face," Trent snarled.

"Fine, but be warned, if you ever cross me again, I'll—"

"You'll what?" Trent said smugly.

"Cross me and find out. Just remember, you owe me, and one day I will collect. You know what? I'm out of here—for good. I don't want to be anywhere near you." Mathias turned and strode across the yard to the administration building where he promptly quit.

As Mathias sullenly drove home, he thought about how screwed up his life had become. He had no money, no job, and no software app to market. With bills to pay and more on the way, he would have to sell

Reslin Ranch—his childhood home. Worst of all, his grandfather—his last living relative—would soon die without a new heart, which they could not afford.

With both hands gripping the steering wheel, Mathias whispered a brief prayer through clenched teeth. "Almighty God, thank You for this opportunity to increase my faith." He did his best to mean every word but failed utterly.

***

Seven months after the theft of Mathias's software, a cheerful blaze crackled in the Thurstons' fireplace. Darcy and Mathias lounged on cushy oversized pillows at the edge of the hearth. The flames cast a faint blush on Darcy's face. Douglas and Miriam Thurston would be gone another three days, hosting one of their seminars. As usual, Darcy had agreed to house-sit. Christmas was a week away, and the holiday decorations should have set a festive mood, but they did little to lessen Mathias's continuing funk.

"I'll admit this beats freezing to death in a rented double-wide," Mathias said morosely. "I had no idea trailers could be so miserable in winter." After accepting an offer on Reslin Ranch, he and Ward had moved into a mobile home while the ranch was in escrow. Feeling cramped and dispossessed, he had taken to spending as much time as possible at either the Thurstons' home or Darcy's apartment whenever an opportunity presented itself.

Darcy said, "I can only imagine how hard it will be for you to close the sale of your home." Lying on her stomach and resting her elbows on the floor with her chin on her palms, she stared at the blaze. "You still have time to change your mind."

Mathias rolled onto his side to gaze at his fiancée. "You can't be serious. There's no way I can back out of escrow. In three weeks, Reslin Ranch will no longer belong to a member of the Reslin family."

When Mathias had made the decision to sell the property, his grandfather had vehemently objected and had declared that he would rather die than see the house his son-in-law had built pass into the hands of a stranger. His protestations had been curtly overruled.

Mathias's brow furrowed. "Grandfather is number two on the transplant list. What happens if a donor becomes available and I don't have the money to pay for his surgery?"

Darcy patted Mathias's hand. "I know, but I hate seeing you lose something that has meant so much to your family."

"It's not people. It's just property."

A burning log spit a glowing ember onto the hearth. With a fingertip, Darcy flicked it back into the fire. "How was your grandfather, by the way, when you saw him this afternoon at the hospital?"

"Antsy. He hates being an inpatient. Hospitals make him cantankerous. Medically, there's been no change. His heart failure is barely under control, but for the moment, he's stable. Trouble is, I don't know how much longer he can hang on."

"Ultimately, it's not up to him, is it?"

"You're right. I keep reminding myself that God is in control, and I have to trust that everything will work out according to His will. It seems easier when it's your own problems you're dealing with. I feel helpless watching him lie there and fight for breath."

Darcy leveraged herself into a seated position. "I think a cup of cocoa would be nice—with marshmallows. Want some?"

"Okay."

When Darcy returned from the kitchen, she handed a steaming mug of hot chocolate down to Mathias. "Let's hope this will lighten your mood." She sat down on a cushion and wrapped her fingers around her own mug.

"I'm afraid I'm not very good company," Mathias said.

"Want to talk about what's really bugging you?"

"And what would that be?"

"I think you know."

After quitting his job at the mill, Mathias had survived by taking on odd jobs around the county. To find work, he had even visited TruFusion's website and downloaded the app he had created, which had seemed hugely ironic and extremely galling.

Mathias stared at the flames. "You're right. It's Trent. I can't get him out of my mind. I try to keep myself busy, but I keep seeing that smug look on his face. I hate the fact that I can't go after him legally. He was right. Without the source code, I can't prove the application was originally mine. You know, I saw him coming out of Sterling Foods the other day. I had to turn around and walk the other way for fear I'd do or say something I'd regret."

"The sooner you forgive him, the sooner you can get on with your life."

Mathias sat up. "How can I forgive him? He has literally taken everything I own away from me."

"He hasn't taken your dignity, nor has he taken your intellect."

"He might as well have. In seven months, I haven't written a single line of code. It's as if somebody flipped a switch and shut down my brain."

"He hasn't taken me. I'm still yours," Darcy said cheerily.

"Does that mean we're still on for June?"

"If you'll have me."

A lecherous grin sprang up on Mathias's face. "I'll have you right now, if you'll let me."

"Now, now. Behave yourself. You know what we agreed. You'll just have to wait." She sipped her cocoa in silence for a time. "I wonder if we're talking about the same thing when we speak about forgiveness. What's your definition?"

Mathias pondered a moment. "To stop holding a grudge. To forget about what's been done to you."

"Now you see, that's not what I would have said. For me, forgiveness is simply the canceling of a debt. It means the person who has wronged you no longer owes you anything. All accounts are marked paid in full. That includes setting aside any desire for revenge."

"How do you forgive someone who's betrayed you, who's treated you with malice?"

"Jesus forgave Judas and the soldiers who nailed him to the cross. I think we can aspire to follow His example. I'll tell you what I think forgiveness doesn't mean. It doesn't mean trusting. Trust must be earned, and that can only happen after the wrongdoer has repented. It doesn't mean liking. Liking is an emotion. Just as Rule 37 says, pure love is a choice. We can choose to love our enemies even though we don't like them. And forgiveness doesn't mean forgetting. How can you forget a wound? It's virtually impossible. No, in my mind, forgiveness only means that there's no longer a debt owed by the person who's wronged you."

"You make it sound easy. The damage he's done is beyond appalling. You're saying all I have to do is set aside any hope of getting even?"

"Basically, yes. And it's not me who says this. It's a commandment, remember, not a request."

Mathias rolled over onto his back and stared at the ceiling.

Darcy bent down and planted a quick kiss on his lips, but then promptly pulled away when he reached for her. She waggled her finger at him as a reproof. "Not until after we're married."

***

"I can't believe you guys have been married six whole months," Ward said.

"I can't believe it's been a year since you got your new heart," Mathias replied.

"Yep, one year to the very day." Ward proudly rubbed the front of his chest where his shirt covered his surgical scar.

"I'm so pleased you agreed to celebrate with us," Darcy said. "So how do you feel, one year later?"

"Better than I deserve." Ward looked around. The Reslins' modest bungalow still smelled of mulled wine and cinnamon. Many of the Christmas ornaments were still up, as were several New Year's Day decorations. "I'm a little sore when I move wrong. It's a pain remembering to take my immunosuppressants, and the steroids make my face fat. Otherwise, I've been granted a new lease on life." He regarded the spartan work area in the far corner of the room where a desktop computer and a gooseneck lamp sat atop an undersized table. "That's new," he said as he looked to his grandson with hopeful expectation. "Are you back to programming?"

"I am. I have an idea for an app that I believe has potential. I'm going to call it Update. Actually, the concept came to me while I was remembering your surgery. People kept calling me, wanting to know how you were doing. Then I thought, wouldn't it be handy if there was a way to keep multiple people in the loop without calling each one individually?"

Ward frowned. "I don't use them myself, but aren't there a ton of social networking sites for that very purpose?"

"There are, but my program will be specifically tailored to aid people with medical illnesses. Before a friend or relative can log in to see how a patient is doing, they'll be given a case-specific password. The app will include resources explaining medical terminology, sites to visit to learn about a wide variety of conditions, a social messaging area, and links to places where they can send cards, flowers, or gifts. I haven't decided yet, but I think I might also include links to the health-care providers' websites so people can get to know them."

"I assume you believe this app will be profitable?" Ward said.

"This time," Mathias commented with a modest grin, "I'm not doing it for the money. I'll earn a small income, but not a fortune. It's my way of paying it forward. Hey, you're the one who keeps telling me that's what my faith demands of me. Why are you smiling?"

"Because it would appear I've kept my promise."

"What promise?"

"The promise I made to your mother to help you become the man she wanted you to be. She would be so proud of you, just as I am."

The lump that formed in Mathias's throat made it difficult for him to respond.

"Tell me, Ward," Darcy said, interrupting the silence, "how are things working out, now that you're back at the mill?"

Ward nodded. "It still galls me working anywhere near what's-his-name."

When Mathias stiffened, Darcy, who stood behind her husband's chair, laid a hand on his shoulder.

"Otherwise," Ward continued, "I'm doing okay. Leonard and I have discovered we both love to fish. Next week, he's going to introduce me to ice fishing."

Mathias gave his grandfather a quizzical look. "You and Mr. Doyle are on a first-name basis?"

"Turns out we have a bunch of things in common." Ward stared at the fire glowing in the pellet stove. "He too has a grandson who needs looking after."

Before her husband could offer a retort, Darcy said, "How's your double-wide working out? Anything else need fixing?"

"Not since you guys replaced the water pump, which is doing fine, by the way. I never thought I'd enjoy living in a trailer, but with the new insulation underneath, it's warm and snug, and it suits me fine." He shifted in his armchair to glance out the window. "Guess the storm they've been yapping about is rolling in. Must be time for me to head on out."

"Before you go," Darcy said, "there's something I'd like to show you. Excuse me a second. I'll be right back." She disappeared into the bedroom.

In her absence, Mathias leaned forward. "Grandfather, I need to talk to you, but not now."

"What's up?" Ward said.

"It's time you and I had another conversation. I can't seem to pull myself out of this—whatever it is. I don't know what to call it. I should be happy or at least content. My marriage is great. Darcy is amazing. We purchased the Silver Rose from Douglas and Miriam, and the business is doing well. I never saw myself working as a shopkeeper, but actually, it's kind of fun. Who knew that I'd like dealing with the public? But despite all that, something is wrong."

"What seems to be the problem?"

"That's what I wanted to talk to you about. I don't know. It's like something is holding me back. Sometimes I get this gloomy feeling, like there's an anchor on my soul. I'm starting to worry. I was hoping you could help me sort it out."

Darcy returned and stepped forward to position herself between her husband and her grandfather-in-law. She cuddled a teddy bear in her arms. "There's something I need to tell you both. Guess what it is?"

"You're entering your second childhood?" Mathias suggested.

Darcy smacked her husband with the teddy bear. "Guess again."

Ward tilted away to keep from getting hit as well.

Darcy's face lit up with a brilliant smile. "I'm pregnant."

"For real?" Mathias leapt out of his chair and threw his arms around his wife. "Fantastic! Are you… Is everything—"

"Relax," Darcy said. "Everything is fine. We're both fine."

Ward stood as well. He lovingly laid a hand on Darcy shoulder. "Congratulations. This means I'll be a great-grandfather. Do you know yet? Is it a boy or a girl?"

"You're kidding, of course." Darcy formed a wry smile. "I just found out yesterday."

The three of them talked excitedly for a while. Then Ward looked out the window again. "It's really coming down. I should be going."

"We are so glad you could stop by," Darcy said.

Ward leaned forward to kiss his daughter-in-law on the cheek. "Again, congratulations, and thank you for brunch. It was a fine meal." He then wrapped Mathias in an affable bear hug. After offering a final blessing on the house and its occupants, he retrieved his coat from the rack beside the door. Fully bundled up, he headed out into the midday storm. Before closing the door behind him, he looked back at Mathias and mouthed the words "I'll call you."

Mathias nodded.

Once they were alone, Darcy stepped up behind her husband to wrap her arms about him. Enclosed in her embrace, he rotated to face her. "A baby, huh?"

Darcy smiled. "Are you ready for this?"

"Are you?"

They gazed into each other's eyes for a time, then Mathias said, "Why me? You could have had any boy you wanted."

Darcy gave a teasing chuckle. "You were the easiest one to catch."

"I'm serious. What made you choose me?"

Darcy thought for a moment. "It's hard to say."

"I am your husband. You can tell me anything."

"No, I mean it's hard to put into words. I just knew you were the one. I don't believe in fate, but I do believe in Providence. You are my destiny. Once I figured that out, everything fell into place. I love you, Mathias Tyrone Reslin. It's that simple."

"I love you, Darcy Lynn Reslin."

***

Half an hour after Ward had departed, a knock sounded at the door.

Arianna Finkel, Abraham's sister, stood on the front stoop. She wore a heavily insulated coat, a woolen cap on her head, a bulky scarf around her neck, and thick gloves on her hands. With a layer of snow covering her from top to bottom, she resembled a Jewish snowman. She offered Mathias a pleading look. "We need your help," she said with great urgency.

"Come in. Tell me what's going on." When he opened the door a bit wider, a gush of frigid air surged into house.

"I'd best not. I'm a mess."

"We're used to it. Hurry, it's freezing outside."

Arianna stepped inside and hugged her arms close to her body.

Mathias saw that she was shivering. "What's wrong?"

"You know Abe and I volunteer for search and rescue? A call came in. There's a snowmobiler stranded somewhere up toward Starfall Mountain. He called in on his cell phone to report that he'd crashed. His machine is totaled. He's also injured, but we don't know how badly. His cell phone cut out before he could describe his wounds."

Mathias scowled. "Do you know where on the mountain he might be? There's a lot of open country up there."

"We lost communication before he could say. Somebody's gotta go up and find him."

"What about Abe?"

"He's out of town."

"Hank Garland?"

"He's out calving on his dairy farm. We couldn't reach him."

"Todd Havers or his son Richard?"

"Visiting friends. You're the only one I could think to ask. I know you are not an official member of search and rescue, but you've helped in the past. Everyone else is gone or unavailable. I realize this is a major imposition, but he could be dying."

"I don't have a snowmobile," Mathias protested.

"You can use Abe's. It's out front in my truck. I even made sure the gas tank was full. Here's the key." Arianna held out her hand.

Mathias hesitantly accepted the key. "Are you convinced this guy's in a bad way—that he can't wait till the storm subsides?"

"He didn't sound good, that's for sure."

"I don't know." Mathias looked to his wife, who had just emerged from the kitchen. He could tell by the set of her jaw that she'd been listening and that she shared his apprehension. "What do you think?" he said.

Darcy nodded a hello to Arianna. When she returned her attention to her husband, there was a look of resignation in her eyes. "I think you don't have a choice—Rule 4."

"If your neighbor asks for help, give it." It was one of the rules his father had stressed most often. Mathias turned to his wife. "If I go, will you be okay?"

"Don't worry about us." Darcy put a hand to her abdomen. "We'll be fine. Just remember to come home."

A questioning look spread across Arianna's face. "Are you?"

"Yes," Darcy declared happily. "Six weeks."

"Wow. Gratz. You'll have to tell me all about it." Arianna faced Mathias and waited.

"All right. I'll go. Let me suit up."

Mathias stepped into the bedroom to put on his cold-weather gear. As he thrust his legs into his ski pants, he could hear the two women jabbering excitedly in the living room. By the time he finished adding layers, he was beginning to perspire. He returned to the living room, where he kissed his wife. "Are you sure you're okay with this?"

"We'll be fine."

Arianna seemed tremendously relieved. "Thank you."

"Anything else I should know?" Mathias said to Arianna.

"I can't imagine what it would be."

"Did this guy happen to give his name?"

Arianna hesitated. "Trent Blaine."

Mathias froze. "You should've mentioned that up front."

"If I had, would you have said yes?"

"Probably not."

"That's why I didn't."

A chorus of dissimilar thoughts struck Mathias simultaneously. Word would get out if he refused to aid a stranded victim, regardless of his identity. His reputation would be trashed. Once before, he had survived a blizzard. He knew all too well the dangers that awaited him. How could he forget; his two missing toes served as a reminder. Finally, there was no assurance his rescue attempt would end well. In the backcountry, anything could happen. Who knew what tragedy might befall his nemesis.

In the final analysis, he was forced to conclude that he had no choice. He headed out into the teeth of the storm.

***

Abraham Finkel's older model snowmobile lacked the power of the Osbornes' sleeker machines. It lugged going up hills and faltered when he pushed its engine to the limit. Mathias found he was able to drive at top speed only on familiar trails where he could see far enough ahead—which was rarely.

As he ventured into the vast expanse of forest that surrounded Starfall Mountain, he tried to imagine where Trent might have gone. The storm had erased all traces of human activity. New-fallen snow covered everything. Heavily laden branches drooped to the ground. A thick layer of hoary crystals coated the trunks of trees on their upwind sides. Plumes of snow spewed out from beneath the snowmobile's tread. A man afoot would have sunk in up to his waist. To Mathias, it seemed that no human being had ever passed this way before.

While puzzling out where Trent might have gone, Mathias decided to rank potential destinations according to their appeal. Certainly, different snowmobilers might have different preferences, but the method seemed logical. Hell-Roaring Glacier and Rocky Point where favorite sites, but they would be far too treacherous after a storm. After giving the matter additional consideration, he settled on Sawbuck Ridge. Trent would probably head there. Besides, of all the sites on the mountain, the ridge was Trent's favorite.

The freezing wind whipped against Mathias's face, chilling his nose and cheeks. Falling snow stung like needles flung against his skin. His goggles iced up repeatedly, forcing him to steer with one hand while he used his other hand to clear his vision. Trails he had traveled multiple times became unrecognizable. Twice he got lost and had to backtrack to find his way.

Worst of all was the bitter cold. It leeched through his boots and gloves. Previously frostbitten fingers and toes ached with a deep pain that penetrated to the bone. His teeth chattered, and the tip of his nose grew numb.

To keep his mind off his ordeal, Mathias focused on what he would do if and when he found his nemesis. He envisioned a variety of cruel scenarios. One in particular seemed appealing. He would taunt his betrayer. Steering just out of reach, he would force Trent to beg for rescue. In another, he saw himself watching from a distance, waiting for his enemy to succumb.

Two-thirds of the way to Sawbuck Ridge, the sun abruptly came out. The storm had broken temporarily. Judging by the sun's position, it was an hour past noon, which surprised Mathias. He had imagined it to be much later. He thought about checking his cell phone to confirm the time, but that would entail stopping to dig into his hip pocket. Instead, he continued on.

Without gales of drifting snow to cloud his vision, he made better time.

When the trail ahead widened for a space, he had a chance to look up. The sky overhead was gray blue, the color of his wife's eyes. A shard of guilt speared his consciousness. He recalled something Darcy had said. "Love is a choice, not an emotion. You don't have to like your enemy to love them." Her words brought to mind their discussion regarding forgiveness.

With all his might, Mathias struggled to ignore the voice preaching inside his head, but it was no use. It whispered in his ear, "How can you call yourself a follower of Jesus if you refuse to do what He says?"

The snowmobile burst out from the tree line at the base of the ridge. He raised his goggles to improve his vision. Upon scanning the terrain, he could find no sign that anyone had been there. After settling his goggles back into place, he took off for the far side of the bowl, just to be sure. As he cruised across the hillside, he glanced up. Along the top of the ridge, he saw something that scared him to the core of his being. A ten-foot wall of snow overhung the crest, like the eaves of a house. The breath caught in his chest. At any moment, millions of tons of snow might break free and come crashing down. The Forest Service would have rated the risk of an avalanche above extreme. He slowed his machine to a crawl to reduce the noise and diminish the vibrations imparted to the hillside.

Terrified by the predicament that had overtaken him, Mathias started to turn around, but a bright flash caught his eye. The sun had reflected off a metallic object a hundred yards away. He eased in that direction.

A snowmobile lay crumpled up against the trunk of a lodgepole pine, its undercarriage bent almost to a right angle. A human body lay beside it, just inside the tree line.

Alerted by the sound of Mathias's approach, Trent tried to sit up. "Oh, hell, it's you," he said as Mathias climbed off his machine, leaving the engine running.

"If you'd like, I can head back and send someone else. How badly hurt are you?"

"A few ribs are busted. I'm not sure about my ankle. Otherwise, I'm right as rain."

"Can you stand?"

"Not sure. Haven't really tried."

"Well, let's try now, shall we? We need to get you out of here. Let me rephrase that. We need to get *us* out of here." Mathias eyed the top of the ridge, then he stepped over to help his nemesis to his feet. Mathias raised Trent's arm to settle it across his shoulders.

Trent grimaced in pain. Trent attempted a smile. "You should've seen me." His voice registered barely above a whisper. "I almost made the top."

"You idiot. With that snowy overhang up there, what were you thinking?"

"Hey, that's part of the fun. Coming down, I was going way too fast. The crash was epic. You would've been impressed."

"No doubt."

With Mathias supporting most of Trent's weight, they slogged their way to Abe's snowmobile. Mathias signaled his intention to settle Trent on the padded seat in the forward position.

"What are you doing?" Trent protested. "I was hoping you would drive."

"I'm not sure you can hang on. I'll sit behind you and reach around to steer. That way, hopefully, you won't fall off."

"This doesn't mean we're going steady or any such thing, does it?"

"Not a chance." With Trent scooted as far forward as possible, Mathias climbed on behind him.

"Why are you doing this?" Trent said over his shoulder. "I thought you didn't like me."

"I don't, but I've forgiven you—for everything."

"What do you mean you've forgiven me?"

"For the hurt you've caused, not just to me, but to my whole family—for all the damage you've done. Far as I'm concerned, you don't owe me a thing. We are even. All debts are canceled." As soon as the words left his mouth, Mathias felt a sense of relief, as if a weight had been shed from his shoulders. The sensation was amazing, but there was no time to dwell on it.

He shifted the snowmobile into gear and gingerly eased forward. The machine responded even more sluggishly than before.

"You came all the way up here just to tell me that?"

"No, I came all the way up here to save your life." To Mathias, it seemed they were barely inching forward, which was fine so long as they kept moving.

They were halfway across the face of the mountain when a shot rang out, or that's what it sounded like to Mathias. He looked up and, to his horror, noted that the top of the ridge had shifted. "Avalanche!" he screamed.

He squeezed the snowmobile's clutch and downshifted two gears. When he gunned the engine, their speed increased, but not nearly enough. The powdery crest at the top of the incline had begun to separate from the frozen base beneath. As if in slow motion, the berm began sliding down the mountainside.

Keeping one eye on the ridge, Mathias steered toward the point where the trail began its dissent into the valley. He figured that if he could make the tree line there, the forest would slow the avalanche's advance. He would have disappeared into the trees immediately except they were too close. In videos, he had watched avalanches rip forests apart. The mass of snow that was breaking loose would snap full-grown trees like matchsticks. His only hope was to outrun the catastrophe headed in his direction.

When Trent looked up and realized what was happening, he screamed at the top of his lungs, "Go go go!"

Mathias revved the engine until he feared it would explode.

Slowly at first, and then with relentlessly increasing speed, the wall of snow slid downhill. The faint rumble that had accompanied the first slippage became a howl and then a deafening roar.

Mathias looked back. Thousands of tons of snow were chasing him down the mountainside. They weren't going to make it. It might be close, but unless he could coax more speed out of the snowmobile, they were doomed.

He leaned forward and yelled in Trent's ear, "Grab the handlebars! You're driving."

"What?" Trent bellowed, making it plain that he too was terrified.

"This machine can't go any faster. It's carrying too much weight. There's no reason both of us need to die. Just remember, as soon as you get to town, send help. I don't care who you find. Just send someone. Promise me you will do that."

"I will!" Trent yelled back.

A sense of peace enveloped Mathias when Trent's hands replaced his own on the grips. He relaxed his body as he slid off the back of the snowmobile. After tumbling head over heels several times, he sat up. When he cleared the snow from his goggles, he realized he was only sixty yards from the tree line. He began furiously swimming and clawing in that direction. He made it a third of the way.

Just before the avalanche caught him, Mathias's hand touched a fallen tree buried beneath the snow. It seemed to be about six inches in diameter. There was no telling its length. Instinctively, he wrapped his arms and legs tightly around the log, hoping it would buffer the avalanche's fury. With immense determination, he embraced the tree as fiercely as he could. His last image before being swallowed up in a cloud of white was Trent disappearing into the forest.

The tumbling and churning seemed to go on for minutes, but in reality, it probably lasted only a matter of seconds. Then the log collided with something solid, jarring Mathias to the bone. A second impact tore the tree from his grasp. Without an anchor to stabilize his momentum, he was swept along. Rolling over and over, he had no way of telling which direction was up.

When the world stopped spinning, he opened his eyes. To his amazement, he found that by the time the avalanche had reached him, most of its forward rush had dissipated. He had nearly made it out. He also discovered that he was buried up to his neck with only his head and one hand free. He had no idea where the log he had embraced had finally come to rest.

Mathias's ears rang, and he could breathe, but that was about it. When he tried moving his arms and legs, they felt like they were encased in granite. He sensed that he was mostly upright, with his body pitched forward slightly. One leg seemed to be sticking out at an odd angle but did not feel broken.

He wriggled and struggled with all his might, but to no avail. He could not bust loose. He was trapped. When he tried yelling for help, his loudest pleas were muffled by masses of snow, as if the world around him had been soundproofed. After several minutes, it became clear that his only hope of survival would be for someone to come along and rescue him before he froze to death.

Mathias began to pray, first that his deliverance would arrive at any second, but then when his mind drifted, he began praying for his grandfather, his wife, and his unborn child. The realization that he would soon be a father brought a whirl of emotions—anticipation, awe, trepidation, and joy. His first reaction was that he wasn't at all ready to be a dad. Then he realized he might never have that chance.

With every ounce of strength he could muster, Mathias fought to free himself from his icy prison. He struggled until his muscles cramped up and forced him to quit. He bent his head forward and tried to bite the snow, which accomplish nothing.

Gradually, he lost feeling in his legs up to his lower abdomen. He imagined himself as a fly trapped in amber. Then his awareness began slipping away. The shivers were mild at first but then became uncontrollable. As when he had been overtaken by the blizzard, hypothermia was settling in. To keep from panicking, he forced himself to recount conversations he and his grandfather had shared. By reliving their life together, he was astonished at how much their relationship had changed.

His musings on relationships sent a jolt of inspiration rocketing through Mathias. He would have leapt for joy if he hadn't been frozen solid. He had found the answer to his mother's question, "What is the purpose of life?" From out of nowhere, he had gleaned the truth, and it made perfect sense—well, perhaps not from out of nowhere.

He tried freeing himself again but couldn't.

Several times, he repeated the question and answered it aloud, just to test how it sounded in his ears. "The purpose of life is to afford every individual an opportunity to develop an intimate, personal relationship with his or her Creator."

His elation lasted perhaps another fifteen minutes until he drifted off. An hour later, he awoke, fuzzy-headed and disoriented. The numbness had ascended to the middle of his chest.

Above the wail of the wind, he thought he heard voices, but it was probably his imagination. A marvelous sense of peace flowed over him as he slowly lost consciousness.

The End

EPILOGUE

ive years after the fiercest avalanche in Rockridge's history, a man stood at the podium of a mega church in Fort Worth, Texas. He had been invited to speak as a guest lecturer at a seminar entitled "A Comparative History of Christian Theology." The schedule listed him as the next to last speaker. A thousand people had attended the first day's presentations. Virtually all had returned for the second and final day.

The man spoke simply and from the heart. He had committed himself to telling the truth, openly and without reservation. As a result, segments of his message had been difficult to hear.

He had spoken about his early childhood and his dysfunctional parents. He had told how his mother had cheated on her husband and then abandoned her family. The speaker had mentioned the pain of losing his mother when he was two years old. He had talked about his father's violent temper and the abuse he had suffered. When describing the beatings, he had spoken bluntly about the agony of having a studded belt flail the skin off his back. The audience had winced in sympathy. Many had cried.

The speaker had gone on to tell about his formative years in school and how he had never felt worthy—how he had never seemed good enough, either in his own eyes or in the eyes of his classmates. Quite a few in the audience had nodded in agreement when he had recounted the burden of realizing he was worthless, that he would never amount to anything or accomplish anything worthwhile. Others had fidgeted uneasily when he had talked about the shame of always being in trouble and how suffering punishment for doing wrong was preferable to being ignored.

The audience had reacted most strongly when he had laid out the betrayal he had committed and how his disloyalty had literally ruined his friend's life. Holding nothing back, he had detailed squandering the money he had gained from selling the software application he had stolen.

But then the tenor of Trent Blaine's presentation changed.

He described how, having just turned twenty-one, he had gone snowmobiling alone because no one would go with him. He told about the terror of being stranded in the wilderness, injured and thinking he was about to die, knowing that his life had been a complete waste. Worst of all, he said, was realizing that in the final judgment, he would be held accountable for all the wrongs he had done.

With a quaver in his voice, he then recounted how he had been given a second chance, not as recompense for anything he had accomplished, but because of the great love of another. He had been rescued despite his failures and shortcomings simply because someone cared.

Trent stood with both hands gripping the podium. He looked out at the audience, and despite the tears of remembrance that moistened his eyes, he smiled and proclaimed, "Greater love hath no man than he willingly lay down his life for his friend. I stand before you today as a testimony to the power of forgiveness. My life changed the day I was rescued because that was the day I accepted Jesus Christ as my Lord and Savior.

"I became a new man when I invited Jesus into my heart. He took away my shame. He took away my pain. He gave me hope and a reason to exist. He can do the same for you, if you will let Him."

Facing the auditorium, Trent said with deep admiration, "We are blessed to have a very special guest with us this afternoon. I am proud and honored to call him my friend. Ladies and gentlemen, allow me to introduce the man who saved my life and then saved my soul, Mathias Reslin."

Thunderous applause filled the lecture hall as Mathias rose to his feet in the first row. Before ascending to the dais, he turned to Darcy and blew her a kiss. He then smiled at his daughter, Melissa, and her younger brother, Zachary.

After greeting Trent with a brotherly hug, Mathias strode to the lectern, but before beginning, he looked down at his grandfather, who was seated beside the children. "Thank you," he whispered, "for everything."

"You're welcome," Ward mouthed back.

Gazing out across the sea of faces, Mathias began, "Ladies and gentlemen, it is an honor to be with you this afternoon." He paused for emphasis before continuing, "If you will permit me, there's a very important question I'd like to ask you. I suspect it's one you may never have considered before. My question is this: What is the purpose of life?

RESLIN'S RULES

1. Never buy anything you can't pay cash for.
2. If you don't know what you're doing, say so.
3. If you make a promise, keep it.
4. If the neighbor asks for help, give it.
5. Don't talk when you have nothing to say.
6. When offered something, take as much is you need, not as much as you want.
7. Never kick a grizzly unless you can run faster than the guy next to you.
8. Always tell the truth, especially to yourself.
9. Never spend all your money.
10. Never bet what you can't afford to lose.
11. Live the way you want to be remembered.
12. Know where the potholes are if you plan on driving at night.
13. Every man lives in the house he builds.
14. Don't smoke unless you're on fire.
15. Take responsibility for the choices you make, especially the bad ones.
16. Be kind to others; one day, they could serve on the jury at your trial.
17. If lost in the woods, don't run around and get more lost.
18. Never tell folks your dog don't bite. When he does, they'll hold you responsible.
19. Fix what you can. Don't worry about what you can't fix.
20. Treat a man with respect unless he means to do you harm.
21. Always save a little bit for later.
22. Forgive others when they wrong you, and don't forget to forgive yourself.
23. Always leave the dinner table wanting a little more.
24. Never turn your back on a guy holding a knife.
25. When the time comes, put your own horse down. Farming it out doesn't make it easier.

26. Every action has consequences, good and bad. Try to predict what they will be.
27. Never borrow money to buy something that can break down or stop working.
28. Remember to give thanks, even if you don't feel like it.
29. Always do your best, even when you don't need to.
30. Never take the biggest slice of pie.
31. Never send a text message without reading it over first.
32. It's okay to give to someone. It is not okay for them to take.
33. Take care of your tools like they're the last you'll ever own, and they will be.
34. Treat every crisis as an opportunity to be a better person.
35. Do what's right, not what's convenient.
36. Never leave just one sheet of toilet paper on the roll.
37. Remember that real love is a choice, not an emotion.
38. It's hard to get where you want to go if you don't know where you are.
39. To live long, laugh often and love much.